MORE ADVENTURES WITH RODNEY RATHBONE!

How to Beat the Bully Without Really Trying

The Call of the Bully

SCOTT STARKEY

REVENGE of THE BULLY

A How to Beat the Bully Novel

A PAULA WISEMAN BOOK
Simon & Schuster Books for Young Readers
New York London Toronto Sydney New Delhi

SIMON & SCHUSTER BOOKS FOR YOUNG READERS
An imprint of Simon & Schuster Children's Publishing Division
1230 Avenue of the Americas, New York, New York 10020
This book is a work of fiction. Any references to historical events, real people, or real places are used fictitiously. Other names, characters, places, and events are products of the author's imagination, and any resemblance to actual events or places or persons, living or dead, is entirely coincidental.
Text copyright © 2014 by Scott Starkey
Cover illustration copyright © 2014 by Tim Jessell
All rights reserved, including the right of reproduction in whole or in part in any form.
SIMON & SCHUSTER BOOKS FOR YOUNG READERS is a trademark of Simon & Schuster, Inc.
For information about special discounts for bulk purchases, please contact Simon & Schuster Special Sales at 1-866-506-1949 or business@simonandschuster.com.
The Simon & Schuster Speakers Bureau can bring authors to your live event. For more information or to book an event, contact the Simon & Schuster Speakers Bureau at 1-866-248-3049 or visit our website at www.simonspeakers.com.
Also available in a Simon & Schuster Books for Young Readers hardcover edition
Book design by Krista Vossen
The text for this book is set in Bembo Std.
Manufactured in the United States of America
0815 OFF
First Simon & Schuster Books for Young Readers paperback edition September 2015
2 4 6 8 10 9 7 5 3 1
The Library of Congress has cataloged the hardcover edition as follows:
Starkey, Scott.
Revenge of the bully / Scott Starkey.
pages cm
Summary: Rodney Rathbone tries to live up to his reputation as a reluctant hero when he earns a spot on his school football team—along with his archnemesis—while trying to regain his girlfriend Jessica's trust and survive his mother's new job as the restaurant reviewer for a local paper.
ISBN 978-1-4424-5677-8 (hc)
[1. Middle schools—Fiction. 2. Schools—Fiction. 3. Bullying—Fiction. 4. Football—Fiction. 5. Heroes—Fiction. 6. Ohio—Fiction. 7. Humorous stories.] I. Title.
PZ7.S7952Rev 2014
[Fic]—dc23
2014011733
ISBN 978-1-4424-5678-5 (pbk)
ISBN 978-1-4424-5679-2 (eBook)

Dedicated to my son, Jake

Acknowledgments

Since my first book was published in January 2012, two constants have made my experience as a writer both effective and rewarding. The first is the many letters and messages from parents, teachers, librarians, and especially children. Their kind words let me know that my stories are making a difference and serve as tremendous motivation to keep the adventures coming.

The second is the continued help of my friend, Lloyd Singer. He's been with Rodney every step of the way. During the entire process his creative insights, strong edits, and sound advice have had an immeasurable impact.

CONTENTS

Chapter 1

WELCOME TO MIDDLE SCHOOL

The front doors of Garrettsville Middle School loomed before me. I paused and tried to swallow but my mouth was too dry. I had been so nervous about starting middle school that I had missed the bus. What a morning. I watched my dad drive off and forced my legs forward, slowly. I made it to the first step. . . .

"Yo, Rodney!"

I turned to my right. Rishi was weaving between students, almost slamming into a bike rack as he rushed toward me. We were best friends and this was the first time I was seeing him since returning from summer camp over the weekend.

"How was it?" he yelled before even reaching me. Without waiting for my response, he continued, "My summer was great. I'm going to tell you everything that happened. On the first day of summer I couldn't find my shoes, right? So I went outside barefoot. Do you know what happened next? You know my neighbor's dog, Boris? Real big, right? Do you know what real big dogs leave on the lawn? You guessed it. I stepped in a big pile of—"

"Rodney," someone interrupted, "whadya do this summer?"

I looked to my left. It was Josh, legendary school bully turned unlikely summer-camp friend. Even though I was standing on the first step, he towered over me wearing that confused expression that came so easy to him.

"Uh, I went to Camp Wy-Mee," I answered. "Remember? You were there." I thought I saw some recognition in his eyes. Either that or he was focusing on a big late-summer fly that buzzed by.

Rishi knew nothing of Josh and my recent relationship breakthroughs. After all, Josh and his evil sidekick, Toby, had spent every day at Baber Elementary threatening me last year. It was only at summer camp—without Toby by his side—that Josh and I had actually hit it off. Not knowing this, Rishi continued, "Hey Josh, I thought Rodney got you sent to military school. Escape already?"

Great. Rishi was doing what he does best . . . getting me into hot water. Before I could explain that Josh's parents had decided against military school, I spotted a face coming our way that I hadn't seen in over two months. It was still as beady-eyed and ugly as ever. Toby walked over and whacked Josh on the shoulder. "Ready to give Rathbone a first-day-of-school beating?"

Josh was indeed ready for something. His eyes narrowed

below his big forehead. I'd seen that look before. He was about to charge! My stomach gurgled. Would he fall back under Toby's control? Was I about to get crushed in the next few seconds?

Again Toby whacked Josh's shoulder. "Come on, big guy. I know you're just itchin' to pound someone. Who's the most annoying kid in the world?" Toby looked in my direction and smiled his crafty sneer. "I know how badly you want to unleash some pain, Josh, so go on. Do it!" For added emphasis, he poked him in the chest.

"Raaaaagghhhhhnhhh!"

I flinched as Josh exploded, but instead of me, he grabbed Toby by the shoulders and spun him halfway around before hurling him through the air. The whole thing took about a second.

"Awesome!" Rishi hollered as Toby landed in a bush.

"Did you see him fly, Rodney?" Josh asked, grinning.

"Yeah, Josh, he flew."

"Like a birdie!" Josh clapped his hands together.

"Listen, Rishi," I whispered as we watched Toby fumble about in the bush, "Josh and I became buddies at camp. You know? In other words, he's not our enemy anymore."

I thought this might surprise Rishi but he accepted the news as if it was nothing. "Nice."

"What's going on out here?" a deep voice demanded. The three of us looked up. A big man stood above us gnawing on a pen. He wore a black baseball cap and black collared shirt, both covered in gold letters that spelled

G-MEN FOOTBALL. "Did you just throw that kid into the bush?" he asked Josh, plucking the pen from his mouth and using it to point at Toby.

I was nervous about the big kids in middle school and didn't want my new bodyguard expelled before we even got inside the building. I tried to come up with an excuse. Josh, however, beat me to it. "Yeah, I chucked him! Wasn't that cool?"

Ughhh. This was it. Josh was a goner.

Mr. Football was still looking at the bush and I cringed as he opened his mouth. "That has to be over ten feet away." He looked back at Josh and a slight smile touched his mouth. "Let me see your muscles, son." Josh flexed his biceps. "Holy smokes! What do you have in those arms, grapefruits? Man, they could be cantaloupes!" Now his smile stretched from ear to ear. He wedged the pen back in his mouth. "You got to be the toughest-looking kid I've ever seen."

"*He's* even tougher," Rishi said, pointing at me.

"Phtttt!" The pen flew out of the guy's mouth and hit me in the forehead. "This . . . um . . . student is tougher than him?" he asked Rishi.

"And faster, too." Rishi grinned. I was ready to clobber him on the head.

"Fast and tough. Can't teach speed!" The guy clapped his hands together and looked at the sky. "Ohhhh. This could finally be the year we beat Windham! What are your names, boys?"

"Rodney and Josh," I answered.

"No. Tell me your full names."

Rishi stepped in again. "Allow me to introduce you to the one and only Rodney Rathbone and Josh Dumbrowski."

"Rathbone and Dumbrowski," he growled. "Dumbrowski and Rathbone. Now those are *football* names! Boys, I'm Coach Laimbardi. I've been looking for players like you."

He'd been looking for us? Why couldn't I just walk in through the front door like everyone else? I'd just finished an insane school year followed by an even crazier summer. I wanted peace and quiet . . . a nice life. I pictured a little cottage in the country by a secluded lake with birds circling overhead. I could get a dog. I'd name him Sam and he'd sit by my side in the evenings while I played harmonica on the front porch. . . .

"Dumbrowski!" the coach barked. My cabin vanished. "You ever play fullback?"

Josh gave his usual response. "Duhhhh."

Coach Laimbardi clarified it for him. "Can you hit?"

"I CAN HIT!" Josh shouted back.

"That's good, because a fullback does a lot of hitting."

Josh grinned. "A lot of hitting? School's gonna be even better than camp, right, Rodney?" Well, at least he'd remembered where he'd been the last seven weeks.

I couldn't answer, though. I was too busy trying to come up with an excuse for why I couldn't be on the team. Before I could think of something—I'm allergic to getting crushed?—Rishi grabbed my shoulder and the coach's attention.

"Now take a good look at this one. Give Rathbone the ball and you'll win every game."

Nothing like added pressure on the first day of school. I enjoyed playing football with my friends but playing on a real team against a bunch of guys twice my size wasn't my idea of fun. Why couldn't the captain of the chess team have seen Josh toss Toby? Unfortunately, it was Coach Laimbardi, and judging from the look on his face, Rishi's buildup of me was getting to him.

"Yeah, I think you're right," the coach answered slowly. "I can see the headline of the *Weekly Villager* now. 'Rathbone Rumbles for 100 Yards.' Looks like I got a new tailback. Of course last year's starter, Trevor Tarantola, he's not going to like it. No matter, tough kid like you no doubt relishes a little heated competition. Isn't that right?"

All I relished was to be home hiding under the covers.

Coach Laimbardi clapped his hands. "All right, boys. Practice starts tomorrow. I'll see you two in full pads at three p.m. sharp." He walked off mumbling something about beating Windham.

"Awesome," Rishi exclaimed. "You're the new starting running back!"

My head was spinning. If things weren't bad enough, what happened next sealed my fate. Toby, who had crawled out of the bush covered in dirt and leaves, growled, "Yeah, definitely awesome. I can't wait to see what my *big* brother, *Trevor*, and his buddies on the football team do to you."

I watched him limp off. How had this happened so quickly? I'd gone from chicken to dead duck in a matter of seconds. Rishi elbowed me. "We haven't even walked in the front doors yet and we got to see Toby go for a ride." He wore a gigantic grin. "Even better, you just took his older brother's starting spot on the football team. Nothing like beginning the school year with a bang!"

I wanted to tell him I preferred starting with a whimper but I kept my mouth shut. We were entering the building and I needed to concentrate on not getting lost. Rishi and I said, "See you later," and split up in search of our lockers. My stomach was in a knot as I walked the strange hallways but a few kids I knew from Baber Intermediate said hi and I began to relax. By the time I found my homeroom I was feeling better—until I saw who was placed next to me. It shouldn't have been a surprise, since homerooms were arranged alphabetically.

As I sat down at my desk, Kayla Radisson's voice sliced into my ears. "I heard *you* had a big summer."

I glanced over. It's kind of interesting seeing faces after a few months. She looked different. Maybe she had changed her hair or something. One thing was the same, though. Her face still wore its usual nasty expression.

I stared at her without responding because I really didn't know what to say. Kayla was best friends with Jessica, who I hoped was still my girlfriend. I was afraid I had ruined the relationship because of something that happened at camp. Impatient as always, Kayla demanded, "So how many girlfriends do you have now?"

"One."

"If you're referring to Jessica, the answer is none. Back in June I told her you weren't worth waiting for all summer. She could have dated any number of better-looking guys than you, but no, 'Rodney this and Rodney that,' and the whole time you're off at camp having a great old time chasing every girl you see."

"That's not true at all!" I told her. "I didn't chase anybody."

"Want to know what *I'd* do to you if you were *my* boyfriend?"

"Not really," I said with a shiver.

She scowled and wagged her finger in my face before stopping it an inch from my nose. "Watch it!"

I was about to defend myself again but thought it best to keep silent. Satisfied that I was "watching it," Kayla lowered her finger and continued. "Now, like I said, I warned her. I was like . . ."

She went on for a bit more before our homeroom teacher thankfully interrupted us with attendance.

This wasn't good. Kayla only confirmed what I already feared—that I had probably lost Jessica. I shook my head. I still couldn't believe the bizarre turn of events on my last day of summer camp. Jessica, perhaps the best-looking girl I knew, had been brought along by my parents as a happy surprise for me. We hadn't seen each other since the day I asked her out at the end of the school year. When she spotted me at camp she ran right toward me to give me a hug. I can still picture her long blond hair blowing in the breeze, her arms outstretched as her eyes smiled into mine.

I'd love to pause the image forever, but I can't. The image always moves on to the next moment when Jessica clunked heads with Tabitha and Alison, two girls I knew from camp who were also running toward me. Turns out all three claimed to be my girlfriend that day. Jessica rode the whole way home in my parents' car with her arms folded staring out the window. She didn't speak to me then and still wasn't speaking to me, even though I tried calling her a few times. . . .

"You there!"

I jumped, startled. "Me?"

The homeroom teacher sat at her desk before an empty classroom. "It's Rathbone, isn't it? Are you waiting for an invitation? The bell rang. Go to first period. Go on. Go!" I had been so lost in thought I hadn't even noticed.

The hallway was jammed and very different from elementary school, where my former teacher, Mrs. Lutzkraut, had insisted that we walk in silent, orderly lines. Here, kids were everywhere, all talking and laughing and moving. It was chaos and I was bumped and jostled so many times that I wondered if I was already at football practice. I had history first period, Spanish second period, and math third—and of course none of the classes were near my locker. I tucked some notebooks under my arm and squeezed past the big bodies and unfamiliar faces.

I found a stairwell that led up to the second floor and down to the basement. It was also crowded. I could tell by the way everyone smiled and joked around that they knew each other. Meanwhile, I was still pretty new to Garrettsville and felt like a complete stranger—until I spotted a vision coming down the stairs. Maybe it was my imagination but the loud voices seemed to go silent as Jessica approached. I saw some older boys looking at her and elbowing each other. I knew this was a chance for me to fix things.

Then she saw me.

Her eyes hardened, but at least she didn't run away screaming. It was now or never. "Hi," I said. "I hoped I'd see you."

"Well, now you've seen me. Do you mind moving?" she asked, sounding scarily like Kayla. "I don't want to be late."

"Jessica, just give me a second. I know what happened the other day looked terrible, but I wasn't dating those two girls. . . ."

She rolled her eyes, again reminding me of Kayla. This was getting spooky. "Listen," I continued, "I think those girls were impressed that I saved Camp Wy-Mee. Seriously, I dreamed of you the whole time I was away!"

Her eyes lost a little of their glare and I began to see the real Jessica returning. "That was the worst moment of my life," she said.

"I can imagine. I am so sorry. I wish it never happened, but I promise you, you're the only girl that I—"

"That's him!" a girl yelled excitedly.

"There he is!" Another girl giggled.

Three girls in matching black tank tops and gold skirts looked my way. "It *is* him!" the third girl gushed. I glanced over my shoulder expecting to see some famous singer but grew alarmed when I realized they were definitely talking about me. The one in the middle, who was slightly taller than the other two, and much taller than me, stepped forward.

"We heard all about you. This is Sarah and Mindy. I'm Josie, captain of the cheerleaders, and I heard you're our new starting running back."

"Ummmm," I mumbled.

"He's a little cutey," Mindy said.

Josie pinched my cheek. "I like running backs."

I began to wheeze.

"We'll see you around," Josie said, smiling and giving me a wink.

I watched them walk up the stairs. "What were we talking about?" I asked Jessica.

"I can't imagine what I ever saw in you! You're horrible."

"But Jessica, I don't know them. They—"

"Leave me alone, Rodney." She whipped out of the stairwell into the crazed corridor. I gulped down a feeling of sorrow. The day had barely begun and I had hit rock bottom.

"Crack!"

I felt a jarring sensation in my arm as my new note-books flew into the air. They smashed against the ban-ister and the loose-leaf paper exploded. I should never underestimate just how low rock bottom can get. A slick voice behind me yelled, "Fumble!" followed by a round of laughs.

I wasn't eager to see who had knocked the books from my arm and for a moment I watched some of the paper float down to the basement. Reluctantly, I turned around. Five or six big guys were laughing at me. One of them stepped forward. "A running back needs to hold on to the ball." I wondered how everyone knew about my new football career already. I took a better look at the guy talk-ing and swallowed down my breakfast. I was looking at a bigger, nastier version of a face I'd come to know and despise.

I didn't really need the introduction but got it anyway. "I think you know my little brother, Toby." He jerked his thumb behind his back. Toby stood there smiling. "I'm Trevor. *Starting* running back. I hear you've come to take my spot."

Not wanting to give him any extra reason to dislike me, I said, "Me? No. I've always kind of pictured myself sitting comfortably on the bench. You know, come to think of it, I'm actually quite gifted at filling water jugs. I'm sure that—"

Trevor's smile vanished and his hands closed on my shirt. "Stop talking. You think I don't know all about you,

Rathbone? You think my runty brother here hasn't been begging me to hunt you down and pulverize you for months?"

"Uhh."

"Truth is, I never listen to the annoying shrimp. . . ." Toby's smile turned to a scowl but I was too preoccupied to enjoy it. His monster brother continued, "Now I see what he's been talkin' about. You just come waltzin' in here like you own the place, thinking you're the baddest. Thinking you can take my spot! Thinking all the cheerleaders are gonna like you! I don't care what you did in that nursery school last year, you're in middle school now and I'm going to be real happy showing you just how *bad* bad can be. I'll see you at practice, loser." He let go of my shirt before adding a not-so-gentle shove.

The group took Trevor's cue to leave. I got a few hard shoulders as they walked off. Toby lingered for a second. "This year's going to be a lot different from last year. I can't wait." He cackled a little and took off up the stairs.

I stood watching him go, now suddenly alone. As I scrambled around in a meager effort to get my books back together, a poster on the wall caught my attention: THIS IS A BULLY-FREE ZONE!

Great, I thought. *Too bad bullies can't read.*

Chapter 2

A SURPRISE ANNOUNCEMENT

Luckily, the rest of my first morning at Garrettsville Middle School was wonderfully uneventful, except for the occasional congratulations on my new football career. It wasn't until lunch in the cafeteria that I found out how everyone knew about my rise to stardom. Holding up his phone, Rishi explained, "I posted on Facebook, Twitter, Pinterest, Flickr, Instagram, and Tumblr that you're the new starting running back."

"You forgot smoke signals," I said.

"And this morning," he continued, "I wrote a couple of blogs. Plus Dave and I are making a rap video for YouTube tonight. Rodney, you'll be a star when I get through with you."

"Look Rishi, I don't really want to—"

"Don't worry, you're not imposing. I don't mind putting in some legwork for a friend, but remember, as your agent I get ten percent of your earnings."

"School athletes don't get paid," I reminded him.

"Until now. I already have calls in to Nike and Gatorade. Oh yeah, keep Friday night open."

"Why?"

"You're making an appearance at the mall."

"No I'm not. I—"

"Relax, all you got to do is sign a few autographs, kiss a few babies, remind the kids to eat their veggies. You know, the all-American athlete stuff."

I groaned. Once Rishi got going there was no slowing him down. My friend Slim, who was sitting at the table with my other friends from last year, Dave and Greg, interrupted my thoughts. "You sure he's harmless?"

"Rishi? Of course he's—"

"Not Rishi," Slim whispered, motioning to the newcomer sitting in our midst. I looked over at Josh. He was attacking his sandwich like a lion mauling a zebra.

"Just keep your hands away from his mouth while he's eating," I cautioned.

Slim sat on his hands and let out a nervous giggle.

It was good to eat lunch with the guys. I'd made new friends while away at camp but I'd missed the lunchroom laughs. Being back with them even made me feel better about the second half of the day, which turned out pretty normal—until I got back home, that is.

★ ★ ★

"I just saw your texts," my dad yelled excitedly to Rishi as we walked in the front door. "You made the football team, Rodney. Great job!"

My mom stood behind him. "I'm not sure I like this whole football thing."

I didn't like it either. I knew Trevor would get me sooner or later so I was more than ready to accept my mom's removing me from the team.

"But since you seem so talented at it . . . ," she continued. *What was that?* ". . . I've allowed your father to convince me to let you keep playing."

My dad nodded at me with a grin. "That's what dads are for."

My mom said, "Well, it looks like we now have two reasons to celebrate. Rodney, I have something to tell you and we're going out to a fancy French restaurant where I'll make my announcement."

"Sound's great. Which one are we going to?" Rishi asked.

My mom looked at him. I could see by her face that Rishi hadn't been on the guest list but she swallowed and said, "We're going to Chez Pierre."

"Awesome." Rishi smiled. "Good thing I'm wearing my fancy first-day-of-school shirt."

Unlike Rishi, I was surprised my family was going out to an expensive restaurant. During the summer my dad had taken a good-paying job with a developer called Vanderdick Enterprises. Everything was fine until the company decided to bulldoze my summer camp to build a shopping mall. I kind of stopped it from happening and they fired my dad. Luckily, he had just gotten another job, only it was part-time—in a mall of all places—and money was a bit tight.

I was thinking about this as we piled into the car. Penny brought me back to more immediate concerns when she said, without looking up from her iTouch, "I can't believe you're playing football, Rodney."

Neither can I, I thought.

Rishi said, "I may have had a little to do with it—"

"That makes sense," Penny interrupted. "Rodney would be too scared to join the football team himself."

I glared at her. My sister could be a nasty little thing, and to make matters worse, she was the one person in the world who had me figured out.

"Penny," Rishi said, "you're a cute kid. Having a brother like Rodney must be difficult. Jealousy's natural. If you ever need to talk it out, I'm here for you, okay?"

She gazed at him in disbelief before muttering, "What a dope."

My mom turned around from the front seat. "That's not nice, Penny. Now children, about my announcement. I've been wanting to get a job since moving here last year and I just found out this week that I landed the most amazing one imaginable."

"It's a very difficult job to get," my dad added. "Very prestigious."

"You're going to have your own TV talk show?" Rishi asked.

"No, I am—"

"You're going to be a scout for the Cleveland Indians?" Rishi tried again.

"No, I'm—"

"The next secretary of state?"

"Rishi!" My mom held her finger to her lips. "I am the new food critic for the *Cleveland Plain Dealer*. It's the city's top paper."

"Food critic?" Rishi shouted excitedly. "What's a food critic?"

My mom took a deep breath and explained, "A food critic goes to a restaurant when it opens and writes a review about the restaurant. If it's a good review, more customers will come than if the critic hates the restaurant."

"Tell them the best part!" my dad said.

"In order for me to sample as much food as possible, I'm allowed to take people with me. Everyone can order something different and I'll just sneak a taste from each of your plates."

"Not *that* part, Gloria," my dad whined. "Tell them the *best* part!"

She smiled. "The entire bill is paid for by the newspaper."

"Can you believe it?" my dad shouted.

"This is awesome," Rishi blurted. "We'll be eating like kings!"

"Just one thing," my mom cautioned. "Don't mention

our real last name or they'll know I'm a critic and treat us differently. You see, there was an item in today's paper announcing that I'll be handling restaurant reviews from now on."

"Won't they treat us better if they know you're a critic?" I asked.

"Yes, but then the review won't be accurate."

"So you're like a secret agent?" Rishi asked.

"Sort of, I suppose. Just remember not to mention Gloria Rathbone."

"Who's Gloria?" Rishi asked.

"Me. Got it?"

He winked at her as we pulled up at the restaurant. "Got it, Gloria."

My eyes took a minute to adjust to the darkness of the dining room. When they did, I noticed white table-cloths, wood paneling, and lots of candles. My skin started to break out in goose bumps from the freezing air conditioning.

"Good evening," said a man in a tuxedo. "Welcome to Chez Pierre." He said it kind of snooty like we weren't really welcome.

"We have a reservation for Smith," my mom said.

The man looked down at his ledger and made a face. "Smith is a party of four."

"Now it's five!" Rishi said proudly.

"Quite. I'll show you to your table."

We followed him to the back of the restaurant where he stuck us between the men's room and ladies' room.

"We don't need to use the bathroom," my dad said with a frown. "Perhaps we could sit at one of *those* tables?" He pointed to the many available ones in the front of the restaurant.

The man made a fake apologetic face. "Oh, I'm sorry sir, those are reserved."

My dad turned dark red. "Didn't *we* have a reservation? Didn't you just read 'Rathbone' back there in your little book?"

"Donald!" My mom tried to shush him.

"What, Gloria? Oh, sorry. I meant Smith."

The man's eyes got real big. "Rahthbone . . . Gloria . . ." He gripped the back of a chair to steady himself. "Oh sir, you're absolutely right. I have a wonderful table for you. It overlooks the river. I think you'll like it. Madame, let me help you to your chair. Are these your children? Very handsome." He patted Penny on the head. "You light up the restaurant like a spring day." He turned sharply, snapped his fingers at two waiters, and made a couple of frantic-looking gestures. "Right this way, right this way."

My dad, Rishi, Penny, and I were all smiles. My mom wasn't. "You've just ruined the review. They know who I am now."

"What? No they don't."

As my dad answered, a waiter slid a glass of champagne in front of him. "Compliments of the house."

"Ah, thanks." My dad turned back to my mom. "Honey, they're just reacting to my powers of persuasion."

She frowned slightly and opened the menu. As my dad looked it over I noticed his hands begin to tremble. "Gloria, these prices! Are you *positive* you got the job?"

"Relax, Donald. Stop being silly. We need to figure out what everyone's getting."

Before we had a chance to read any further, the waiter sprinted to the table like an Olympics finalist. He launched into a grand speech describing all sorts of food. I soon lost interest. All I remember is something about an *S* car going, which made no sense, and then something about sweet bread.

Rishi smiled. "That's what I want. I like bread and I like sweets. And I'll have the filet mignon . . . medium rare."

"Very good, sir."

"I'll take the *S* car going and the duck," I said.

The waiter smiled at my parents. "What sophisticated eaters you have with you."

My dad put down his champagne long enough to answer, "We try our best to expose them to the finer things."

"I'm quite sure," the waiter said. "Now, what can I get for the rest of the table?"

Everyone ordered and the waiter walked off. I noticed that my mom was smiling slightly at Rishi and me. It seemed like she found something funny, but instead of talking she turned back and listened to what my dad was saying about the beautiful view.

I smoothed out the white tablecloth in front of me, leaned back in my chair, and took a sip of my Coke. I could get used to this. I realized that my mom really *had* gotten a dream job—except that she had to go home and write a review. I, on the other hand, just had to eat fine food. Ah, to be the son of a food critic! Finally, here was something I could enjoy that wouldn't put me in great physical danger.

Yeah, I never learn, do I? Being the son of a food critic was about to land me in the middle of the most dangerous adventure of my life. Not knowing what awaited me, however, I raised my Coke glass and said, "To Mom, getting the best job in the world."

The glasses clinked and we were all smiles—until the appetizers arrived! The waiter placed a small white plate in front of me with six slimy looking gray things on it. "What's this?" I almost shouted.

"Escargot."

"What is it?"

"Why, it's snails, of course," the waiter said, smiling.

Rishi and Penny laughed. Rishi said, "You're turning green, Rodney! Maybe I'll give you a piece of crust from my bread."

The waiter plopped down a plate in front of him. "Your sweetbreads, sir." It didn't look like any bread I'd ever seen. Rishi queasily looked up. The waiter, wearing a slight grin, said, "I've never served sweetbreads to a boy your age. Children don't often enjoy cow throat. Have fun."

It was my turn to laugh.

Fortunately for both of us, the steak and the duck were really just steak and duck. We also loved the flourless chocolate cake and the other desserts. By the time we got up to leave we were stuffed. My dad, who had almost licked his plate clean, had to unbutton his pants on the ride home—which any food critic would have to agree is the sign of a good meal.

I should have fallen right to sleep that night but something a lot heavier than the chocolate cake weighed on my mind. Tomorrow would bring football practice, and along with it my new enemy, Trevor. Plus Toby was itching for a fight, Rishi was trying to make me famous, and the girl I liked wasn't talking to me. Some first day of school. As I drifted off to sleep I thought about the one important lesson I had learned. Escargot is French for gross and never, ever order sweetbreads!

Chapter 3

TWIN PROBLEMS

"You there. You paying attention?"

It was Mr. Scab, my wood shop teacher. I had been staring at the clock on the wall for half the class, hoping against hope I could slow down time. It was the last period. Football practice was just minutes away.

Mr. Scab banged on my desk. "What's your name?"

"Um, Rodney."

"Well, Um-Rodney, I once chose not to pay attention during wood shop. Do you know what happened?"

"No," I squeaked.

"This!" He held up his hand. I swallowed as I looked at his missing pinky. "Think that's bad?" he continued. "Want me to remove my glass eye?"

I was trying to decide if he was serious when the bell rang. I headed down the hall, relieved that Mr. Scab hadn't lost any body parts while talking to me.

Unfortunately, my relief was short-lived. I was heading to football practice. My stomach gurgled louder and louder with each step. It was the second day of school and I would soon be helmet-to-helmet with Trevor and his buddies. I rounded the corner. Coach Laimbardi was standing in the crowded hallway outside the gym arguing with a woman. He motioned for me to come over.

"Rodney, I got some bad news. The nurse says you need to have your parents fill out a permission slip and bring in a record of your physical. Sorry, but it looks like you won't be able to make practice."

No practice? I almost jumped up and down. Finally, some good luck. I let out a deep breath.

"Rodney!" a man's voice shouted from down the hallway. "*There* you are!"

I turned around—along with every other student—to see my dad waving his arms and heading my way. I sort of waved back thinking, *Please go away*.

"Young man, do you know that person?" the nurse asked.

A crowd of kids began to gather. Great, they would all know I was the one with the weirdo dad. "He's my father," I eventually admitted.

"Excellent!" Coach Laimbardi hollered.

"Rodney," my dad called out as he approached us, "I thought I'd come down and watch your first practice."

"So you're my new star's dad? I'm Head Coach

Laimbardi." I watched the two shake hands. "You know, now that you're here, you could sign Rodney's release and he'll be able to prac—"

"He will still need a copy of his physical," the nurse interrupted. I was beginning to like this nurse.

"Don't worry," my dad offered, "now that I have a little more time on my hands I was able to go on the district website and read all the requirements to play interscholastic sports. I got the physical right here! I got his mouthpiece and jock strap, too. You know where this goes, son?" He held up the jock strap.

"Dad, I know where it *goes*," I whispered. By now all I heard was the sound of kids laughing. I couldn't bear to look up.

"Well done, Mr. Rathbone!" yelled Laimbardi. "Active parents make all the difference. Now Rodney, go see Assistant Coach Manuel and get fitted for your pads. I'll see you out on the field. Mr. Rathbone, it was a pleasure meeting you."

"Thank you, coach. And Rodney, I'll pick you up after practice."

"Whatever," I muttered as I walked off to get fitted.

"Wait," my dad suddenly shouted from down the hall. "You forgot something." *Please no*, I thought, but sure enough I turned around to see my father waving the jock strap high above his head. Luckily, only about two hundred other kids seemed to notice.

★ ★ ★

Twenty minutes later I found myself walking out of the tunnel under the gym toward the football practice field. It was my first time wearing football pads. Besides what my dad had brought me, I had on a helmet, shoulder pads, rib protectors, hip pads, a tailbone pad in the back of my pants, thigh pads, kneepads, and a mouth guard. "That's all you got?" I had asked Coach Manuel. I liked the idea of being covered in a modern-day suit of armor—especially when I got to the field and saw I was the smallest kid on it.

"Rodney, this is awesome!" Josh barked at me. "I can't wait!" His eyes sparkled from inside his helmet. Now *there* was a football player. While he might have been younger than some of the other guys, he was one of the biggest.

"All right, take a knee over here!" Coach Laimbardi called out. We all huddled around. I could feel sets of eyes staring at me through face masks. Some were friendly. Many were not. Coach Laimbardi cleared his throat. "As most of you know, we've been having a tough time the past few years. We haven't had a winning season in over twelve years. Even worse, we haven't beaten . . ." He paused and his face scrunched up into a wretched expression. "We haven't beaten Windham in seventeen years."

"Eighteen," Coach Manuel corrected him.

Laimbardi scowled at us for a minute. "You hear that? Eighteen years of misery! Whoever said winning isn't everything never played football. That numbskull certainly didn't have to endure the jokes and ridicule of

Coach Bill Belicheat. He's always . . . picking on me."
He shook his head and looked at his feet. I thought I
saw his lip quiver. His eyes looked damp. "I just want to
beat Belicheat and Windham once before I retire." After
a moment his voice sounded strong again. "I was beginning to believe I never would beat them, but yesterday I
saw something wondrous. Something that told me the
black cloud that's been hanging over Garrettsville might
finally be lifting."

I noticed Josh glance up at the sky with a confused
look on his face.

Coach Laimbardi, who had stopped in back of where
we were kneeling, placed his hands on Josh's and my
shoulder pads. He turned to the rest of the team and
announced, "Let me introduce you to our new starting
backfield—Rathbone and Dumbrowski. They have just
the kind of toughness we've been lacking around here!"
Thank God he didn't notice my knees beginning to
shake under all that padding. "I can't wait to see them in
action," he continued. "In fact, let's not wait any longer.
Now, I know we don't scrimmage the first week . . ."

That's good, I thought to myself.

". . . but I'm willing to make an exception. We have
enough guys here today from last year to run some plays.
Let's see what the new guys Rathbone and Dumbrowski
can do. Trevor, take the defense out to the twenty-yard
line and let's get started."

I watched Trevor's helmet nod. Then, with a wicked

look, he pointed at me and mouthed the words, "You're mine."

I had an urge to puke but pictured bits of last night's fancy French dinner getting caught in my face mask and managed to keep it down. In a fog, I followed the other offensive players as we made our way onto the striped field. I was about to get crushed and torn apart. Noticing several small groups of students filing into the stands did little to make me feel better. A familiar voice rang out from one of the spectators. "Go get 'em, Rodney!" It was Rishi, sitting with my dad. He waved and held up his phone. "Don't worry, this takes great video!"

I walked into the offensive huddle. Apart from Josh, the other faces were unfamiliar. I was relieved to see they weren't menacing. In fact, many of the guys smiled down at me through their face masks. A bunch of them were as big as Josh and I assumed they were the offensive line. One of the biggest, a tall black kid with a friendly smile, stuck out his hand. "Welcome to the football team."

I shook his big hand and breathed easier. "Thanks."

"No, let us thank *you*. We're sure glad you're joining the offense, Rodney. My name is Joe. I'm the center. JJ and AJ are your tackles, and Philip and Frank are the guards. We're the offensive line."

I couldn't believe it. These guys were nice and seemed genuinely happy to have me with them. Not only that, each player was bigger than the next. As I had learned with Josh, it's good to have big friends.

Frank said, "We heard all about you last year, of course."

"Yeah," AJ added. "I still can't believe someone attacked the McThugg Brothers and lived to talk about it."

JJ blurted, "I still watch your flight off the Ravine of Doom on YouTube!"

Joe smiled. "Like I said, we were all real happy when we heard you were joining us. You see, we were kind of hoping you'd be able to help us with some of our problems."

The good feeling in my chest was replaced by a tight, uncomfortable feeling. Their faces had lost the smiles of a moment ago and now they looked frightened. "You see, Rodney," Joe explained, "we've been getting bullied quite a bit by a real mean group."

The tight, uncomfortable feeling in my chest was quickly replaced by difficulty breathing and a racing heart. This was getting worse by the second. These guys were a head taller than me and a hundred pounds heavier. What group could possibly be nasty enough to bully *them*? And what could I possibly do about it?

Over the pounding of my heart I heard myself ask, "It's Trevor and his gang, right? Are they the cause of your problems?"

Joe looked surprised and almost laughed. "If it was Trevor, I could handle it. These guys are much worse. I'm talking about—" He stopped short and looked from side to side before making sure it was safe to continue. Finally he whispered, "I'm talking about the Windham team."

"Two in particular," JJ added. "Twin brothers."

"Exactly," Joe said. "They come over here after school—"

"Oh, no!" JJ gasped, staring at the sideline. "They're here." The huddle collectively shuddered. I snuck a peak. You couldn't miss the twin giants!

"So can you help us?" Joe asked.

Trevor had wandered by and was waiting to hear my reply. Suddenly I was living out my worst nightmare. At Baber Intermediate, I had built a reputation as a kid who feared no one—despite the fact that I'm pure coward through and through. It was all by accident, of course, but now I realized that none of my past victories meant much in this new, larger world. If I acted afraid, my whole "Rodney reputation" would vanish. Once it was gone I'd be the number one bully target in Garrettsville. Heck, maybe all of Ohio. I had to pretend to be tough, but how?

Before I had a chance to answer, Coach Laimbardi shouted, "All right! Let's run a play!"

"We'll talk about Windham later," Joe said.

For the time being I was safe—but for how long? Another kid, in a number sixteen jersey, cleared his throat. He'd been quiet up until now. "We'll run a basic sweep. Sound good to you, Rodney?"

"Huh?" I was so busy worrying about my reputation that I had forgotten about football.

"Oh, hey, my name's Hector. I'm the quarterback. I broke a state record last year."

With a star quarterback, maybe we wouldn't have to

run the ball that much. "A state record. That's great," I said.

"Yeah, I broke the record for getting sacked the most times in one season. Seventy-nine—thanks to this great offensive line. That's twenty-two more times than Johnny 'Pancake' Stevenson. I just regained feeling in my feet last week."

I glanced over at the offensive line. Joe and the rest of the guys looked sheepish. No one was arguing.

"I'm not planning to throw the ball this year," Hector continued. "Not once. Good luck running it. But with these wimps blocking for you, well I just hope you get the bed with the window."

"What window?" I asked. "What bed?"

"At the hospital, man. So you ready?"

"You sure know how to motivate a guy," I grumbled.

He ignored that. "I'll flip you the ball. You run around the right side. Let's go. The snap is on two."

I grabbed Josh. "You stay in front of me, and if anyone comes near me, you hit him, okay?"

"Yeah!"

Josh was my only hope for survival. I was already wondering which state record I'd be going for—most broken bones or wettest pants. I shook off further thoughts.

Hector stopped walking to his spot behind the center and headed back toward Josh and me. He seemed to want to remind of us something. When he got within a couple of feet, Josh took two steps, lowered his shoulder, and flattened him to the ground. "I done what you said, Rodney!"

Hector lay gasping on the field. "So much for the feeling in my feet returning . . ."

I knelt down. "Sorry about that. Josh is kind of new to the sport."

"It's okay," Hector wheezed, "I'm used to it. I was going to remind you to try to run out of bounds. Trevor and the defense love to pile on top of the runner."

I looked in Trevor's direction and shuddered. He and the rest of the defense were staring hungrily at me. To help set the mood, some band kids in the stands struck up a tune that sounded a lot like the theme from the movie *Jaws*.

I had just made up my mind to bolt home when Hector yelled, "Hut! Hut!" The gold-and-black bodies in front of me collided with a crunch. I watched in horror as my golden offensive line fell to the ground, offering minimal resistance to the black shirts that swarmed in my direction. Hector just managed to get the ball away before being swallowed up. The ball flipped through the air several times in my direction and I grabbed it without thinking. The black shirts growled and swarmed onward.

Josh smashed the first two but Trevor sprinted by him as Josh wrestled with a third. Two more frightening linebackers were a step behind Trevor. They all looked like sharks ready to feast on some foolish swimmer. The band's choice in music made perfect sense.

And that's when my instincts, my ultracowardly, ultra-chicken instincts, swept through me and took full control over my nervous system. My legs spun into action. They must have looked like two whirlwinds in a cartoon. I ran hard to my right—away from Trevor. I would have run straight to the sideline but a defensive end ran out in front of me. Knowing that I was about to get crushed between four thugs, I turned hard and sprinted down the field away from the horror behind me. My fear was giving me bionic speed.

"That's my boy!" I heard my dad shout as I flew by.

I was making a run like I did at field day the year before and was going in for the touchdown! The wind was rushing through my face mask as my feet tore down the right sideline. The old Rathbone luck was still with me—until someone dove at my legs. Jumping instinctively to my right, I plowed straight into two gigantic kids standing on the sideline. Their heads banged together as all three of us flew into the air. I was the first to land and watched the other two hit the ground with deafening thuds.

Rishi charged down from the stands. "That was great!" he shouted. "You hit them like a bowling ball smashing two pins. I got it all on video."

The two guys I had clobbered weren't as pleased. As they staggered to their feet, covered in mud and grass and rubbing their heads, I realized it was the Windham twins! Towering over me, one of them growled, "I know you did that on purpose." He spit some dirt from his mouth. "Too bad we can't properly introduce ourselves with so many witnesses around, but we'll be seeing you soon enough. Bart and Bruno, remember those names."

Still dazed from the collision, I watched them walk off.

"Rathbone! That was the best run I've seen in years!" It was the excited face of Coach Laimbardi staring down at me. "In a real game, the spectators won't be right next to the field. Unlucky. But with you handling the ball, I see big things for this team. Big things."

"Super job, son!" my dad yelled from the sideline as I rose to my feet.

Joe clasped my shoulder. "I *knew* we could count on you to take care of those guys."

"Me too," JJ added. "It's great that you have our backs! Finally, someone who's not afraid of anything."

Boy, was I glad my sister wasn't around to hear that one!

Chapter 4

A BIZARRE LESSON IN ROMANCE

The start of school can be a nerve-racking time for a kid. While my first couple of days probably surpassed anything experienced by my classmates, I can't say I was surprised. Trouble knows how to find me. For instance, how many people get thrust into the role of football savior on a team where half the players want to tackle them? Or find three cheerleaders flirting with them—right when they're trying to win back their girlfriend? Or worst of all, witness their dad running around school with a jock strap in his hand?

Well, you get the idea. It was all pretty much business as usual for me. But by the end of the first week, I began to realize my life had taken a turn that even I couldn't have imagined in my wildest dreams. I looked around one day and saw that things were . . . good. Thanks to the incident with Bart and Bruno, I was barely getting threatened in the halls and without

Josh by his side, Toby was keeping his distance.

The place where I really noticed a difference was at football practice. I was doing all right and starting to enjoy it. I figured the best thing to do was run right behind Josh as much as possible. And it had been working. He was able to handle Trevor and the middle linebackers, hammering them so hard that they toned down their ferocious assault on the field. Coach Laimbardi loved it. After practice one day he said, "You know, Rathbone, I've never had a running back that uses his lead blocker as well as you."

"Thanks, Coach."

"Yeah, a lot of times players run away from protection and get tackled." He certainly didn't have to worry about *me* running from protection. "Keep up the good work, Rathbone."

"I'll try."

"Yeah, Coach, he's playing good," Trevor's voice sounded from behind me.

With my helmet on, I hadn't seen him approach. Laimbardi nodded his head in agreement before turning his attention to Coach Manuel and walking off.

"Hey Josh," Trevor called out, "someone was just looking for you. He said one of the janitors needed help exploding something."

Josh immediately tore off in the direction of the school building. I got a sick feeling in my stomach. This wasn't good. Trevor watched him disappear, muttering,

"What a loser." Then he slapped his hand down hard on my shoulder pad. "I wanted to have a little talk without Frankenstein around to protect you."

Was Trevor really going to start something right in the middle of football practice?

"Listen, Mr. Football Star," he began, "enjoy the ride, but don't kid yourself into thinking that I'm not going to get ahold of you. I would right now, if Laimbardi wasn't here. Trust me, we Tarantolas have no problem waiting for the best time to strike."

"Actually, you kinda got me already," I said. He looked confused so I continued, making it up as fast as I could. "It's the suspense of waiting, you know. Just ask anyone who's been killed. Waiting's the worst part. It would be so much worse for me if you waited, um, say twenty or thirty years."

Trevor shook his head before responding. "My brother Toby said you had a smart mouth. He wasn't kidding. You know, part of me appreciates that, though. Really. But another part of me, a bigger part, can't stop thinking of the joy your squeals of pain will bring me. Besides, you took my spot as running back and I'm not forgiving that!"

"Why not? You're still the starting middle linebacker."

"True, Rathbone, true. Coach says defense wins championships. But *I* know that offense gets the girls. I was *this* close to kissing Josie." He held his fingers an inch apart in front of the bars of my mask. "Then you

38

show up and she hasn't spoken to me since. I've been really depressed." He shook his head. "And you know, there's only one thing that can get me out of this funk. Can you guess what that is?"

I had a pretty good idea, especially since he was twisting the front of my jersey and pulling me closer. He said, "You know, maybe now isn't such a bad time after all, Rathbone. The school psychologist says I need to find an outlet for my anger issues. He advised me not to bottle up my feelings. . . ."

"Have you tried yoga?"

"Do you punch people in yoga?"

"No, but my mom showed me how to do the downward dog. Here, I'll show you." I attempted to pull away but Trevor only pulled me in closer. I watched his other hand form a fist. The coaches had conveniently wandered off. Josh was still back at the school. How had the field gotten so empty? Where would he punch? If he went for my face mask he would probably break his hand. Would he aim at my stomach instead?

Before I found out the answer to my last question, my chicken instincts took over. "What if I can get you a date with Josie?"

His fist lowered slightly. "I don't need a slimy runt like you to land me a lady. She already went on a date with me during the summer."

"What happened?"

"We had a great date. Super romantic."

"Candlelit dinner?"

"Nahh, we went to see the demolition derby."

"You think a demolition derby is romantic?" I asked.

"All right, maybe it's not as romantic as professional wrestling, but that's why I bought her dinner."

"Well, that part sounds nice."

"Yeah. The hot dog had a little dirt on it, but it gets dusty at the track."

I almost pointed out his stupidity but decided to play along. "Certainly sounds like a special evening," I lied. "The track dust is part of the ambiance. Besides, I've always felt that dirt adds a nice smoky flavor to meat."

"Exactly!" he said, nodding. "You get it."

"So after this clearly wonderful date, what happened?"

"I don't know!" He let go of my jersey and put his hands into the air. "I texted her a couple of days later to see if she wanted to go cow tipping at the old Smith farm. She never wrote back and when I try to talk to her she avoids me."

I had to ask. "What's cow tipping?"

"You city boys don't know nothin' about a good time. Cow tipping is when you sneak up on a sleeping cow and push it over. They wake up mad and you run away. Good thing you moved here from the city. You've been missing out on the finer things in life."

"So I see . . ." Afraid he might still need to unleash his anger, I added, "What about me getting you a second date?"

He looked at me for a moment, thinking.

"Tarantola!" Coach Laimbardi called from the other side of the field. "Bring in that tackling dummy." I glanced down at the large red pad lying on the grass.

Trevor lifted the back of my jersey and hollered, "Don't worry, Coach, I got the dummy right here!"

Then, so only I could hear, he added, "You get me that date with Josie and maybe you'll avoid a date with my fists." With that, he gave me a jarring shove to the ground and walked off the field.

After a pretty quiet week, my life had returned to normal.

Chapter 5

PULLED INTO
A MEETING

In the days that followed I did everything possible to ask Josie about a second date with Trevor, but there was a problem. Jessica. She still wasn't talking to me and the last thing I needed was for her to see me with Josie— or to hear about it from someone else. Three different times I had approached Josie in the hallway only to have Kayla pop up out of nowhere and give me one of her knowing, angry looks.

I finally got my chance late one morning while Jessica and Kayla were outside for gym. Josie had been excused from gym for a week after a particularly nasty split during cheerleading practice. I noticed her alone in the library and decided to bring up a different nasty split.

"So," I began, "I heard from Trevor that you won't return his phone calls."

She stuck her finger down her throat and pretended to throw up on the floor.

"Oh come on, he's not so bad," I said.

"He took me to a drag race. Me! Do you know how gross it was?"

"It was a demolition derby, and he *did* buy you dinner."

At the mention of the infamous hot dog, Josie's face twisted into such a disgusted expression that I really did expect her to throw up. She limped off toward the bathroom.

I had my work cut out for me. Before long, Trevor would run out of patience. For the time being, however, I was safe.

Or so I thought. Later that same day, Rishi, Josh, and I were walking home from school, joking around and enjoying the beautiful September afternoon. Josh began to lag behind but I was used to that. A crack in the sidewalk was enough to distract him. Rishi was in the middle of a story when I began to notice a car engine idling in back of us. I could also hear tires crunching very slowly over sandy gravel. The hair on the back of my neck stood up. This was all too familiar. Last year, my crazy teacher Mrs. Lutzkraut and her nutty friend Long Nose had followed me all through my neighborhood. Were they inching along with me now? It couldn't be! Mrs. Lutzkraut was supposed to be "resting" for a few months in a place called Shady Pastures.

I glanced back slowly. There was a car following us all right, but it was a black limousine.

"Ooof," I gasped, colliding with something soft yet

solid. I found myself eye-to-eye with the buttons on a beige dress shirt.

"Are you's Rodney Rathbone?" a deep voice asked. I peered up at an enormous man. He had a big face that matched his large belly. A large strange man asking for me by name. Definitely not good.

I was about to run off screaming. I turned to Rishi and whispered, "Let's get out of here."

Instead, Rishi took a step closer to the stranger. "To answer your question, yes, this is Rodney Rathbone, but you'll need to talk to me. I handle all his business affairs."

Another man was climbing out of the limo. He wore a bright ugly shirt and tilted hat. He looked at Rishi. "What are you, his lawyer?"

Rishi looked unfazed. "I prefer agent. Rishi Singh, at your service." He handed both men his card. "What can I do for you?"

Ugly Shirt said, "I like this kid. He's good with da words. You like him, Cheese?"

The big guy, who I guessed was named Cheese, grunted. I couldn't tell if it was a yes or no grunt.

Ugly Shirt said, "Look kid, the guy we work for wants to talk to Rodney. My name's Willy and this here is Cheese. Whadaya say we take a little ride downtown?"

The idea of a limo ride with these two seemed like the worst idea in the world.

"Sounds great," Rishi said.

"What?" I squeaked. "Listen, it looks like a nice car

and all, but we prefer to walk. Nice day and besides—"

"That's right," Rishi cut in, "my clients are in training." He motioned to Josh, who had finally caught up with us. "Josh, meet Mr. Cheese and Mr. Willy."

Josh yawned.

Willy continued. "Anyway, you's can walk then. Walk on down to Mama's Restaurant. It's under a mile away. No reason to be afraid—"

"I ain't afraid of nothin'!" Josh barked.

"*Dis* is da one I like," Cheese said, pointing at Josh.

"That makes sense. He's like a mini you."

"Who you callin' mini?" Josh snapped, taking a few steps toward Willy.

"The Boss might want to talk to this one too." Willy laughed. "We'll see you at Mama's. You know where it is?"

"Yes," said Rishi, looking at his phone. "You can tell Mr. Boss we should be there in twenty minutes."

"It's not Mr. Boss. Boss isn't his last name. He's the boss, because he owns the restaurant, and he don't like to be kept waiting, so make it quick." The two of them climbed into the back of the limo and drove off.

What did they want with me? And who was this Boss? I had lots of questions but knew one thing for sure. No way was I heading to this meeting. I went to take the left toward home.

"Where are you going, Rodney?" Rishi asked.

"Home."

"What do you mean? We have a business meeting in fifteen minutes. I told you my hard work would start to pay off. One of the town's big shots wants to meet you. He must be important if he's called Mr. Boss."

"Look Rishi, something feels a bit strange about these guys. I have homework and my parents will expect me . . ."

"No they won't. I just texted your father that you're eating over my house. This, Rodney, is called opportunity. And what kind of friend, what kind of agent, would I be if I let you take the turn toward home? What do you think, Josh?"

"Huh?"

"See? He understands. Now, let's go." And of course, against my better judgment, I followed.

As we rounded onto the main street in town Rishi shouted, "Look, there it is." He pointed to a building with a green awning over a white-tile entranceway. Above the awning was an unlit neon sign that read, MAMA'S. In the window was another sign: OPENING SOON. It was only when we got closer that I noticed a smaller sentence below: AND YOU'S BETTER SHOW UP.

I glanced up and down the street hoping to spot a convenient police car. The only car was the black limo parked in front. I could hear its engine rattling, cooling down. Otherwise, the street was empty. Second, third, and fourth thoughts swept my mind but before I had a chance to voice them, Rishi and Josh walked into the restaurant. Once again, I had no choice but to follow.

Inside it was dark. A few beams of daylight shined in through the slats of thick wood blinds. A couple of green lights hung above a wood bar that ran the length of one side. Twenty or so tables dotted the room. I noticed a bartender with rolled up sleeves and a bald guy with some gray hair above his ears and heavy, black-framed glasses. He wore a jogging suit and sat at a table writing something in a big book. Besides them, the room was empty.

"Here we are," Rishi announced.

"You Rodney?" asked the guy at the table.

"No, I'm his manager."

"Well the Boss only wants to talk to Rodney." He looked at Josh and me and asked Rishi, "Which one of dem is Rodney? The runt or the big guy?"

The scared, shaking runt, I wanted to answer. "Me," I volunteered.

"Good." His glasses made his eyes seem twice as big as normal. "Go back through that door."

"I usually do most of Mr. Rathbone's business planning," Rishi began. "I'd better talk to Mr. Boss with him—"

"You'd better sit!" the guy shouted. "And it's just Boss. None of this Mr. Boss stuff. Got it?"

Rishi didn't answer. Instead he climbed onto a bar stool and tapped the wood bar. "I'll have a stiff one."

The bartender just stared at him.

"Make that a Coke," Rishi said, smiling.

The bartender reached for a glass and looked at Josh. "What about you, big fella? What can I get you to drink?"

"A drink," Josh said.

While this brilliant exchange was underway, Cheese and Willy stepped out from the back room. "All right, enough gabbing. The Boss is waiting. Come on, Rodney."

Rishi called out, "Don't sign anything without me reviewing it first!"

The guy at the table muttered, "Dis kid," and shook his head. Then he looked up at me as I passed by with Willy and Cheese. His big eyes behind his glasses were blank and told me nothing of what to expect on the other side of the door. To be honest, I was as curious as I was scared.

The old, heavy door swung open. A man who I guessed was the Boss sat behind a huge wooden desk. His hair was dark brown and slicked straight back. A smile broke across his wide, clean-shaven face. "Rodney, thank you for accepting my invitation here this afternoon."

"What, I had a choice?" I said as I sat down in one of two leather chairs facing the desk.

The Boss laughed. "You a funny kid, Rodney. I heard you had a big mouth. I like funny people. They make me laugh. Watch this. Hey Cheese, what kind do I have in the drawer?"

I heard Cheese inhale noisily. "Provolone."

The Boss clapped his hands together. "Man's a genius. Can sniff out a slice of cheddar from thirty paces."

At least I now knew how he got his name, but that's all I knew. How did this Boss guy know *my* name, and that I had a big mouth? How did he know anything about me? I was about to find out.

"So Rodney, I guess you're wonderin' why you's sittin' here today."

"The thought crossed my mind."

"Well, first let me say that all of us is big fans of yours. Them McThuggs have been quiet for a year. Now, we can certainly handle those boys, but you know handling problems can be, shall we say, bad for business. Also, I hear you're the new running back on the G-Men. I like football."

I was about to ask how he knew I was the running back when he said something that really shocked me. "Anyway, the real reason you's here is your mother."

My mom? I hadn't seen that coming. Did she think I should get a part-time job or something?

"She's the new food critic for the paper," he continued, "and we is opening a new restaurant here. Do you know what a restaurant needs to be successful?"

"Good food," I answered.

The Boss shook his head. "No."

"Good service?" I tried again.

Looking impatient and kind of angry he shook his head again.

"Nice decor?" I tried. "Reasonable prices?" I spat. I didn't like the change in his expression.

"You obviously know nothin' about the restaurant business, kid. Why should we waste our money hiring an expensive chef or fancy-pants decorator?"

"Because people come here to eat?"

"No, they come here because someone tells them it's good. Someone they trust. Someone like a food critic. Someone like your mom."

"You want my mom to write a good review for your restaurant?"

"Ah, a quick learner."

"But she's not going to write a good review if you don't have good food."

The Boss smiled at me. It wasn't the kind of smile that made you feel all warm and fuzzy. He said, "Why do you think you're sitting here, Rodney? Just to chat? I got my own bratty son at home to annoy me. Your mom *will* write a good review, because you're going to convince her to."

I understood. I understood I was in big trouble. "My mom doesn't listen to anything I have to say. She's not—"

"I told you that I like football. I wanted my son to play, but he spends all his time on music, composing some phonies."

"Symphonies?"

"Yeah, that's it. He wants to go to this joint called Juilliard. I say what about Ohio State?"

"Go Buckeyes!" I added, trying to stay on his good side.

The Boss nodded. Then his forehead creased and his eyes went cold. "But I didn't bring you down here to talk about the Phil Moronic Orchestra. I want to talk about your career. Now, you get me a nice little restaurant review in the *Cleveland Plain Dealer* and I'll see you get whatever you want, on or off the field. Let's just say I got connections in dis town. You understand, Rodney?"

I nodded, though understanding what he was saying did little to lift my spirits. The Boss smiled wide and banged his palms on his desk. "Now we's coming to an understanding. Conducting business, you could say. I know you're gonna get us that good review. You do that and we're friends. You don't, and, well . . ."

Willy spoke up. "Let's just say it's healthier to be on the Boss's good side."

"So, Rodney," the Boss continued, "do you want to be friends?"

"Uh, I can't think of anything better." How I managed the lie with a straight face I'll never know.

"Rodney?"

"Yes, er, Mr. Boss?"

"Not Mr. Boss. I hate when people say Mr. Boss! It's just Boss. Now, where was I?"

"You were yelling at me that we should be friends."

"Right! So listen . . . you're not going to go talking about our business, are you? That's not what friends do."

"I won't say anything," I promised.

"Well that's good. Not that anyone would listen. We is pillars of the community."

My nervousness was building and since my well-being depended on the success of this restaurant, I asked, "What kind of food are you going to serve?"

"Russian Italian, like I had growing up."

"Russian Italian? Who'd want to eat that?" It was out before my slow brain had a chance to filter it. His eyes darkened and I scrambled to recover. "I mean, it's just that I never heard of mixing Russian and Italian. I . . ."

"What, you never had borscht parmesan or cabbage pizza?" the Boss asked. "I ate it every day. I got a Russian dad and an Italian ma."

Just the thought of eating that made my stomach gurgle and I could taste my lunch in the back of my throat.

"Great stuff. The kinda food that puts hair on your chest." He looked over at Willy. "Give Rodney a menu." Willy took a sheet of paper off a shelf and stuck it in front of me. "Now," the Boss continued, "tell me dis don't make you hungry."

I started reading the menu.

Herring Parmesan

Pigs Feet Parmesan

Poached Fish Parmesan

Matzo Balls Parmesan

"So, what do you think?" the Boss asked.

That I'm as good as dead. There was no way my mother

was going to give this place a good review. Instead, I managed, "Interesting."

"Want to try some of it?" Willy asked.

Before I had a chance to scream "No!" there was a knock at the door.

"What?" the Boss yelled out.

The bald guy with thick glasses stuck his head into the room. "Sorry to bother you, but I can't take it no more."

"What's the matter?"

"It's Rodney's friend, the little one. He's driving me nuts. He won't shut up about how much money he can make us."

"Oh yeah?" the Boss asked. "Well bring him in. I think Rodney and I are done with our talk. Right, Rodney?"

I didn't answer, and I didn't pay attention as Josh and Rishi joined us in the back room. I was too busy thinking about the Boss and what to do next. He hadn't exactly *said* anything bad, but somehow I got the feeling he could make my life miserable if I didn't go along with him. Plus I didn't trust Willy or Cheese or those other goons out front. . . .

"Have you set a marketing budget?"

I looked up. Rishi was talking excitedly. Everyone in the room was staring at him like he taught advertising for a living.

"Never mind da budget for now," the Boss said, "what do you think of our slogan? And our website?"

I realized in shock that Rishi was sitting in the Boss's seat behind the desk. They had placed a laptop in front of him. Rishi looked at the computer screen and read out loud, "*Eat at Mama's, or else.* Yeah, well it's catchy and all, but maybe—"

"Check out our social media campaign," Willy added.

Rishi read, "*Like us on Facebook, or else.* Well it's a good start. Maybe we could tweak it a bit. Have you considered any e-blasts? Do you have a Twitter account? Are you running any other promotions, like coupons to build a following? Have you been in touch with the local papers? Let me take a look at your press release . . ."

"Rishi, are you ready?" I asked.

"Just a minute, Rodney. I need to add some color to this web page . . ."

"You know what?" the Boss said to Cheese and the other guys. "I kinda like these kids. They got smarts. Maybe we can put them to work. What do you think?"

Rishi looked up at him from the laptop.

"Yeah, it's a good idea," Willy answered. "They can start hanging flyers around town. You know, spread the word about the restaurant opening."

I knew that getting in any deeper with these guys would be a real bad idea. I said, "As much as we'd love to spread the word, we have a lot of schoolwork . . ."

Rishi opened his mouth to back me up—or so I thought. "Don't worry, Rodney. I can handle two jobs. You're still my priority. We'd love to get more involved.

Is it too soon to talk about compensation?"

The Boss laughed. "Again with da money. Don't worry. We pay very well."

Rishi looked so excited I thought his eyes were going to pop from his head. He turned to Josh. "What do you think? Want to make some money?"

"I like money," Josh said.

That seemed to decide it. The Boss reached out his hand and Rishi gripped it, only too happy to shake the hand of his new employer. "And now," the Boss said, looking down at Rishi, "the first order of business."

"What is it?" Rishi asked, grinning.

"Get outa my chair!"

Chapter 6

BEET LITERATURE

"May I try the herring-stuffed ravioli?" my mom asked the Boss. I sat squeezed between the two of them, our backs to the wall of the restaurant. As the large plate passed in front of me I noticed the ravioli was gray and wet. My mom took a bite. "This is the worst meal I've ever tasted!" she shouted. The Boss gave me an evil look. "Help," I tried to shout, but nothing came out. My mom took another bite and gagged. "It's awful!" This time the Boss grabbed his fork and . . .

I awoke so suddenly that it took me a few seconds to realize I was safe in my bed. My heart was beating fast. It was pitch black and the house was silent. I guessed it was a few hours before dawn. After a minute I began to relax and forget about the dream . . .

Relax? Safe in my bed? Who was I kidding?

Yesterday's meeting with the Boss shot through my brain. I immediately craned my neck to glance out the bedroom window, half-expecting that Cheese guy's big face to be peering back at me. There was no one there but I realized that these new people in my life were no dream. I had watched enough old movies with my dad to know that someone like the Boss could be more dangerous than any schoolyard bully from my past. Just the kind of thought a coward like me needs in the middle of the night.

Later, at breakfast, I was still nervous and jumped when my mom shut the silverware drawer. My dad smiled, folded his paper, and looked at me. "Rodney, it's totally normal to be excited." His eyes twinkled.

I put down the piece of buttered toast I was about to bite and swallowed nervously. My dad and I viewed the world rather differently. The fact that Penny was smirking did little to ease the tension.

"Why should I be excited?" I asked.

"It's Friday," he said.

"Yeah?"

"And tomorrow's Saturday," he continued.

I was getting impatient. "And the day after that is Sunday. I know how it works."

He speared a sausage off a plate in the middle of the table. "You realize what Saturday is, don't you?" Was he just talking about enjoying the weekend? I doubted it. I took a sip of orange juice. "Don't you remember? Tomorrow is your first football game."

I almost spit the juice in his face. Game tomorrow? I had been so caught up with Mama's Restaurant and Trevor's love life and trying to win back Jessica that I had forgotten about the game. I wasn't ready to play an actual football game!

"You'd better finish your toast," my dad said, interrupting my panic. "You need to start carb-loading. Also drink lots of water. I can't wait to see you play. I bet the whole town is going to be there."

"*Everyone* will be watching you," Penny added, her devious grin widening. "Rishi's made sure of that."

"That's right. You'll be the star," my dad said, missing my sister's attempt to elevate my panic level. She was doing a great job.

"I have your jersey all ready for you," my mom added. "It's folded over there." I looked at the black jersey with the gold numbers. I could feel my heart beating harder.

"Number twenty-eight, just like Curtis Martin," my dad said proudly. Curtis Martin was my dad's all-time favorite New York Jet.

It was all too real. I was going to be on the big stage. Ready to blow it in front of everyone. I grabbed my stomach. "I don't feel so good."

"That's just butterflies. You step on the field tomorrow and all your problems will vanish."

My stomach twisted again. Butterflies? More like giant vultures!

"Can you pass the sausages?" my mom asked my dad.

As the large plate moved in front of me I suddenly remembered last night's dream. I couldn't take it anymore and bolted from the kitchen. The last thing I heard was my dad tell her, "Look at him practice sprinting. That boy is a born football star."

Josh and I walked into school from the bus and I realized that I didn't know which problem to worry about first. Just a couple of days ago I thought my life had taken a turn for the better. Lurking disasters were part of my past, I had told myself. Yeah, right! Now I was so overwhelmed that I walked straight to my locker, making no attempt to talk to Josie about Trevor. I didn't even want to talk to Jessica about me. Girls would have to wait. I was taking some books out when Rishi stuck his head around the open locker door. "You're going to have to take care of the back basement hallway."

I had no idea what he was talking about and didn't care. "Not now, Rishi."

As usual, he ignored me and went right on talking. "I've already covered the front of the building, the gym, and two stairwells, not to mention half the telephone poles in town."

He thrust a roll of masking tape and some flyers into my hands. I glanced at the papers. EAT AT MAMA'S—HOME OF THE WORLD'S BEST BORSCHT PARMESAN.

"World's best?"

"Rodney, don't get bogged down by the details. We're building excitement."

"What's borscht anyway?" I asked, looking at a gross picture.

"I don't know. I Googled it last night. It's something made with beets."

Josh had joined us. "I can beats things up," he shouted, denting the locker with a punch.

Rishi turned to him. "I read another interesting fact about beets last night. One that you might appreciate."

Josh cocked his head.

"Apparently, if you eat enough beets, your poop turns red."

It was a rare moment when Josh grasped a concept immediately. "Red poop!" he yelled. He clapped his hands together and laughed and laughed. Eventually he gained control of himself and, turning around, noticed a group of girls walking our way. "Guess what I learned?" he asked them.

The five stopped and stared. "What?" one asked.

Josh proudly announced his new fact. Four of the girls let out a simultaneous "Ewwwwwwww!" and hurriedly walked on, but one lingered. It was Wendy Whizowitz. I didn't know her too well but I knew she was considered to be the smartest girl in Garrettsville Middle School. She was also the tallest . . . just about the same height as Josh.

"Interesting," she observed, before asking, "Did you

read my paper on cow chips and their impact on home-steaders, or do you just find the large intestine fascinating like me?"

Josh managed a nod. I caught an elbow from Rishi.

"Yes," Wendy continued, "as I suspected. Of course, it's really an interesting point you bring up. If a beet can have that kind of effect on the digestive tract, are there other underlying benefits in the process? Maybe we could do an experiment. We could create a colon health breakthrough and publish our findings. Would you like to be my coauthor?"

Josh managed another nod.

"Nice. I'm Wendy Whizowitz. I know you're Josh Dumbrowski. I'll be at your game tomorrow. I was going to spend the day reading *Moby-Dick* again—"

"Hahaha," Josh interrupted.

"You find Herman Melville humorous too? So many people miss the subtle comedy in his prose. Want to walk me to my first class? We can talk beets and nineteenth century lit."

Josh shot Rishi and me a puzzled look before heading off with her. Rishi smiled. "Maybe Wendy's got a friend for you, too, Rodney."

"Yeah, that's just what I need." I looked at the flyers in my hand. "Listen, Rishi, I've got too much going on right now. I can't get involved with this restaurant thing."

"Hey, I know you're busy. Big day tomorrow and all that." For once he sounded reasonable—which lasted for about a second. "Don't worry," he continued, "I've got you covered. I already have a reporter from the *Akron Beacon Journal* assigned to do a write-up on the game. I sent him several photos of you to use in the spread."

"Photos? What photos?"

"Who's the best cameraman you know? Hey, I also sent him one that your mom showed me from Camp Wy-Mee. You know, the one of you in a dress."

"What?" I wanted to strangle him.

"We need to emphasize your playful side. You can come across very serious sometimes."

"Rishi," I began to growl.

"See? You're doing it now. Anyway, you made a deal to work for the Boss. After history class you pass the back basement hallway on the way to music. Just hang three of them down there. Make sure they're eye level. Do you like the graphic? I had trouble finding a good picture of borscht."

I glanced again. "It looks like a bucket of vomit. How's that going to build excitement? It's more likely to scare people away."

Rishi frowned. "I'm not an artist. It's all we got. Anyway, can you hang them?"

"Okay," I finally agreed. "I'll see you at lunch."

Rishi smiled. "Let's hope they're not serving beets."

After history class, my head hurt as I pondered the list of horrors facing me. For about the hundredth time in my life I thought about running away to some far-away place, only I knew that the first person I'd meet in Faraway Land would either be the town thug or some local evil mastermind. At least here in Garrettsville my enemies were familiar and after a year in Ohio I was learning the good places to hide out. In fact, this quiet back basement hallway seemed like an ideal location.

I hung the first flyer above a clogged, dirty water fountain. I figured that anyone who'd drink from it might actually enjoy Mama's disgusting food. I moved along, sticking up another flyer about twenty feet down the hall. I was putting up the third flyer when I noticed some boy pull down the first one. "Hey!" I yelled.

He turned toward me and I immediately felt bad I had shouted at him. It was a quiet kid I'd noticed a few times around school. He was always drawing in a notebook and wore the same hooded sweatshirt every day. The first time I saw him he was sitting on the floor outside my history class leaning back against the lockers. I remember he glanced my way and I thought there was something sad about him. I had tried to say hello but he had quickly shifted his attention back to whatever he was drawing.

Now, in the basement, he stared at me for a moment before backing away, the flyer still in his hand. I decided not to say anything. Besides, maybe he enjoyed Russian-Italian food!

I continued down the hall, still thinking about the quiet kid. Just yesterday I had seen him getting teased by some students in Mr. Scab's class. I was glad I hadn't said anything mean just now. Anyway, it wasn't his fault I was having a bad day.

And with that thought my day got a whole lot worse.

"Hanging out with the rats in the basement, Rat-bone?"

I looked up. It was my old enemy, Toby. I hadn't seen him coming down the stairs at the end of the hall. "Land in any bushes lately?" I asked.

He gave me a big smile. "That's right, keep joking. I've been waiting a long time for my revenge and the wait will soon be over. *Real* soon." He chuckled.

I realized with horror that he actually looked happy, like a child about to open a birthday present. I had never seen him like this. Usually he just frowned. He turned and practically skipped into the basement gloom.

All through music class his words echoed in my head. On one hand, I doubted he would do anything. His brother Trevor was depending on me for dating advice and Josh and I were best buddies now. On the other hand, I knew Toby too well. He was the mastermind behind all my problems last year with Josh. Even worse, over the past few days I had noticed him hanging out with some pretty tough-looking kids. Was he about to set them loose on me? Had he talked his brother into crushing me on the football field tomorrow in front of all Garrettsville?

At lunch I sat down with Rishi and Slim but the

image of a mysteriously happy Toby had ruined my appetite. I pushed my tray of greasy nachos in front of Slim. "Go ahead, you can have them."

"Thanks!" he said, smiling, ready to attack the cheese-covered mush.

"Did you hang the flyers in the back hallway?" Rishi asked me.

Before I could respond I saw the kid with the gray sweatshirt slowly walking up to us. He always ate alone, so I was surprised to see him approaching our table. Was he actually going to say something? Maybe apologize for taking the flyer down? When he reached me he removed a piece of paper from his notebook and placed it on the table. It was the flyer, only he had sketched a perfect drawing on it of what I guessed was borscht parmesan. The drawing was in full color and looked as good as any painting I had seen in a museum back in New York City. You could even see steam rising from the food! It looked so good that it actually made me hungry. Slim whimpered as I took back my nachos.

Rishi, looking over my shoulder, shouted, "This is brilliant. Great job, Rodney, enlisting an artist to help us market the restaurant. I should have thought of it myself! Are you going to introduce me?"

"Uhh . . ." I faced the kid in the sweatshirt. "Hi, I'm Rodney. This is Rishi. My pouting friend over there is Slim." Slim gave a little wave.

The kid looked scared but eventually managed a quiet, "I'm Pablo."

"Pablo, I like that name. I like your work even more." Rishi grabbed Pablo's hand and started shaking it. "Come, sit with us. You drew that picture just this morning?"

Pablo nodded. "It took about ten minutes."

"Ten minutes! Did you hear that, Rodney?"

I nodded. I smiled. I noticed a slight smile begin to form on Pablo's face.

Rishi said, "Pablo, do you think you could do some more food drawings for me?"

The next thing I knew, Rishi and Pablo were deep in conversation. It was hard to catch everything they were talking about, especially since Pablo spoke so quietly, but I did hear him say something about converting the image to a digital file and I could tell Rishi really liked that.

"Pablo," Rishi said, grinning, putting his hand on the kid's shoulder, "I think this is the beginning of a beautiful friendship." Then he looked around. "Hey, where's the flyer?"

Josh was holding the drawing to his face and sniffing it. In all the excitement I hadn't seen him walk over to us. "What are you doing?" I asked.

He didn't answer. Instead he stuck his tongue out and started licking the picture. A stream of drool fell from his mouth to the floor.

"You'll have to pardon our friend . . . ," Rishi started to tell Pablo, but it was too late. The sight of a drooling giant towering over the table was too much for him.

"Where'd he go?" Slim asked.

I pointed to a shaking gray hoodie in the corner of the cafeteria.

"Don't worry," Rishi remarked, "I'm sure we'll be seeing quite a bit of Pablo. In fact, Rodney, you'll be seeing him tomorrow."

"Huh? What are you up to, Rishi?"

"I just hired him to sketch your first touchdown! I wonder if the *Akron Beacon Journal* uses freelance artists. . . ."

Slim must have noticed my face turn white as I remembered the game. "Can I?" he asked.

"Take them!" I shouted. With all the vultures flying around my stomach, the last thing I needed was a pile of soggy nachos.

Chapter 7

MY FIRST BIG GAME

My dad was right about the whole town coming down. The stands were packed. Half the crowd wore black for Garrettsville, the other half blue for Streetsboro. Black and blue. Not a promising sign. My stomach tightened and I glanced at the four porta-potties behind the end zone. Hopefully I wouldn't have to make any sudden visits.

I decided to turn my mind to more pleasant thoughts and tried to pick out a familiar face or two in the stands. The first one I spotted was the Boss. Not so pleasant. He was flanked by Cheese and Willy. All three wore dark sunglasses and mean expressions. The seats around them were empty, as if everyone felt their menacing presence.

Everyone except one kid. I watched as Rishi walked right up to the three toughest guys in the bleachers with a big smile on his face. He blabbed to the Boss for a couple of minutes and showed him something on his iPad. The Boss removed his sunglasses, stared at what Rishi was showing him, and eventually nodded approval. Rishi immediately took out his phone and was about to sit down when Willy gestured for him to beat it.

I figured I had about another minute before the game started so I scanned the crowd one last time. I spotted my parents and Penny. My mom waved. My dad looked proud. Penny stuck out her tongue. To their left I noticed Kayla and Jessica. Kayla saw me and also stuck out her tongue. This was getting ridiculous. At least Jessica made a little smile before flipping her blond hair and staring off. Two rows in back of them sat my former principal, Mr. Feebletop. He wore a New York Mets hat and gave me a big thumbs-up. I also noticed that Wendy Whizowitz had come out to support Josh, which was nice, except her head was buried in a book. Dave, Slim, and Greg sat nearby. Below all of them, under the bleachers where no one could spot him, sat Pablo. I gave him a little wave and was happy to see a hand pop out of his gray sweatshirt and wave back. In fact, seeing him and my other friends and my family gave me a feeling of relief.

Until Coach Laimbardi approached from the sideline and I remembered I was about to play my first big game in front of everyone I knew.

"Good to see you boys so excited," he said. He was either joking or blind because the team was staring at the ground in silence. He continued, "I've been waiting for a day like this for several years. Who else is ready to go win a football game?"

Hector coughed, AJ whimpered, and Joe dejectedly kicked his cleat, trying to dislodge some caked mud.

"That's the spirit!" Laimbardi continued. I began to realize he was serious. He took a step closer to us and stared into our eyes. "You know our game plan, right? The one that almost guarantees victory?"

A no-lose game plan? That sounded promising.

"Just hand the ball to Rathbone and get out of his way!"

Just hand the ball to Rath . . . What?

"Go get 'em, Rodney!" Coach Laimbardi shouted. "Hands in! G-Men on three. One-two-three!"

I caught myself glancing back at the porta-potties as a barely audible "G-Men" wafted into the fall Ohio air.

There's nothing like starting a game with an exciting, memorable play. Ours saw Hector toss the football back to me, as we had planned. It floated in the air for just a second but to me it seemed to hover there for ages.

I had heard that the game slows down for great athletes and they have time to do extraordinary things while the average player sees the game quickly and barely has time to react. And here it was, slowing down for me. But instead of calculating some brilliant play, all I could think about was everyone watching me. The thought sent a nervous shudder through my body—and my fingertips—just as the football arrived. Still in slow motion I watched it slip from my hands.

"Fumble!" I heard a defender scream.

I gasped and tried to dive after it but my knees turned to Jell-O and I fell to the grass. The only other person nearby was Josh. "Get the ball!" I hollered. Amazingly, he reacted quickly and picked it up. "Run!" I yelled. He took a couple of steps but the Streetsboro defenders had broken through the line. The first tackler ran full speed into him. It was a jarring blow. I watched the Streetsboro kid go flying backward and land hard on the packed dirt. Josh, on the other hand, had barely moved. Unfortunately for Streetsboro, the hit had clearly left him angry.

"Run!" I yelled again, only this time it was a warning to the other team.

Ignoring me, the next tackler, a big, tough-looking linebacker, dove at the enraged grizzly bear in their midst. Josh caught him in midair and body-slammed him to the ground. Seeing this, the rest of the Streetsboro team stopped dead in their tracks. Their coach screamed them on but Josh looked so ferocious they refused to go near him.

At this point, Josh could have walked the length of the field and strolled into the end zone for a touchdown. Instead, his crazy temper made him hurl the ball at the closest Streetsboro player. It bounced off the kid's backside and rolled toward me. I gulped. A chance to redeem myself! I picked it up and darted forward, managing to cross the line of scrimmage before the defense attacked and tripped me up. I'd gained about five yards.

Some people in the stands cheered, but most just looked confused. The Streetsboro coached hollered at the refs and called time-out. We shuffled over toward our sideline. Josh was still breathing hard but starting to calm down. I was unsure of what to expect from Coach Laimbardi. Yeah, I had gained a couple of yards, but I had also fumbled.

I needn't have worried. "Now *that's* how you play football," Laimbardi said, grinning. "I like the way you two think. Being unpredictable is a gift. Look how rattled you got Coach Laundry and his players. Keep it up." He called over to Trevor, "I hope you're taking notes."

I thought I saw a puff of steam shoot out from the ear holes of Trevor's helmet.

"Did I get a home run?" Josh asked.

"Ha ha! Good one," Coach answered. "You two crack me up. What a duo!" As he walked away I heard him say something about Mack and Byner.

I was surprised by how quickly halftime rolled around. Streetsboro had scored a second-quarter field goal and the score was 3–0. Before heading to the locker room for the break I was joined by a couple of my friends on the field. Rishi seemed oddly nervous.

"You're holding back, right?" he asked. "Saving

everything for the second half, right? I get it."

I was about to ask why he cared so much when my parents and Penny came up to us. "Rishi," my mom asked, "who are those three men you were talking to in the stands?"

"What men?" he lied.

"*Those* men," my mom answered, pointing right at the Boss, "and why are they wearing pinstripe suits at a football game?"

Before he could answer, the marching band started heading our way. "I've got to go join the team," I said. "Enjoy the game. See you all later."

As it turned out, however, there wasn't much to enjoy. The second half dragged and dragged. Late into the fourth quarter we still trailed by three. With every passing second I felt more desperate to win. I felt full of energy. I had stayed right behind Josh for most of the game and avoided getting smashed to pieces . . . except for one hard hit that left my ears ringing. But now wasn't the time to worry about injuries. Now was the time for a hero! For the first time, I knew I could do it.

We had the ball and were down to our final play. We lined up. This was it. My nerves were on overload. Hector snapped and flipped the ball to me. Luckily the defense seemed unusually slow to react and I bolted through the line without being touched. I couldn't believe I was in the open field! Seeing the end zone ahead, I ratcheted up the speed. Only the Streetsboro safety could stop me now but instead of running me down, he just watched me run by. Evidently he and the whole team were in awe of my blazing speed. I was going in for the touchdown. I really *was* hero material. Why had I ever doubted myself? As I crossed into the gold-painted end zone I knew that Jessica was somewhere in the stands watching me save the game for Garrettsville. Just like all my favorite players, I spiked the ball and turned, ready to soak in the cheers of the adoring crowd.

I was met by silence. It was oddly terrifying. My first thought was that I was in some bizarre dream. Finally the crowd erupted—into screeching laughter. All I saw were fingers pointing at me. I quickly checked to see if my pants were still on.

The line judge walked over and picked up the ball I had spiked. "That was some run, son," he said. "Too bad the other team called time-out just before the play got off."

I hadn't heard the call because of the dumb ringing in my ears! Feeling like a fool, I walked back to the huddle through the howling Streetsboro defense.

"Classic Rathbone!" Trevor called from the side.

The game ended a few minutes later. Streetsboro held on for the 3–0 win.

I avoided looking into the crowd. I didn't want to see any more smiling, laughing faces. At least I'd given them something to enjoy. Trailing Coach Laimbardi, we shuffled back to the locker room. Losing the game was bad enough, but playing the role of town bonehead . . . well, I felt pretty low.

The rest of the team and I sat down on the wooden benches with our helmets resting by our feet. I wasn't looking forward to the speech I knew was coming. Was he going to yell at us? At me? I kept my eyes fixed on a pattern in the blue linoleum tile floor. Coach Laimbardi walked into the middle of the locker room.

"Boys, that was spectacular!" he cheered.

Huh?

"Coach Manuel, when was the last time we lost by only three?"

"Five years ago."

Coach Laimbardi blotted his eyes. "You boys have made me very happy today. Well done! A three-point loss. I think I'll be heading out with Mrs. Laimbardi and treating myself to the surf and turf tonight. I'll see you Monday. Game ball goes to Rathbone! Enjoy the rest of your weekend!"

We changed back into our street clothes. Coach's speech had an uplifting effect, and while I had to deal with the typical "Nice run, Rodney!" comments, I recognized that it was okay to laugh at myself. In the end, the whole team was cracking up about the famous "Time-out Touchdown." I joked around with everyone as they filed out of the locker room and was actually starting to feel pretty good when one word sent a shiver down my spine.

"Scram!"

It was the unmistakable voice of Cheese and it was directed to the few kids still left talking to me. I turned around to face him. Cheese was well over six feet tall and looked about as wide as our entire offensive line. The remaining teammates took one look at the oversize visitor and bolted. Cheese called out, "Da coast is clear."

The Boss and Willy walked in. Followed by Rishi! Satisfied that no one else was in the locker room, the Boss stared down at me and shook his head. Something told me the words "Better luck next time" weren't about to spring from his lips. He got right to the point.

"Your friend here"—he motioned at Rishi—"ain't doing you no favors."

Rishi spoke up excitedly. "I still say it will put you on the map."

"It'll put me in the poorhouse!" the Boss shouted. "I'll go broke."

I was completely confused. "Can somebody please tell me what's going on?"

"Sure," the Boss growled, "I'll tell yuh. This little joker is about to cost me a boatload of money. He talked me into the dumbest thing I ever did. He said I should run a full-page ad for Mama's in tomorrow's daily paper. We sent it out right before da game."

"What's so dumb about that?" I asked.

He was ready to explode. "What's so *dumb*? The ad

promises that once we open, Mama's gotta give away a whole day of free food for each G-Men loss between tomorrow and the grand opening. That's still weeks away! I'll go out of business before we even get going."

"Why did you agree to THAT?" I shouted, suddenly realizing that Rishi had just upped the pressure in my life by about a million percent.

The Boss looked just as panicked. "I *agreed* to this cockamamie plan—"

"Cockamamie!" Cheese interrupted. "Dat's a funny word."

The Boss snapped his finger. Willy ran over and smacked Cheese on the head.

"Ow!"

The Boss continued, "I agreed to this cocka . . . this *crazy* plan because your dopey friend told me it was a lock! He said you's was the best football player in America or something."

The two of us turned and faced Rishi. My "friend" was pacing in the corner of the locker room talking on his phone. After a minute he hung up and walked over to us. "I've got good news and bad news."

"What's the bad news?" I asked, wondering whether I'd ever see my family again.

"The paper's already gone to press for tomorrow. The ad is running. There's nothing we can do to stop it."

We all looked at each other. "Yeah?" the Boss finally asked. "So what's the good news?"

Rishi smiled proudly. "I was able to get us great placement. We're on the back cover. Everyone from here to Cleveland will see it tomorrow, Mr. Boss."

Without warning, the Boss kicked the lockers so hard that Cheese and Willy jumped as high as Rishi and me. "Don't call me Mr. Boss!" he yelled at Rishi. Then he glared in my direction. "You better make sure dat team of yours don't lose no more games."

"But the G-Men haven't won in like a hundred years!" I tried to explain.

"Then go out and hire a hundred coaches. I don't care if you gotta drop out of school and train the team round the clock. No more losses, ya got it? And you," he shouted, returning his anger to Rishi, "you'd better make me lots of money with all your marketing stuff."

"Don't worry, Mr. Boss."

Willy and Cheese cringed. I wanted to jump in a locker and hide. The Boss stared down at Rishi and took a deep breath. Finally he just shook his head. "Let's go, boys."

The three of them left. Rishi stood smiling at me. "Wow."

"Wow?" I fought off an urge to strangle him. "What were you thinking with that ad?"

Still smiling, he put his hands up. "Rodney, relax. You're talking to Rishi, remember? Have I ever put you in a bad spot?"

My face felt funny and I wondered if I was developing

78

a twitch like my old teacher, Mrs. Lutzkraut. Rishi continued, "Don't let the Boss's temper get you worked up. We're right where we want to be."

"I want to be home—safe, sound, and watching TV."

"Come on, I know you're enjoying this as much as me. Besides, you'll be famous after tomorrow."

"Listen, Rishi, I . . ." Suddenly my face definitely began to twitch. "Famous? Rishi, what did you do . . . ?"

"Well the ad needed a picture to go along with the part about the G-Men, so I kind of used a photo of you."

My heart stopped. "Not the one from camp of me in a dress!"

Rishi laughed. "No, a good one I took of you at practice. Boy, Rodney, you have to learn to trust me."

Trust Rishi? I couldn't think of anything scarier if I tried.

Chapter 8

GARRETTSVILLE IDOL

"Rodney, get up!" my dad yelled, pushing open my door. "It's a wonderful morning!"

"Huh?" I yawned.

"Hurry! Get dressed and come down to breakfast."

I hadn't seen him this excited since he found out Garrettsville had a Dairy Queen. "What's the rush?" I asked.

"Rush?" he echoed back. "I've been waiting all morning for you to get up."

I was about to ask why but he was gone in a flash. I pulled on my jeans and a T-shirt and shuffled down the stairs. Penny pushed her way past me going up the stairs. She looked glum.

"Rodney, Rodney, Rodney. It's all I hear." She turned at the top of the stairs. "We both know this popularity stuff isn't going to last."

She seemed even more annoyed at me than usual. What

had set her off? I rounded into the kitchen and found the answer. My mom and dad were staring at a newspaper on the kitchen table. "Isn't this exciting?" my mom gushed without taking her eyes from the paper.

"Isn't what exciting?" I started to ask but my dad interrupted me.

"Put on some shoes. We've got to head down to the newsstand before they're all gone!"

"Before *what's* all gone?"

"This!"

He held up the back page of the newspaper. A familiar-looking kid in a black-and-gold football uniform stared back at me. I took a step closer and saw there was a reason the kid's face looked familiar. It was *me*! Taking up almost the whole page! In the picture I held my helmet in the crook of my arm. Several of my teammates were small and out of focus in the background but I was as large and sharp as could be. My hair was wet with sweat and I was staring off, looking serious and confident. Storm clouds hung dramatically low over the horizon. I definitely looked the part of football hero . . . I'd give Rishi that.

My mom was smiling proudly. "You look so handsome and grown up. And look, the caption says, 'Rodney Rathbone, G-Men Football Star.' I want to mail a copy to Aunt Evelyn. Go with your dad and get some more. Hurry!"

Sunday mornings are usually a quiet time at my house

but today everyone was telling me to hurry. I ran down the driveway after my father. He was almost pulling away as I jumped in. "Be sure to get plenty of copies!" my mom called after us.

As my dad and I drove downtown I kept thinking about the full-page ad in my hands. What would this mean for me? Yes, it was pretty cool to see myself occupying the back page of the newspaper, but what would happen in school? What would the rest of the team think of me being singled out? I knew that Trevor wouldn't appreciate it. Just last night I had come to the conclusion that I needed Trevor more than ever if we were going to win the next few games.

Win the next few games. I was so caught up in the picture of me that I had forgotten about the Boss. My stomach tightened into a knot. For the first time I let my eyes drift down to the writing below the photo:

WE GUARANTEE THAT G-MEN FOOTBALL WINS EVERY GAME BETWEEN NOW AND THE GRAND OPENING . . . OR DINNER'S ON US!

It was signed, THE GANG AT MAMA'S RESTAURANT.

I gulped as my dad pulled into a spot. He was in a rush to get out of the car but I lingered, thinking that my sister had been right earlier. Thanks to Rishi's dumb ad, everything would be coming to an end real soon for me.

Unless, of course, no one paid attention to it! A wave of relief suddenly washed over me. How silly I had been.

The rest of Garrettsville probably wouldn't even notice the ad.

"There he is!" someone screamed. "It's Rodney Rathbone!"

"I saw him first," another voice chimed in. They were all holding newspapers.

My dad stood outside the car and held up his hands to the gathering crowd. "People, people, calm down. There's plenty of Rodney for everyone."

What? As I slid down in the seat I heard him continue, "I just spoke to Rodney's agent this morning and there will be a formal autograph session this afternoon. In the meantime, the father of the football star would be very happy to sign your newspapers!"

His smile stretched from ear to ear. At least one Rathbone was enjoying himself.

Any hopes that the advertisement would go unnoticed in school the next day were dashed before I even had a chance to walk through the front doors. Standing on the steps, quite near where my horrible, hated football career had begun, I was met by Rishi handing out newspapers to a throng of students.

I was about to yell at him when my worries were replaced by an unexpectedly pleasant surprise. Fifteen or so girls stood clearly waiting for me. "I like your picture, Rodney," said one girl who I didn't even know. I think she was blushing. My pulse quickened. My mom had said

I looked handsome, but moms always say that.

"Errr, thanks," I replied.

"Can you sign mine?" asked another girl.

I liked the attention, but then I saw Jessica among the group and my knees buckled. A number of hands helped prop me back up. I regained my composure as our eyes met. My face got hot and I smiled at her.

Kayla stepped between us. My smile sagged. "Don't think some fancy camera work and media attention is going to get you anywhere," she scolded. "We know what you're all about. Don't we, Jessica. Jessica?"

Jessica stepped around her and returned my smile. "I don't want to be late for class. We'll be at your next game, Rodney."

What? Really? Wow! I love football! I felt dizzy. The day was actually turning out really good.

For some of us. Kayla, on the other hand, stamped her foot and I noticed her face redden. She turned to follow Jessica but Rishi sprang up in her way. "So you think my camera work is fancy?"

"Grrrrrrgghhhhhhhh!" She roughly pushed past him.

"Yup, she likes me," he said to me. "Maybe I'll ask her out to Mama's. With all the great PR work I've done for him, I bet the Boss would let us eat for free."

"For free?" I shouted. "You and everyone else in Ohio will be eating for free! There's no way the G-Men can win a football game, and besides, what 'great PR'? He hates both of us right now. Remember that little meeting in the locker room on Saturday?"

"Rodney, he's just excitable. Everything's going perfectly."

"Perfectly?"

"Yeah, perfectly. He just offered us another twenty dollars each to put up more flyers around town. Where else can we make that kind of money?"

I had to admit he had a point, but there was a problem. I knew my mom and dad wouldn't want me hanging around someone like the Boss, and they definitely wouldn't want me taking money from him. I had decided not to tell them . . . for now.

Suddenly Rishi uttered words I never thought I'd hear leave his mouth. "Anyway, Rodney, money isn't everything." I realized he wasn't joking when he added, "Just look around you."

I did. Everyone was happy and smiling. A couple of students were still waiting patiently for my autograph. Maybe Rishi was right. Maybe he *did* know what he was doing.

"And don't forget," he added, "I'm the one doing the heavy lifting around here. You have it easy. I even let you skip yesterday's autograph session. All *you* have to do is win a few football games. Now, which way did Kayla go?"

I didn't notice. For a split second I had locked eyes with Trevor—the one person who had me worried. And judging from the look on his face I had every reason to be concerned. "Talk to you later, Rishi," I said. If he replied I didn't hear him. I had to take care of something important.

Trevor never walked straight to class in the morning. He would visit his office first, otherwise known as the second-floor bathroom. Today was no different. I followed him up there and watched the door close behind him with a heavy thud.

I'd never been in the second-floor bathroom. Of all the bathrooms in the school, this one had the toughest reputation. I'd heard tales whispered on the bus of the things that had gone down in there over the years. Horrible stories. Stories that convinced me to make the nurse's bathroom my toilet of choice.

But Trevor was in there and I figured Trevor, our best football player, was the one guy who had a slight chance of saving me from the Boss. I hesitated before going in. What if he picked a fight because of all the attention I was getting? After a few minutes I decided it was a chance I'd have to take. I gulped, said a prayer, pushed open the door—and was immediately struck in the face.

Only not by Trevor's fist. It was worse. Perhaps the most awful smell I'd ever inhaled choked me and made my eyes water. Trevor, who was washing his hands, saw me in the mirror. "Like that, Rathbone?" he laughed. "Onion rings. I love 'em, but whooooooo-eeee!"

I pulled my shirt up over my nose. "Good game yesterday. The defense played great."

"What?" Trevor asked. "I can't hear you through your shirt."

It was clearly a trick. Without lowering my shirt I repeated what I had said. This time he just shrugged and added more soap to his hands. "I didn't see *myself* in the paper after the game," he finally answered. "I saw this other guy. Then I saw all these girls lined up to see this other guy. And then, then I got mad, but I remembered what the school psychologist is always telling me, so I didn't punch the other guy. Plus there were some teachers walking around. I figured maybe one day I'd get this other guy alone. And look—what do you know? The other guy is standing right in front of me."

"Where?" I almost shouted, but Trevor didn't look like he would appreciate that. He had finished washing his hands and was now drying them by making fists. I considered bolting. Then I remembered a trick I had used on bullies in the past. Sometimes the smartest thing is to just pretend you didn't hear their threats. "I think we're playing Mantua next week," I said, lowering my shirt from my nose. "Think we can win?"

"Rathbone, we never win."

"But maybe we could start winning." Wow, my trick had worked. Just for good measure I threw in a compliment. "You're our best player, Trevor. You could really get the team going."

"I'm quitting."

The shock made me inhale sharply. After spluttering

and wiping my watering eyes, I managed, "What? You can't quit. You're too good." What I wanted to say was, "You can't quit or the Boss will make Beet Parmesan out of me!"

"Rodney, I played football to impress the girls. Josie won't even speak to me. My heart's not into playing anymore. You know how it is . . ." He looked more depressed than fearsome. "I'm done with football," he continued. "You even said you'd get me a date. How's that going? Not too good, I bet."

This was horrible. Every time I mentioned Trevor to Josie she'd go, "Ewww, he's gross," and start in about the demolition derby date. There was no way I could get her to go out with him.

Trevor stared at himself in the mirror for a few long seconds. Then he turned to me and took a step closer. The mean, scary look was back in his eyes. "Yeah, Rathbone, there's not much point to playing anymore, is there? Looks like there's only one thing left to make me happy." He cracked his knuckles and stepped closer still.

I'm not sure if it was the threat of Trevor's fist or picturing Cheese lurking outside my bedroom window but my mouth took over. "Trevor, guess what I came in here to tell you?"

He paused.

My mouth continued, "I got you a date with Josie next Saturday night."

"Rodney, that's the best thing anyone's ever told me.

I owe you! I'll do you any favor." He grabbed my hand and started pumping it up and down. Good thing I'd seen him wash so thoroughly.

"Any favor?" I repeated. "Just try to win next week. Josie said she'd love to see the G-Men win at least one time while she's head cheerleader."

"Don't worry about me. I'm going to make sure we win. Hey, you're not lying to me now, are you?" His grip tightened.

"I never lie," I lied. "No, Josie said she couldn't wait."

His hand released mine and he actually tousled my hair. "Rodney, you're the best." He turned back to the mirror. "Do you think I need a haircut?" He smiled at himself then made his hand look like a gun and fired it at his reflection. "You know what? It doesn't matter. I look good either way. See you at practice, Rathbone."

He walked out. As the door clicked shut, reality kicked in. What had I just gotten myself into? There was no way Josie was going out with Trevor on Saturday.

My life was beginning to stink worse than this bathroom!

That afternoon I sat staring out my bedroom window. How was I going to set up a date between Josie and Trevor? I kept trying to come up with a plan but it was no good . . . I was drawing a blank. I knew deep down that this problem was way beyond anything my brain could figure out. It called for someone so shrewd, so devious, so manipulative that even the C.I.A. would fear him.

"Rishi," I said into the phone, "I need your help."

"That's what I'm here for. What can I do? Contact the papers for interviews? Speak to the Boss about expanding our role?"

"No, not that. Just listen for a second. I have to get a date with Josie next Sat—"

"Holy smokes! Josie? The cheerleader? I thought you still liked Jessica . . ."

"Rishi, I—"

"Oh, I get it, you're trying to make Jessica jealous. Sneaky, Rodney, sneaky, but I like it. I could make a video of the date and e-mail it to her."

"Rishi, you're not listening to—"

"I'll get the Boss to hold a private dinner for the two of you. Lots of candles. You should order Josie strawberries. No, lobster. Hmmm, I got it—chocolate-dipped strawberries! No, chocolate-dipped lobster."

"Rishi!" I snapped. "I don't want to go on the date with her. I'm talking about Trevor."

There was a pause. "You want to go on a date with Trevor?"

"No!" I tried again. "I want *Josie* to go on a date with Trevor."

"Why would you possibly want that?" Poor Rishi was having a hard time following me. Finally he just said, "If you're looking to hook someone up on a date, I can think of a guy with dark flowing hair, skin the color of the most delicious caramel, a legendary personality . . ."

"Listen, I kind of promised I'd help Trevor, that's all. He was real upset about Josie. Plus it will make him play better. Remember, we need to start winning football games."

"But you're the star player!"

"Rishi, you're beginning to believe your own publicity."

"That's true. See how good I am?"

"Anyway, football isn't tennis. It's a team sport and I need Trevor to get the defense going."

"Okay, I get it. Do you still like my idea of holding the date at Mama's Restaurant?"

"Yes, that's great. I knew I could count on you to get this going."

"All right, Rodney. I'll call the Boss right now. Besides, I want to check with him to see if he has more work for us."

"Has he paid you yet for all the flyers we hung?"

"Well, not yet, but I know he's good for it. Anyway, like I was saying, by the time I get through with that place, Mama's will be the most romantic spot east of the Mississippi. Talk to you later!"

Rishi was a good help but I was still in trouble. I had a place for a date but no way to get Josie interested in Trevor. None of my other friends would have a clue of what to do.

I glanced up at the bulletin board above my desk. I'd hung pictures there from my summer at Camp Wy-Mee. It was only about a month ago but it seemed a world away. There was a picture of Mr. Periwinkle and me sitting under his favorite beech tree. Next to it was a picture of our cabin, Loserville. I was standing in the middle surrounded by all my friends. As I looked at their faces I felt a little sad. I wondered if there was such a thing as campsickness. Besides Josh and me, Stinky was in the picture. I could see his wet armpit stains. Next to him, Thorin held an aluminum baseball bat high above his head pretending it was a sword named Orcrist. Next to him was my best friend in the bunch, Fernando. He was wearing a silk burgundy robe smirking at the camera. Next to him—

Fernando!!!

I fell out of my chair. Why hadn't I thought of it sooner? Fernando was a world-class expert on romance and girls. He would know what to do about Josie! I pulled open my drawer and rustled through a bunch of papers looking for the Post-it with his number. Right before search-panic set in I found it stuck to a brochure from Camp Wy-Mee.

With sweaty fingers and a racing heart I hit the numbers. If there was anyone who would know what to do it was Fernando. It rang and rang. Eventually the message clicked on. "Hellooo. You've reached the voice mailbox of . . . *Fernando*. I am currently doing something exciting and romantic, but if you'd leave your name, number, and text me a picture, I'll be sure to call you soon. Adios, for now."

Beep. "Fernando, it's Rodney . . ."

I launched into my problem, giving him all the major

details. Five minutes later my phone rang. "Rodney, it was great to hear your voice, and even greater to hear that you are still searching high and low for adventures. You were right to call me. This sounds like a job for Fernando. I will be there Thursday evening."

"Don't you have school in Canton on Friday?" I asked.

"On Friday I will have school in Garrettsville."

"How will you do that? You're not enrolled here."

"Leave that to Fernando. I need time in your school to get the feel. I want to meet this Josie and I'll need to see Trevor. There is work to be done. You just get your parents ready for my visit. I'll be arriving Thursday and leaving Sunday. This will be a weekend to remember. Now, I go!" Click.

I hoped it would be a weekend to remember for all the right reasons. Even so, I trusted Fernando and began to feel better about things. For the first time all day I actually relaxed and stretched out in the chair, letting my eyes wander back to the bulletin board. Next to the camp pictures was a big blank space where last year's calendar had hung. "What the heck," I thought, getting up and grabbing something off the bed. "It's not every day you're a football star."

The picture of me on the back page of the paper took up half the bulletin board, but darn I looked good! In fact, I was so busy admiring myself that I barely noticed Penny burst out laughing when she walked by.

Chapter 9

VISITING DAY

I stared out the classroom window thinking about everything going on in my life, including Fernando's upcoming visit. As I stared, I noticed that the trees beyond the school fence were beginning to turn bright red and orange. I wouldn't have seen that last year locked in Mrs. Lutzkraut's gray class, where the shades were forever drawn. Mrs. Lutzkraut. She was my greatest enemy—worse than the Boss and Trevor combined. Luckily, she was in Shady Pastures and couldn't bother me anymore. I guess after the bulldozer incident at Camp Wy-Mee . . .

"Rodney?" Mr. Witlacker's voice interrupted my thoughts.

"Yes?" I asked my history teacher.

"What's your take on the reading? What do you think of the Trail of Tears?"

Huh? I hadn't heard a word. Trail of Tears? Tears . . .

"Uhh, it was sad?" I managed. I knew I was about to get in trouble for staring out the window.

"Wonderful answer, Rodney! I think sadness summarizes it beautifully. Maybe you can follow up with some specifics about the Cherokee."

Cherokee? I couldn't think of anything. Wait . . . "It's an SUV, made by Jeep, right?" A few kids giggled. Kayla whispered with a nasty smile, "Nice going, genius."

"Excellent, Rodney," Mr. Witlacker nodded.

"Huh?" Kayla blurted. "Jeeps have nothing to do with Native Americans and Andrew Jackson. Rodney wasn't listening! He was staring out the window like a zombie." There were a couple of more giggles.

"Kayla," Mr. Witlacker continued, "I can see how you might have missed it, but I believe Rodney was trying to take our conversation to the next level. The horrible treatment of the Cherokee has weighed heavily on our nation. As a result, we see that an American car company has used their tribal name as a form of social apology. That was your point, right, Rodney?"

"Exactly."

"You see, Kayla?"

I turned to face Kayla. She was shaking in her seat and ready to blow.

Mr. Witlacker smiled at me. "I drive a Cherokee, by the way."

"It's a nice looking truck, sir," I said.

"It's got air-conditioned seats."

"Uhhhggggg," Kayla groaned, snapping her pencil in half.

Boy, Rishi, I thought, *you sure can pick 'em.*

Beep. The classroom phone rang. Mr. Witlacker picked it up. "Hello? Yes, he's here . . . Oh? Okay . . . bye."

Mr. Witlacker looked at me. "Rodney, you're wanted in the principal's office. Bring your things."

Bring my things? That meant I wasn't returning. Some kids in back of me went "Uh-oh" and Kayla added, "Good! You're in trouble. Why don't you drive a Cherokee down to the principal's office . . ."

Mr. Witlacker frowned. "That's enough, Miss Radisson."

Was Kayla right? Was I in trouble? What had gone wrong now? My mind scrolled through all the pos-sibilities. When nothing came up I let myself breathe a sigh of relief.

Had I known what was coming, I would have escaped down my own Trail of Tears and never looked back.

Things didn't start bad. The secretary in the office said, "Hello Rodney, have a seat on the bench. Your mom is picking you up soon for the doctor's appointment."

Oh, so that was it. But what doctor's appointment? Maybe she mentioned it the other night. Must be a checkup. I probably wasn't listening.

As I sat on the bench outside the office, I smiled to myself thinking about all the times last year outside Mr. Feebletop's office. He would have called me in and started talking about the New York Mets. Stepping into his office was like visiting the Baseball Hall of Fame, with signed posters on the walls and everything. I craned my neck around and peered into my current principal's office. The walls were empty. The office was neat and sparse. The desk was almost completely bare. No autographed baseballs. Only a computer, a stapler, a person staring at me, a pen . . . Yikes!

"Can I help you?" It was the first time Dr. Elizabeth Stone had said anything to me. I'd seen her before standing in the hall looking serious. She was just as serious now. Her hair was pulled into a tight bun and her face was as emotionless and blank as her office.

"Um, no. Sorry to be looking in. I was just curious."

Her face didn't move. "You're that Rodney Rathbone I've heard so much about."

"Yes, I am." I puffed up my chest a little. Sometimes my reputation was a good thing.

"I hear you're pretty active in the community."

"I try to get involved." *Why be modest?*

"That impresses some people. Do you know what impresses me?"

"No."

"I appreciate students who follow the rules. Students that work hard and make academics their priority. The stories I hear about you and that restaurant . . ." She paused and straightened the pen on her desk. "The stories tell me you have a lot of other things going on. Perhaps you don't share my priorities."

So much for my reputation. "Well I—"

x

97

"I'm not interested in what you have to say. I'm interested in the decisions you make from this point forward. Now, I need to return to work. Please remove your head from my doorway."

I didn't have much time to ponder Dr. Stone's warm and fuzzy advice before my mom showed up and signed me out. One second I was sitting in class, the next I was driving to a doctor's appointment I didn't even know I had.

We made our way through town and then headed out toward the country. As we drove along I decided to ask my mom about Fernando visiting. I was happy when she said it was okay. She was hesitant at first but seemed glad that I was maintaining a camp friendship. While discussing Fernando, I told a couple of silly stories from camp. Mom told me a few of her own childhood summer stories. They were pretty funny and the ride went by quickly. After a while I just looked out the window at passing cows and farms. "Mom," I finally asked, "what doctor am I going to all the way out here? I don't remember you saying anything about a checkup and I definitely have never been here before."

She smiled but didn't say anything. For a moment I studied her face, watching her round sunglasses reflecting the road.

"Uh, Mom?"

"Rodney, you're really going to enjoy today."

"I'm going to enjoy the doctor's?"

"Rodney, I got a phone call, and let's just say you're going to have a special surprise today."

My heart started beating a little quicker. "You know, Mom, contrary to what you and Dad believe, I don't like surprises."

"Oh, come on, Rodney, everyone likes surprises."

"I never like them, and they never turn out good."

"You didn't like camp?"

"Well, that was different. I wound up liking it, but that was because—"

"Oh, stop your worrying. Look, we're here."

We made a sharp turn through a large iron gate onto a long tree-lined driveway. The sun was shining and the sky was blue, but something felt a bit off as we approached the brick building looming at the end of the drive. My mom pulled to a halt in front of the main doors and a guy in a white shirt approached the car. "Hello, ma'am," he said. "May I take your car?"

"Valet service." My mom smiled. "How nice."

As we got out and the valet drove off I suddenly realized that maybe she was taking me on a surprise restaurant review. Before I had a chance to ask, two guys in uniforms ran out the door. One of them turned to my mom. "Have you seen Johnny?"

"Johnny? You mean the valet?"

The man didn't answer. Instead he shouted into his walkie-talkie, "Johnny's mobile."

The other man said to us, "Don't worry, we'll get your car back."

"He's not the valet?" my mom asked, beginning to sound alarmed

"No, he's a patient. But he's an excellent driver."

Before my mom could say anything the two men sped off in a van, kicking up gravel and leaving us standing in a cloud of dust. "I guess we might as well go in," she suggested after a minute, looking a little uneasy.

"Mom, *what* is going on?" I asked. "Where are we?"

Just then, a guy carrying a clipboard and wearing thick black glasses walked over to us. "What's all the commotion?" he asked. "I'm Dr. Pecans. May I help you?"

My mother stared at him for a minute before asking, "Are you *really* Dr. Pecans?"

"Yes, I am. You must be Gloria Rathbone. We spoke on the phone. And this must be the famous Rodney Rathbone. Please, come upstairs to my office. Oh, and welcome to Shady Pastures."

My mom and I sat in two leather chairs facing Dr. Pecans, who was seated at his desk. To his left was a wall completely covered with books. Behind him was an open window—which I was ready to jump out. My mom and her surprises.

Dr. Pecans looked directly at me when he spoke. "I'm so glad you could make the trip out here on visiting day. I so appreciate it. I think it will make such a positive difference in one of our patients . . ."

I stood up and shouted, "I know who you're talking

about! I also know there's nothing I can do to help her. I'm definitely the last person on earth she'd want to see, and I . . ."

Dr. Pecans raised his palms to me and motioned for me to sit back down. "Rodney, let's just talk for a second. So, you realize that you're here to see Mrs. Lutzkraut." Hearing the name out loud caused me to shudder. "Now Rodney, you are aware that Mrs. Lutzkraut suffered quite a disappointment during the summer."

"Yeah," I said.

"From what I understand, she was about to become a millionaire when some, uh, young person caused a change in her fortunes."

I smiled, remembering how I had ruined her plans to bulldoze Camp Wy-Mee.

"When she transferred here," he continued, "all she could do was mutter *your* name." Dr. Pecans looked at me with an accusing eye. "Over and over, day and night, Rodney, Rodney, Rodney . . ." He trailed off and stared out the window, his lips still mouthing my name. Finally he remembered us sitting there and spun around. "It was awful!" My mom and I jumped. He settled down and took a deep breath. "Anyway, that's all over now. To speak frankly, we recently had an unexpected breakthrough. I believe our dear friend is well enough to return to society."

My mom grabbed my knee. "Isn't that wonderful, Rodney?"

My mouth just kind of hung there and I felt like I needed to visit the bathroom.

Dr. Pecans said, "I can see you're happy to hear it!"

Happy? This guy was clueless. I decided to set him straight. "Mrs. Lutzkraut belongs here," I said. "She's evil, and if you think she's made some great recovery, she's fooling you. Trust me, I know her. And I have no idea why I'm even here. She hates me—"

"Rodney, that's not true," my mom cut in. "She always told me how much she adores you." She turned back to Dr. Pecans. "She may come across as a bit stern, but she's a very dedicated teacher. She even stopped by our house one time when she had some concerns about Rodney's difficulty socializing. Not too many teachers would take the time to do that."

I remembered the visit. "Mom, she was secretly threatening me and plotting my end . . ."

My mom shook her head. "Rodney, the only thing she was plotting was a wonderful summer for you! You loved Camp Wy-Mee. She's done so much for you. Now's your chance to help her in return."

This conversation was going nowhere. I tried one last time. "Mom, I have no problem helping people. I'll help at the soup kitchen. I'll make valentines for veterans. I'll talk to anyone else here. I'll even go for rides with Johnny downstairs. Just don't make me see Mrs. Lutzkraut!"

"Rodney," Dr. Pecans interrupted, "many times we

act most hostile to the people for whom we feel the greatest emotional interest."

Huh? I had no idea what he was talking about.

"If you've had difficulty with her," he continued, "it's most likely because she has such strong feelings for you and wants you to do well."

I remembered Mrs. Lutzkraut laughing and high-fiving Mr. Cramps as my canoe and I barreled toward Breakneck Rapids. "Yeah, Doctor," I said. "You really got her figured out." I looked at his diplomas hanging on the wall and noted which universities to avoid in the future.

Dr. Pecans smiled. "So, you'll help her then?"

"No!"

"Rodney," snapped my mom, "you most certainly *are* going to help Mrs. Lutzkraut. I'm sorry, Dr. Pecans. I can't understand why he's acting like this. I'm very disappointed."

Dr. Pecans reached out and patted his desk in some sort of soothing way. Then he said, "Come. It's time we visit Mrs. Lutzkraut. This will be the final test and the main reason I asked you here, Rodney. If she can see you without returning to her former agitated state, then we will know our work at Shady Pastures is complete."

I looked at Dr. Pecans and my mom and realized there was no way out of it. I was about to visit my greatest enemy.

★ ★ ★

Mrs. Lutzkraut's room was in another building. We went outside and passed by a well-kept garden where a number of people were sitting around on benches. One group of men was playing cards. Two women were busy painting. "I think nature is wonderfully therapeutic," Dr. Pecans droned on. "I always try to get my patients outdoors as much as possible. Unfortunately, we've had a difficult time getting Mrs. Lutzkraut outside on a regular basis. When we *do* get her out, we always bring her to the nicest place on the grounds."

"Where's that?" my mom asked.

"Under that magnificent beech tree over there. Sadly, she usually starts grumbling about someone named Percy."

I almost laughed. Percy Periwinkle was Mrs. Lutzkraut's brother-in-law. He ran Camp Wy-Mee and she hated him and his beech tree as much as she hated me. "It seems like a great spot," I said. "I wouldn't give up on it. She's crazy about beech trees."

Dr. Pecans shot me a look.

"I mean, she likes them a lot."

"Anyway," he continued, "for today we will visit your former teacher in her room. I know this visit will go wonderfully well."

I doubted that . . . which secretly pleased me. I knew as soon as Mrs. Lutzkraut saw me she'd go berserk. Dr. Pecans would have little choice but to write a report that kept her safely locked up for a very long time.

We reached her door. It was partly open and a yellow

light shone out into the hall. Dr. Pecans pushed it slowly. I made sure to stand behind him and my mom. While I wanted my evil enemy to behave poorly, I didn't want to get strangled in the process.

"Helga, I have a special surprise visitor for you," Dr. Pecans called softly.

Suddenly I spotted her. She sat in a chair looking as awful and frightening as usual. She didn't see me because her eyes were closed. I watched the lids flitter and open, magnified by her enormous glasses. They immediately stared intently into mine. For the briefest of moments they flashed their familiar glare of pure evil.

And then it was gone.

Her face broke into an enormous smile. "Why, if it isn't Rodney Rathbone! This is a wondrous surprise. Mrs. Rathbone, so nice to see you, too! Dr. Pecans, you sure know how to make this girl happy. How did you know young Rodney was my favorite of favorites?"

I almost fainted. This couldn't be happening. Mrs. Lutzkraut rose and hugged my mom, who had walked over to her. "So nice of you to come, Gloria. It means so much to me."

"We wouldn't have missed it for the world," my mom said with a teary smile. "Isn't that right, Rodney?"

I stood gaping. My brain was just starting to process Mrs. Lutzkraut's latest plot. She was acting completely normal and doing an excellent job of it. In a flash I realized the sickening truth. She was getting out of here.

"Look at him," Mrs. Lutzkraut said, "he's speechless. Come, give your old teacher a hug." I saw her advancing toward me. My feet wouldn't move. I couldn't escape. It was worse than a nightmare. I felt her big, saggy arms reach around me. I wanted to scream but her embrace buried my face. "Reminds me of the hug you gave me at graduation," she purred. Just as I thought I was going to suffocate, she released me.

"Look, Rodney," my mom called out cheerfully, "isn't that your picture?"

For the first time I noticed the walls. It was my picture, all right! Twenty or thirty pictures of me from the newspaper were plastered all over the room.

"Rodney, isn't that wonderful?" my mom asked.

No, I wanted to shout, *it's amazingly creepy!*

Mrs. Lutzkraut sighed. "Oh, I am so proud of him. Little Rodney, a football star."

Dr. Pecans laughed. "When Helga saw the paper the other day, she insisted we buy every copy in town. That's when we decided to give you a call, Mrs. Rathbone." More quietly he whispered, "That's when we knew she was over her obsession with Rodney."

"I see," my mom said.

You see? All I could see was my face staring back at me and it was absolutely frightening. I looked more closely at the walls. A couple of the faces had red circles around them with red slashes through the middle. Even worse, I noticed others looked like they were full of dart holes.

"Mom, she's been throwing darts at the pictures!" I blurted.

Everyone in the room laughed. Dr. Pecans answered smugly, "What an imagination, Rodney. This is an old building. We have mice."

"Who throw darts?" I asked, but it was no good. Everyone was ignoring me. Once again, Mrs. Lutzkraut had gotten her way.

Eventually, Dr. Pecans said, "Visiting hours will be ending soon. I think this little afternoon get-together was just what the doctor ordered . . . which is why I ordered it. Hahaha."

He laughed at his own dumb joke for at least a minute. Mrs. Lutzkraut wore her best fake smile and said, "That is very funny, Dr. Pecans. By the way, why don't you tell Gloria the joke you told me yesterday about the bird and the hippo? And since I heard it already, it will give me a chance to leave Rodney with one *final* hug. What do you say, Rodney?"

I didn't move, but then my mom nudged me forward.

As Dr. Pecans and my mom yucked it up in the corner of the room, Mrs. Lutzkraut gave me another of her smothering hugs, only this time she whispered into my ear, "Dr. Moron over there will be letting me out very shortly. You and I have a lot of catching up to do." Her embrace grew tighter. "Maybe we can start with a vocabulary lesson. Tell me, Rodney, are you familiar with the word 'revenge'?"

Chapter 10

FERNANDO KNOWS BEST

The ride back from Shady Pastures was quiet, silent, and hushed. Did I mention you could hear a pin drop? I refused to speak, I was so mad at my mom. Besides being mad, I was too busy trying to process this latest shock to my system. Like I didn't have enough problems, I could now add Mrs. Lutzkraut to my ever-expanding list of enemies and rivals out to get me. I shook my head "no" when my mom asked if I wanted to stop for ice cream. It was the closest I came to talking.

Yes, my visit with Mrs. Lutzkraut had left me shaken. For the next day or so I didn't really think about anything else beyond the word "revenge" and what form it might take. Even my sister noticed that something was up. "You're making that crying look again," she said. "I hope your friend from camp doesn't notice. He just pulled up in the driveway."

Fernando! I had forgotten he was arriving tonight.

Of course, it was Thursday already. He was here to help me with yet another problem—stopping Trevor from killing me. I needed a scorecard. I ran downstairs to meet him.

My mom had invited Fernando and his parents onto the back deck. I bolted outside to greet my best friend from camp.

"Rodney, you didn't tell me you had such an enchanting mother." Even at night I could see her blush. Good old Fernando. With a little bow to the adults he added, "And now, if you will pardon us, Rodney and I have much to discuss."

Once back in the house and up in my room, Fernando got right to business. As he explained his ideas for how we could get Josie to go on a date with Trevor, the unlikelihood of success became very apparent. The way I saw it, the only two things getting acquainted Saturday would be Trevor's fists and my face.

The rest of the evening I did my best to enjoy Fernando's visit and avoid thinking about my problems, but when the sun hit my window the next morning, it took all my strength not to stick my head under the covers.

"Good to see you're ready to go," Fernando said from the air mattress on the floor. I couldn't help notice that his hair looked perfectly combed. "Fernando cannot wait for the fun before us."

"Me neither," I managed, my hair sticking straight up like a rooster.

"In that case," Fernando said, smiling, "let the adventure begin!"

As we walked to the bus stop, Fernando remarked, "This Garrettsville seems nice. The fresh smell in the air, the creek running through the town, the big trees . . ."

"Yeah, it's great," I said with little enthusiasm. "Big trees." Each time we passed one I imagined Mrs. Lutzkraut jumping out with a dart in her hand. Or Trevor, or Toby, or Cheese, or The Boss. Pretty soon I might have to make a quick getaway from this lovely town!

Fernando was my only hope, at least as far as Trevor. Unfortunately, his plan seemed far-fetched. "Tell me again," I asked, "how do you plan to go around in school with me today?"

"Just take Fernando to the office when we arrive."

I noticed Rishi waiting for us under his big tree at the bus stop. As we approached I wondered how my two friends would get along.

"Fernando, this is Rishi. Rishi, this is—"

You didn't have to worry about awkward silences with Rishi. "Fernando! Rodney's told me all about you! Hey, I hear you know a lot about girls."

"I know a little," Fernando answered with a grin.

Rishi spoke even quicker than usual, asking, "Hey, should I part my hair down the middle or right here? Should I button my shirt all the way up? I've thought about getting a fancy walking stick. Cool idea, right? Should I memorize some French poetry or something? Is that worth the effort?"

The groan of the school bus reached our ears before it rounded the turn in the road. Fernando put his hand on Rishi's shoulder but looked at me. "Rodney, I like how your friend thinks. Rishi will be with us this weekend?"

"Sure. He's already handling the restaurant part of the plan."

"Good, we have a lot of work to do, and we could use a man like him on the team. Rishi, part your hair along here." He pointed at Rishi's scalp. "I always leave as many buttons open as possible. And I love the walking stick idea. May I borrow that?"

We climbed aboard the bus and headed to the back to grab some seats. Rishi asked, "What about the French poetry?"

Fernando recited a line or two. Several girls simultaneously grabbed their hearts and let out a collective, "Awwwwww."

"This guy is brilliant," Rishi muttered in amazement.

Fernando noticed someone sitting in the back of the bus. "Josh!" he called out.

Josh ran down the aisle and put Fernando in a big bear hug. I was beginning to wonder if Fernando had uttered his last stanza when Josh let him go. After gasping for a second, Fernando smiled and said, "Long time no see."

"Huh? You blind?" Josh asked.

"I missed this guy," Fernando whispered to me.

We took our seats and the bus ride was a lot of fun, but I still didn't expect Fernando to be sticking around long in school. When we got there we headed into the office and Fernando asked to speak to the principal. The secretary, without even bothering to look at us, snapped, "Dr. Stone is too busy."

"Excuse me," Fernando asked, picking up a framed photograph from her desk, "surely this can't be your wedding picture?"

"Yes, it is," the secretary answered. "Taken twenty years ago this December."

"But you look even younger now!" Fernando exclaimed.

The secretary smiled. "Let me see if Dr. Stone can squeeze you in."

A minute later she emerged and told us we could head into the office.

Dr. Stone's hair bun was pulled very tight. Her pale, expressionless face told me immediately that she didn't appreciate our visit. She said, "Rodney Rathbone, twice in one week."

"Um, yes, lucky me. So, Mrs. Stone . . ."

"Dr. Stone."

"Uh, yes. Sorry. Dr. Stone, sorry to interrupt you."

"You wouldn't need to apologize if you didn't interrupt."

"Uh, that's true, but . . ."

"Mr. Rathbone, did you know that I was a teacher for seven years?"

"No, I wasn't aware of that," I said.

"Do you know why I left teaching and became a principal?"

I thought for a second. "Because you could help more children if you ran an entire school instead of a single classroom."

"No. I became a principal because there's far less interaction with students. Now, this has been a nice little talk. Good day, boys."

She glanced down at her paperwork. Dr. Stone had about as much personality as the paperweight sitting before her on the desk. I had tried to explain this to Fernando last night. I expected he'd soon be calling my dad to come pick him up, although he seemed as cool and collected as usual.

"Señorita Rosalita," he suddenly spoke. I almost died.

Dr. Stone's eyes glared up from her paper. "I thought our meeting was over, and I believe I've already made it clear how I am to be addressed."

"I was referring to your nail color," Fernando said.

Dr. Stone opened her mouth to say something but instead looked down at her nails.

"A vibrant, exciting color," Fernando continued.

"No one's ever noticed my nails before." Her stern look softened and I thought I saw a hint of something other than her usual frown. "Who are you again?" she asked.

"I am Fernando. Did you get the orchids?"

Dr. Stone pointed slowly over Fernando's shoulder.

"Dr. Stone, I'm here because I'd like to visit your school for the day."

"Well, Fernando, orchids or no, we can't just let random people—"

"I don't want to be a random person. Rodney here told me all about your school. I read about you on the district website. I knew I had to come meet you. I had to." He paused and grabbed his chest. "You are an inspiration. The ultimate administrator! Surely you should be superintendant of the entire district . . ."

"Oh, go on!" Dr. Stone blushed. She patted her hair bun. "Well, Fernando, I have to admit I'd love to have you in my school, but I don't think *your* school would appreciate—"

"Here is my principal's phone number at Crenshaw Middle School. She's expecting your call."

Dr. Stone looked confused for a second, took another look at Fernando's smiling face, and dialed the number. "Yes, hello. My name's Elizabeth Stone and I'm the principal of Garrettsville Middle School . . . Hi . . . Yes, the reason I'm calling is I have one of your students sitting in my office. . . . Yes, his name is Fern . . . Yes, he certainly is . . . I can see that . . . He did? Hahahaha . . ." Dr. Stone was smiling and giggling and occasionally looking at Fernando. "That's right, he wants to visit for the day. So you're fine with . . . well we'll take good care of him . . . Okay, my pleasure . . . bye bye."

Dr. Stone hung up and gave Fernando a big smile. "I'll have one of the secretaries write up the visitor paperwork. I guess you can follow Rodney's schedule."

"May I take my lunch in here?"

She gave Fernando a knowing eye. "Don't push it."

Fernando gave her a quick bow, grabbed my arm, and led me out of the office. As soon as we were back in the crowded hall I spotted Rishi. Fernando, however, had spotted someone else. "Jessica!" he called.

I watched her blond hair spin in our direction. What was he up to now? He must have remembered what she looked like from that one time at camp. Samantha and Kayla were beside her. Samantha saw Fernando and smiled. Kayla saw me and frowned. They waited for us to approach.

"Have we met?" Jessica asked him.

"I have discussed your beauty under the stars. I have seen your eyes looking out the cabin windows over the lake at sunset . . ."

"Don't talk to him, Jessica. He's obviously nuts," Kayla said.

"Who cares?" Samantha pointed out. "I like listening to him."

I spoke up. "Jessica, Samantha, Kayla, this is Fernando. He's my friend from camp."

"Well, I should have known," snapped Kayla. She poked Fernando in the chest. "I bet you're trouble too."

Rishi slid in and said to Fernando, "Ain't she something?"

Fernando smiled. "She has a sharp, quick tongue. Her eyes are fierce and dark, like a raven." Kayla narrowed her fierce eyes and her cheeks took on an angry red.

"I like the way she blushes," Rishi said to Fernando.

"Yes, I can see that," Fernando replied.

Kayla looked more annoyed than usual. "Hey, you two brainless buddies. I'm standing right here. I can hear you. Hell-ooooo. You don't talk about people in front of them. It's considered rude in most cultures."

"Being rude to you is the last thing I want to be," Rishi replied, trying to sound like Fernando. "Let me redeem myself. I wrote this just for you . . ." He put one hand on his chest and the other in the air. He began, *"J'ai besoin d'utiliser la salle de bains—"*

Kayla interrupted. "Am I living in bizzaro world? Is every boy in this school completely wacko? Rishi, go recite your gibberish to someone else. I'm going to class."

Rishi's performance may not have captivated Kayla, but a few other people stood in the hall looking at him. Among them were Josh and Wendy, who were spending more and more time together. "How'd I sound?" Rishi asked.

Wendy said, "The pronunciation wasn't bad but you just told her you need to use the bathroom. How charming."

Josh stood listening. I could tell by the drool buildup that he was thinking hard. Slowly he grabbed his chest like Rishi and said to Wendy, "I need to go doodie."

Wendy laughed. "I love your wit, Joshy, and you're charming, too." She took his arm and the two walked off. Josh had a happy grin stretched across his face.

Fernando was watching them too, looking like a proud father. "This is a very romantic hallway." Shifting his eyes to me he added, "Now it's your turn."

Jessica was still standing there, her blue eyes looking at me as well. My throat dried up and my back began to sweat. The only French word I knew was "escargot" and I doubted Jessica would appreciate me comparing her to a slimy snail!

She broke the silence. "You two talked about me at camp?"

Fernando replied, "He talked about you all the time. I'm going to have to try out this Tunnel of Love at Super Adventure."

"You talked about *that*?" Jessica asked. Her face flashed red. I couldn't tell if she was mad, embarrassed, or both.

"He also said that you were the nicest, coolest, prettiest girl he'd ever known."

"Well then why did those other girls—"

"Alas, that is my fault," Fernando continued. "He spent so much of his time looking sad and missing you, I tried to get those other girls interested in him, to cheer him up. I can see my actions have had the opposite effect.

Look at him now. Notice the pale color in his face, the dark circles under his eyes, the sagging shoulders, that, 'I've given up on life' haircut, the—"

"I think she gets the point," I interrupted.

"Yes, I'm sure she does. In short, he's a miserable wretch. And for that I owe an apology to you both." He bowed slightly. "Please accept Fernando's deepest regrets. Oh, and Rodney has a question for you."

"I do?"

Fernando ignored me. "Jessica, Rodney has been hoping that you'd allow him to accompany you on a stroll from this fine institution to your lovely abode."

"Are you talking French again?" she asked.

Fernando smiled. "Let me translate. Can he walk you home one of these days?"

Jessica glanced down the hall, then at her shoe, and finally at me. "Okay." With that she turned swiftly and headed off to class.

"You're amazing," I told Fernando. "Thanks."

"I owed you that one, my friend. You've always liked her, and I did just what I said, pushed you toward adventure. But maybe, Rodney, it is I, Fernando, who should learn things from *you*."

I thought once again about my troubles. "Trust me, Fernando, you don't want what I got."

He didn't say anything to that but his face looked unusually solemn. After a pause he said, "All right, Rodney. It's time that you took me to our most difficult challenge

118

this morning. It's time for Fernando to meet Josie."

Finding her took a couple of periods, but after wandering through the eighth grade hall we eventually spotted Josie surrounded by her cheerleader friends. Fernando smiled. "Look at them. As beautiful as a Santorini sunset."

"Uhh, yeah, whatever."

We approached the girls. None of them seemed to mind Fernando stepping confidently up toward them. I marveled at him. Walking up to a crowd of girls filled me with fear. I whispered, "Remember, she thinks Trevor is gross."

"I have it under control," he replied. He eyed each girl carefully. "Josie, I presume?" he asked, picking her out. The kid had a sixth sense when it came to girls.

Josie smiled. "Yeah, I'm Josie. Who are you?"

"I am Fernando. I made a special trip to this school to ask you a favor for a dear friend who is too nervous to ask himself. Are you free tomorrow night?"

"That depends. Who is your friend and what is the favor?"

"The favor is to have dinner with him."

Josie shifted her glance to me. She gave me a nice smile and I shuddered slightly. This had to work. I had so much riding on it.

"Sure, I'll go out to dinner. You said this friend was real nervous."

"That is correct," Fernando added.

"Rodney, you look pretty nervous," Josie said with a wink.

Did she think Fernando was talking about me? I immediately tried to act less nervous, and to clarify the situation I said, "I uh, well, um, me? You see, it's not like . . ."

"You're kinda cute when you're mumbling like that."

I didn't know what to say. Fernando continued, "I think you're going to find that your date is quite adorable. So dinner works then?"

Josie smiled at me again. "Sure."

"Great, can you get to Mama's in town tomorrow at seven p.m.?"

"I believe I can manage that."

"Wonderful! You've just made someone very happy." Fernando gripped my shoulder. "Come on, we'd better go."

I stumbled along beside Fernando, feeling numb. The conversation with Josie had gone by quickly and my brain took seconds to catch up. We were around the corner before it all hit me. "Wait!"

Fernando paused.

"She thinks she's going on the date with me!"

Fernando smiled and nodded.

"That's no good!"

"Well, it's certainly better than the truth. There was no way, from your description, that she was going on the date if she knew it was Trevor. Right?"

"Yeah, but, what if she tells anyone? What if Jessica finds out? What if Trevor finds out?"

"Rodney, some people spend their entire existence worrying 'What if this?' and 'What if that?' I have one more quote this morning. Shakespeare said, 'If it be now, 'tis not to come. If it be not to come, it will be now. If it be now, yet it will come—the readiness is all.'"

"What does that mean?"

"I have no idea but it's Shakespeare, so it must mean something important! Now, my friend, go think about those words of wisdom as you attend the rest of the day's classes."

The only thing I thought about the rest of the day was the catastrophe looming on the horizon. At seven tomorrow night, all my worst fears were coming together for dinner at Mama's!

Chapter 11

REPEAT AFTER ME

To my immense surprise and relief, Saturday started great. We drove out to our game against Streetsboro in a noisy yellow bus. Trevor, revved up to impress his date, played tremendously. He tackled, sacked, intercepted, taunted, and offended everything in a blue Streetsboro uniform. He even chased a security guard halfway across the field because the poor guy was wearing a blue jacket! Yes, Trevor was on fire and scored all our points off turnovers—except for the one touchdown of the game. That, amazingly, came from Josh and me. I stuck to my usual plan of running right behind him and this time it worked like a charm.

It was Garrettsville's first win in years. The team dumped Gatorade on Coach Laimbardi and I even exhaled a long sigh of relief when the Boss, sitting in the stands, gave me the thumbs-up. During the game I had noticed a long black car parked by the gate and realized he had made the trip to Streetsboro as an added incentive for us to win.

The bus ride back to Garrettsville felt like a summer festival. Everyone was shouting and having fun ... except me. I knew the day's biggest challenge was still to come. So many things had to go right if I had any hope of pulling off the date between Trevor and Josie. Arriving back at school, we headed straight to the locker room. When Trevor finished changing, I motioned for him to join me in the gym. That's where Fernando met us.

"Trevor, I presume?" Fernando stepped up to Trevor and extended his hand.

"What's with this guy?" Trevor asked.

I wasn't sure how to explain Fernando. Before I had a chance to think of an excuse, my mouth took over. "He's what's known as an international dating consultant."

"A what?" Trevor asked, looking annoyed. "I don't need a doctor."

I ignored him. "His name is Fernando and he has traveled from a faraway land to help us out ... I mean, to help you out, to make sure everything goes perfectly with tonight's date."

Trevor still looked like he wanted to punch someone until Fernando said, "I currently have six girlfriends. Eight, if you count the Smith twins. Do you want my help or not?"

Trevor looked long and hard from Fernando to me. "Sure," he finally replied.

"Good," Fernando said, immediately launching into what he called his Ten Rules of Fine Dating.

It didn't take long for Trevor to stop him. "You want me to wear a tie?"

"Clean shirt, tie. You need to make a positive first impression."

"Rathbone, where did you find this goofball? I already know how to make a good first impression."

I remembered the demolition derby and pictured Josie running out the door screaming into a traffic-filled street. "Yeah," I said, "we've been down that road before and you probably don't need any help, but I want to make sure the date is a success. That's why Fernando's here. Remember, he's an international expert."

Trevor eventually nodded like he understood and I felt better—until I noticed Toby approaching. The fact that he was smiling only made things worse.

"Hey big bro," he said to Trevor.

"I'm busy here," Trevor snapped.

"Oh, well, I just heard some of the cheerleaders talking during the game. I thought you might be curious what they were saying about tonight's big date."

Toby was talking to Trevor but staring at me. I knew what was coming and quickly looked around the gym to see which exit was closest.

"What are they saying?" Trevor asked.

"They're saying that Josie is really excited."

Trevor nodded smugly. "Naturally."

Toby continued, "They're saying she's really excited to be going on a date with *Rodney*, not you."

Trevor's eyes bulged and his face turned dark red. He looked back and forth from Toby to me as if trying to decide who to punch first. *Oh, good*, I thought as Trevor's punch landed on his brother.

"I'm telling Mommy!" Toby yelled with wet eyes. We watched him run off to the parking lot.

"What was he going on about, Rathbone?" Trevor asked. I noticed that his fist was still clenched.

I shrugged. "When does he ever make any sense? Just be at Mama's tonight at six forty-five to get ready for dinner."

"I don't know. Something seems fishy. Speaking of food, I think I'll give you a little taste of my fist so you know what's coming later if this doesn't go the way I want!" He grabbed my shirt and pulled back his arm.

"Trev-oooooooor!" A woman with a scarf wrapped around her hair hollered from just outside the gym doors.

"Oh shoot, it's my mom," he gasped, lowering his fist. "Okay, I'll be there later, to either wow Josie or beat you into marinara sauce."

As he took off, Fernando called after him, "Don't forget the long-stemmed roses!"

I straightened out my shirt and stared at Fernando. "Well, that went well."

"I'll say," Fernando agreed, not catching my sarcasm.

"Fernando sure is glad he came for the weekend. This has been a lot of fun so far."

"Easy for you to say. No thug is threatening to make you into sauce."

"Rodney, things will go just fine tonight. Just wait and see." Smiling, he put his hand on my shoulder. "Besides, I'm sure you'd taste great over a hot plate of linguini."

A few hours later—Trevor's fist still fresh on my mind—Rishi, Fernando, and I approached Mama's door. I felt my anxiety level approach hyper-panic.

We entered the restaurant. Compared to the bright afternoon sun, the room was dark and my eyes took a few seconds to adjust. When I regained my sight, I was met with a stare from the Boss. His eyes were darker than the room. He sat at a table toward the back with Willy, Cheese, and an older lady.

"You're interrupting my dinner."

"Uh, sorry, but we needed to get ready for tonight," I said.

"Tonight?" he asked, clutching a butter knife.

I glanced at Rishi. He stepped toward the Boss. "Don't you remember? I called you during the week about hosting a date for our friend Trevor and—"

"I remember telling you 'no.' I remember telling you I don't need to play babysitter on my Saturday night. I remember a lotta things and none of da things I remember explains why you's standing here."

I couldn't believe the whole conversation. Rishi had told me we were all set. What was I going to do? Trevor and Josie would be here in an hour. I was done for. Now the Boss's attention was suddenly on me. "You're real lucky that game went the way it did . . ."

"Sweetie," the old lady said, reaching out and patting the Boss's arm.

The whole place went silent.

The Boss seemed to shrink a bit as he said, "Ma, don't call me sweetie in front of da boys."

She looked over at us. "Isn't he cute when he gets embarrassed?" She grabbed his cheek and shook it. It made a flapping noise. When she let go, the Boss's face curled up into an ugly, pinched expression. "Sweetie, who are your friends?" she continued.

The Boss flinched at the second sweetie and exhaled sharply. "Ma, they're not my friends. They're some local boys that do a little work for me."

"Now Francis . . ."

Cheese let out a chuckle. "Francis."

The Boss's eyes flamed up and Cheese snapped his mouth shut. The Boss looked over at his mother. "Ma, you know I don't like you using my name."

"Nonsense, it's a beautiful name. It was my father's name. I was just going to say how proud I am that you're taking an interest in helping the local children. Father Nikolai at the church will be very pleased. So, introduce me."

"Well, the big mouth there, that's Rishi. He's real

127

annoying. The other one, Rodney, he ain't as bad. And that one . . . that . . . I don't know dat guy."

Fernando strode forward. "I am Fernando, and this is indeed a pleasure." He took the Boss's mom's hand and bowed in to give it a kiss.

The Boss swung his finger at Fernando's face. "If you wanna keep dose lips you better stop right there."

Ma knocked her son's hand away. "What a little gentleman. What's your name?"

"Fernando."

"Really? I knew a Fernando once. He had such beautiful hair. I used to run my—"

"Ma!"

"Oh, sorry. Sometimes I get lost in my memories. Boys, pull up some chairs. You all look hungry."

The Boss shook his head. "Ma! They're about to scram."

"Nonsense. They're going to have dinner with us and then you're going to help them with their little date."

"I'm not goin—"

"Francis Vladamir!" Ma said the name again but this time it sounded like an order. Her eyes stared at her son.

"Yes, Ma."

We all did what we were told. I felt great relief that the date plan was back on. Unfortunately, I didn't feel so wondrous when I saw what the Boss's mom was piling on my plate. "Here, have some spaghetti and cabbage," she commanded. "I made the sauce yesterday.

You look like you could use a big meal. Eat, eeeeaat."

It smelled great and despite the weird looking cabbages leaves, I couldn't help but dig into the steaming plate. It tasted better than anything I ever had. The sauce on the stuffed cabbage was a kind of sweet, garlicky, tomato mixture and absolutely delicious.

The Boss's mom was clearly happy to see us all enjoying the meal. "You just call me 'Mama,'" she said, smiling, pinching my cheek. "If you want more, ask."

A sudden thought hit me. If this lady was the cook, convincing my mom to write a good review would be a cinch. I wouldn't have to worry about what the Boss would do to me after a bad review. "Are you the cook for the restaurant?" I asked.

The Boss's fork clinked onto his plate. "What kind of son would I be if I let my ma work in the kitchen? I already hired two guys. They're in the back getting the kitchen set up. They came cheap. Since I know I'm going to get a great review in the paper, I figured I could save a couple of dimes." He gave me a leering smile and the cabbage turned in my stomach. "Cheese, bring Rodney in to meet our new cooks."

I followed Cheese into the kitchen. "Dose two are da chefs," Cheese said, pointing, though I didn't see anyone. He didn't stick around to complete a formal introduction. The kitchen door wobbled back and forth to a close.

The kitchen had big stoves and a grill along the back

129

wall. A silver thing to my left held a tray of forks and spoons. I assumed it was the dishwasher. Back by the stoves, behind a row of shelves and pots, I finally spotted two guys. They looked more like loggers or mountain men than chefs. The first guy was sitting on a milk crate, asleep and snoring. His shirt had more grease on it than the deep fryer and his beard reminded me of Santa Claus—if Santa Claus slept in a dirty alley. The other guy looked at me, flicked an ash from his cigarette into the soup, and asked, "You wanna see something cool?"

"Uh, I guess so."

He tossed an onion into the air. Then, grabbing a big knife, he swung at it and yelled, "Samurai!" Unfortunately, he missed the onion, lost his balance, and fell into some pots.

The other guy woke up. "Weasel, I told you to keep quiet. You're interrupting my nap! I'm going into the walk-in where it's quiet." He passed by me, scratching his dirty beard. "I'm Big Earl. You the new dishwasher?"

"Not exactly. I'm—"

He didn't listen. "You'd better get busy on those pots," he ordered, picking his nose. "I like my work environment nice and clean."

I almost gagged.

He opened a large silver door and disappeared into a cloud of cold, frosty air.

"He's going to take a nap in there?" I asked. "Won't he freeze to death?"

"I keep hoping," Weasel said. "The slime in his beard freezes rock hard and spiky. It cracks me up but of course it's best not to laugh at Big Earl."

Weasel went back to chopping onions. The pieces flew all over the counter and the floor. How had I wound up in this situation? I'm not sure if the onions had anything to do with it, but my eyes got a little teary. With these two cooking there was no way my mom would write a good review.

I was just turning around to head back to the dining room when Rishi stuck his head into the kitchen. "Trevor's here," he shouted. "Now the real fun begins!"

The first thing I heard was Trevor yell, "Why is it so dark in here?"

He had a point. The lights were turned way down and one candle was lit at a small table for two. I could barely make out Fernando. He was leaning against the bar sipping a Coke in a tall glass. I decided to position myself behind the bar. If Trevor got mad about something, at least there would be a big wooden obstacle between us.

"Trevor, what could be better than candlelight?" I asked. He looked around, finally spotting me.

While I had been in the kitchen getting etiquette lessons from Weasel and Big Earl, Rishi had convinced the Boss, the Boss's mother, Cheese, and Willy to retire to the back room. That meant the cooking would be left to Weasel! I just hoped the ambiance in the restaurant would impress. Looking at Trevor, I already had my doubts.

"I can barely see," he said.

"Darkness has its advantages," Fernando observed.

"What does that mean?" Trevor demanded. I couldn't tell him the truth, that Josie wasn't expecting him!

"Never mind that for now," Fernando continued. "Rishi, we don't have much time. Hook him up."

Rishi stepped out of the darkness, walked up to Trevor, and began to stick something in his ear. Trevor flailed at him. "What are you doing? Don't touch me."

"Don't get crazy." Rishi laughed. "This is just a little speaker we'll keep hidden in your ear. Josie won't see it. This way, Fernando can speak into a microphone and give you pointers."

"I don't need no pointers."

"Now, now, everyone needs advice sometime. Keep still. I borrowed this from my uncle in the Akron Police Department."

Even through the dim light I could see that Trevor looked a little nervous. "Where's all the people in this place? Where are the waiters?"

"I'll be your waiter this evening," Rishi said. "The restaurant doesn't really open for another two weeks. We have certain pull with the owner."

"Wait a minute," Trevor snarled, "who's cooking the meal? It better not be you, Rathbone."

You'll wish it was me, I thought, but answered, "The chefs are in the back. A real talented pair." I glanced at my phone. "It's almost seven o'clock." I would know soon enough if this was going to blow up in my face.

Fernando stirred the ice in his drink. "Yes, we need to take our places. Okay, everyone, you know what to do."

Rishi positioned himself in the front of the restaurant. Trevor took his assigned seat at the table with the candle. It was under a fake vine of purple grapes that cast a dark shadow over him. Fernando and I slid behind the kitchen door and stood peering through the crack.

At seven p.m. sharp we saw car lights shine in through the window. Moments later a car door opened and we heard Josie's voice. "Yes, Dad, I know. Yes, eight thirty. No, I won't. Yes, I'll let Rodney know that you know where he lives. Okay? What? No, I'm not going to tell him that you're an expert with a blowtorch and a chain saw."

"Sounds like a caring father," Fernando whispered.

"Yeah, he sounds great," I said with a shiver. "Maybe he can give me welding lessons when he stops by with his blowtorch."

Josie walked in through the front doors. I braced for the biggest hurdle of the night.

"Good evening, madam, may I take your coat?" Rishi asked.

"It's sixty-five degrees out. I don't have a coat. Where is everyone? Hey, don't I know you from school?"

Rishi didn't miss a beat and continued like a true professional. "The restaurant isn't officially open yet, however Rodney pulled some strings and . . ."

"That Rodney! A restaurant all to ourselves. How romantic! Where is he?"

"Well, Rodney has come down with a bad case of the shingles and a bad case of poison ivy. Somehow, the two mixed together. He's got sores all over, especially around his mouth. They're oozing and dripping pus. Very contagious. One doctor even mentioned leprosy but Rodney's got his fingers crossed . . . while he's still got fingers."

I had told Rishi to think of a convincing excuse but this was overboard. I didn't need to be known as the king of cooties in Garrettsville.

"Ewwww," Josie said.

"Yes, it's extremely disgusting. Anyway, Rodney is at home soaking his face."

Josie turned to leave and whined, "My dad already pulled away."

"That's a shame, however, there is another gentleman from school who is without a companion. Perhaps you could dine with him this evening." Rishi pointed toward Trevor.

Josie, her eyes fighting through the dim shadows, asked, "What's that thing hanging around his neck?"

"It's called a tie, madam. I think you'll find him a rather sophisticated young man and a most pleasant dinner companion. May I show you to your seat?"

"Uh, I guess," Josie said. "Wait a second. Is that Trevor?"

"Stand up. Tell her she looks nice," Fernando said into the microphone.

I saw Trevor swat at his ear but he stood and said, "You look nice."

Josie said, "Thank you. You, uh, do too."

Trevor smiled and pushed a hand through his hair.

Rishi cut in, "Mr. Tarantola has taken the liberty of ordering you a Sprite. May I pour it?"

"I guess," Josie said.

My eyes had become fully adjusted to the dark. As Rishi poured, I noticed that the room looked really good. With the orange candlelight glow, the paintings of Venice, Florence, and Siberia, the white tablecloths and the long wood bar, Mama's looked just as nice as Chez Pierre or any other expensive place. This could actually work, I thought.

Fernando whispered into the microphone, "Tell her it's wonderful seeing her at a fancy restaurant. That she must have class."

"Wonder why you're at a restaurant," Trevor said. "You must have gas."

Josie wrinkled her nose. "I don't have gas!"

Fernando gripped the microphone and whispered into Trevor's ear, "Tell her you're nervous and you fumble your words—"

"I never fumble!" Trevor barked. "If I was still running back, you'd know it!"

Josie looked completely confused. "Uhh, okay. That was a little weird, but you *did* play great today."

"Thanks," Trevor said.

Fernando whispered, "Tell her you played great because she inspires you when she cheers."

Trevor picked up his Sprite and confidently stated, "I played great because you perspire when you cheer."

Josie's jaw dropped and she felt her armpit. Then she pulled out her cell phone. "I think I better call my dad."

Fernando spun around to Rishi, who had joined us in the kitchen. "Get out there. Don't let her make that call."

Rishi tore out to the table and swiped the phone out of Josie's hand.

"Hey!" Josie snapped.

"Sorry miss, we have a strict no-cell-phone policy at the restaurant. It disturbs the other diners."

"We're the only ones in here. Give me the phone!"

Josie reached out to take it but Rishi held the phone over his head. "I'll just keep it behind the bar until after dessert."

As he went to walk off, Trevor gabbed Rishi, lifted him off the ground, and shouted, "Give the young lady back her phone."

Caught in Trevor's powerful grip, Rishi had no choice but to obey.

"Darn it, she's got the phone," I whispered to Fernando.

He smirked back at me. "Don't worry. That was perfect."

Trevor, sitting back down at the table, repeated, "That was perfect."

"Yes, it was," Josie agreed, now looking at Trevor in a whole new way.

Fernando covered the microphone with his hand. "Rodney, when it comes to matters of romance, you must learn to trust Fernando."

Trevor and Josie were staring into each other's eyes. I felt like I was watching one of my mom's sappy movies.

Still covering the microphone, Fernando whispered, "We're almost there. Trevor has successfully acted the hero. Now if I can just get him to say a line correctly my work will be finished. I'll go with something simple." He picked up the microphone. "Tell her that's a nice dress."

"I know what to say, Fernando! Stop blabbing in my ear! I got the perfect line already."

I smacked my forehead. Josie was now definitely going to think he was crazy, and then he'd blame me for the wire, and then I'd be marinara sauce. I crossed my fingers, hoping his line was good. I watched him lean in toward her and say, "You know, Josie, if you were a booger, I'd pick you first."

"Did you just call me a booger?" she asked.

Fernando and I looked at each other. I was dead.

"Because if you did," Josie continued, "I think that's hysterical."

"You do?" Trevor asked. "I got a million booger jokes."

Josie laughed and for the first time all evening looked completely relaxed. "You know"—she smiled—"I'm kind of happy Rodney got leprosy and you happened to be here tonight."

I had mixed feelings when I heard that but Fernando looked pleased. He turned off the microphone. "My work is done."

"Good," spoke a voice in back of us. I jumped and spun around. Cheese was standing there. "If you're done, you won't mind your little friend taking a walk with me. Rodney, follow me into the office. Boss wants to see you."

I didn't like the sound of that. What had I done wrong? I followed Cheese and soon found myself face to face with the Boss.

"I've noticed how you and Rishi and that shifty other kid operate." He turned his computer monitor around, revealing several windows with security camera feeds of the restaurant. I hadn't been aware I was being watched all evening. "I might need a little more help opening night," he continued. "Want to make some money and bus tables?"

I was beginning to like the idea of making money—only

I knew my parents wouldn't want me working here. Not for the Boss. "Uh, sure," I suddenly said, figuring I could ask my parents later if it was okay. "Opening night must get pretty busy and all."

"It's not just that," the Boss continued. "Some important friends of mine from Chicago called. They said they'd be stopping by that night. I'm going to need to host a special dinner. It has to go well, Rodney."

"Makes sense," I said. "I mean, after all, they're coming a long way. I guess they're excited to see the new place."

More to himself than to me, the Boss said, "Let's hope they like it. Let's hope we make a ton of dough that night so Spats can leave happy." He glanced up at Cheese and Willy. The three of them looked deadly serious—actually frightened.

Willy said, "We all remember what happened to Joey Cranberries."

The Boss shook slightly. "Enough." Then he looked at me. "Beat it."

As I headed back to the kitchen to meet my friends, I began to worry about what I had just gotten myself into. Too bad I didn't have a little voice in my ear like Trevor telling me what to say.

But that wasn't entirely true. Something *had* told me not to agree to work for the Boss. Unfortunately, I had chosen not to listen.

Chapter 12

THE MYSTERY OF
THE EVIL HEAD

Monday mornings are the worst. For me, they usually mean the start of a week spent hiding from bullies and getting yelled at by teachers. It was really bad when I lived in New York and when I first moved to Ohio. Every Sunday night I would lie awake as late as possible hoping I could keep Monday morning from arriving . . . but it always did.

Today, however, was the first Monday in my life that I actually wanted to go to school. Everything had gone great on Saturday with Trevor and Josie, but more importantly, I couldn't wait for what might happen *after* school today.

"I'll be a little late this afternoon," I finally announced, chewing a piece of pancake. I tried to sound as casual as possible.

"Oh?" my mom asked. "Why is that?"

"Well . . ." I paused. I was embarrassed to talk about

it and pushed another piece of pancake through some syrup. I felt my family's eyes on me, so I said it: "I'm going to ask Jessica if I can walk her home."

My mom smiled over at my dad. He put down the paper, beamed back at her and actually reached for her hand.

Penny wasn't as charmed. "Jessica is not going to go out with you. I should know. I sat next to her in the car the whole way back from camp. She kept making a face like she smelled something rotten. But you know, you did smell pretty bad, Rodney. Did you shower at that camp?"

I glared at her.

"Penny," my mom cautioned.

"What?"

"Go get cleaned up for school."

"I'm already dr—"

"Penny?"

My sister huffed and shoved off into the other room.

My dad was still grinning. "Walking a girl home from school . . . that's quite a big step, Rodney. You want to hear about the first time I walked a girl home?"

"No," my mom answered.

My dad shut his mouth. I was glad he didn't go any further. I was afraid he was going to start talking about how things were in his day.

"In my day," he continued, "there were certain things you'd better do if you wanted a girl to like you." I braced myself, ready for one of his long stories. "They're all still true today. The first thing"—he raised a finger in the air—"is to open the door for her. The second"—he raised a second finger—"is to make sure she walks on the inside of the street, away from the traffic. Do you know what the third thing is, Rodney?"

I shook my head no. Surprisingly, I actually wanted him to continue. While he wasn't exactly Fernando, my dad seemed to know what he was talking about.

"The third thing is that you must hold her books for her. Got that, Rodney?"

I nodded. "Yep, hold her books."

My dad smiled. "Rules to live by." Satisfied that his son had absorbed all his wisdom, he turned to his next favorite breakfast-table subject: the weather. "Looks like it's going to be a hot one today."

My mom ignored him and said, "Rodney, I hate to remind you of this, but you have football practice after school. Jessica may not want to wait until you're finished."

I hadn't thought of that and started to feel deflated. My dad jumped in. "Of course she'll wait. Look at him sitting there. He's a Rathbone!"

My mom stared from my father to me. "You're right, honey. He's a Rathbone, all right. With that syrup on his shirt he's the spitting image of you. Now hurry up and change, Rodney."

"But this is the only clean short-sleeved shirt I have."

"Just put on long sleeves . . . and hurry. You don't want to miss the bus and make Jessica walk home alone, do you?"

* * *

The idea that football practice might ruin my plans dampened my spirits slightly, but even so, my face wore a smile as I stepped up to the bus stop. I was confident Jessica would say yes, if not today, then soon. I had another reason to feel good. Trevor had left Saturday night real happy and promised that we were friends forever. For once I didn't have a potential bully waiting for me at school. I paused and breathed in the morning air. My dad was right. Even though it was autumn it felt nice and hot out, like summer.

Rishi was watching me from his tree. "You're smiling, Rodney." He looked puzzled. "What's going on?"

"What are you talking about?" I asked.

"It's just that you're not a morning person. You always show up staring down at the pavement, acting like your dog died, totally serious. It's my job to cheer you up. I'm like your personal cup of coffee."

"I don't always look serious," I said, frowning.

"I guess you're right," he replied. "Sometimes you look like you might cry."

"What? No I don't."

"Sure you do." He pulled out his phone. "Check out this picture I took of you last Wednesday." I snatched the phone and sure enough there I was with wet eyes and downturned lips.

"That's just my allergies, and I'm deleting this photo."

"That's fine, I already uploaded it and have hundreds more just like it."

I sighed and handed back the phone. We both turned around at the deep sound of the bus approaching. Embarrassing pictures or not, Rishi couldn't bring me down this morning. In fact, the good feeling lasted the whole ride and was still there when we entered school. I felt lighter in my step, and, seeing Dr. Stone standing by the front door, I grinned and said in my best British accent, "Top of the morning to you."

She smiled and said, "An exchange student, how nice. Would you like to see how we conduct detention in America?"

"No."

She nodded and resumed staring stonily at the students arriving behind me. Even that didn't squelch my excitement, nor did seeing Kayla standing by Jessica's side. They were in front of Jessica's locker. Rishi said, "Look at them, Rodney, the best two girls in the school."

"Uh, yeah, I agree." *With half of it, anyway.*

We headed over. "I heard about this whole walking home thing," Kayla announced. "Unfortunately, Rodney, today's no good." She put on a fake sad face.

"Why not?" I asked.

Jessica went to open her mouth but Kayla cut her off, as usual. "Because Jessica and I have yearbook club this afternoon. We are staying an hour after dismissal. We have to take the late bus."

"Are you sure you have to stay an hour after school?" I asked.

"Yes," Kayla answered.

"Are you positive?"

"Yes, we're positive."

"Well that's great," I almost shouted. "My football practice ends an hour after school." I glanced over Kayla's shoulder. "Jessica, would you like to meet me here at that time?"

"Okay, Rodney," she said, smiling.

Kayla frowned, but Rishi may have caused that. He had suddenly stepped into her personal space and asked, "Maybe we could double date?"

"Ewww!" Kayla made a gagging face and stomped off, but not before shouting, "Just the thought gives me diarrhea!"

Rishi grabbed my shirt excitedly. "Did you see that, Rodney? I am close to winning her heart."

"Uh, well, you *did* seem to have an effect on her," I said in support.

"So I'll see you after school?" Jessica asked, ignoring my crazy friend.

I smiled and gave her a big nod.

That smile stayed on my face all day. It was there when I got on line to buy lunch and Trevor announced to the crowd, "Sorry everyone, but my man Rathbone goes straight to the front!" I'd felt a little bad about cutting thirty students, but "my man Rathbone" had a nice ring to it. By afternoon, in Spanish class, I actually got a cramp in my cheek from smiling so much. Ms. Noabla criticized my pronunciation—but I just smiled. How could Rishi say I walked around like I was about to cry? Even after football practice the smile was still there! I headed down the long empty corridor toward Jessica's locker. As I turned a corner, I noticed the light from the front glass doors reflected off the shiny floor. It was interrupted by the shadow of a solitary figure. My smile widened still further.

"I was waiting for a couple of minutes," Jessica called out to me. Her voice sounded playful. As I got closer she asked, "What's wrong with your face?"

"Nothing," I answered.

"I guess I never saw you smile before," she teased.

Great. Now she was saying it. I was about to come back with a joke when I noticed her reaching down to lift her backpack from the floor. My dad's rules went through my mind. "May I carry that?" I asked.

"Sure, thanks."

"No prob-lemmmm." My answer came out strained instead of smooth. What did she have in there, a pile of bricks? Lead bars? I went to swing it over my shoulder and fell back into the lockers. In my dad's day, I don't think girls carried so many books! Combined with my own backpack it felt like I had a safe tied to my shoulders. Fortunately, Jessica had started moving down the hall and didn't notice me thrashing about. I saw that she was at the front doors. I had to hold them open for her! I sprinted down the hall and yanked. In my eagerness, I pulled the door too hard and she nearly got bashed in the face. This date was going great so far.

"Sorry about that," I said. "I wanted to hold the door for you."

"That's very nice of you. Just be careful next time. I like my nose the way it is."

"It's a beautiful nose," I gushed. "I mean, I'll do my best."

She rolled her eyes but grinned and we headed outside.

Jessica lived about a mile from the school, which I thought was perfect, since it would give me a lot of time with her. Now that I was hauling five hundred pounds on my back, I wasn't so sure. Plus I had changed into a long-sleeved flannel shirt in the morning. The afternoon sun was super hot and beads of sweat began to roll down my forehead into my eyes. "This is nice," I managed.

"It *is* nice," Jessica agreed. "Hey, did you know Rishi joined the yearbook committee?"

It didn't take a genius to figure out why. "No," I said, adjusting the weight of the backpacks. "He never mentioned anything about it."

"Well, he showed up today with a full portfolio of photos he printed out. Mr. Witlacker, who's the adviser, loved his pictures and made him the head photographer. He seems really interested in photography."

"That's not the only thing he's interested in," I said, wiping some sweat from my forehead.

Jessica laughed. "I think it might be good for Kayla. All

summer she whined about Dave. She was real upset when he told her he didn't like her." I'd forgotten that Kayla had liked my friend Dave last year. "Anyway," Jessica continued, "today Rishi sat down next to her and kept showing her pictures. She wasn't interested and told him to go away, but then she found ones she liked."

I smiled. "Oh yeah? What did Kayla like?"

"She liked the ones of you."

"Of me? I find that hard to believe." I was trying to have a normal conversation as we walked along but my eyes had begun to sting and the world was getting blurry.

"Well, she didn't care much for all the ones *he* showed her . . . ones of you playing football, but then she took his portfolio into her own hands and found ones she did like. Like the ones of you crying."

"What? That was allergies!" I yelled, wiping sweat from my face. I was praying Jessica didn't look over at my watery, stinging eyes. Anyway, it could have been worse with the pictures. At least Kayla didn't find the one of . . .

"Kayla's favorite was the one of you in a dress. She really loved that."

"I bet," I said, trying to laugh. *Wait until I get my hands on Rishi . . .*

Jessica must have sensed my thoughts. "Rishi didn't mean it. She stole it from him. Besides, the two of them seemed to have a lot of fun, and I thought you looked good. Pink is your color."

"I'm glad they found something in common." It was

hard to get mad or stay embarrassed with Jessica by my side, but suddenly something felt wrong. My chicken senses tingled. I spun around and looked back down the block. All I could make out were houses and empty yards.

"What is it?" Jessica asked.

"Nothing. I thought I saw something." It felt like I was being watched, but that was silly. If I told Jessica she would think I was nuts.

We kept walking. Our conversation was light and fun. It had been a while since the two of us had really spoken. I'd almost forgotten how great she was and how smart. Why was this awesome girl walking with me?

I felt a twinge of nerves when the tone of her voice sounded a bit more serious. She said, "I'm glad your friend, uh, Fernando, explained everything about the summer. I feel a lot better now."

"Me too. It was real hard being away from you." *Thank God for Fernan—*

I jumped. Over Jessica's shoulder, fifty feet in front of us, I saw what looked like a strange, creepy figure step out from behind some hedges. It had wild crazy hair, almost like a clown mask. A chill ran down my spine and my right knee buckled. Just as I started to raise my hand to point, the figure slipped back behind the bush.

"You're right," Jessica continued. "The summer was hard. I think the hardest part was that you couldn't use the phone. Don't you agree?"

"With what?"

"Are you listening to me, Rodney?"

"Oh, absolutely. I agree completely." Maybe it wasn't the most graceful recovery, but I was focused on getting as far away as possible from the creepy clown person. "Do you want to switch to the other side of the road?" I suggested.

"No, this side is sunnier."

"Exactly," I said. "I forgot to apply my afternoon sunblock. I burn very easily." I was only half-lying. I couldn't stop sweating and the stinging in my eyes was getting worse.

"You're silly, come on."

I had taken my father's dating advice and made sure that Jessica walked on the inside—away from traffic and closest to maniacs. As we reached the hedge I could actually hear my heart pounding. I held my breath, waiting for a murderous hand to grab us. But nothing happened. We walked right by and I let out a high-pitched wheeze.

"Are you okay?" Jessica asked.

"Yeah, just my allergies again." I fake coughed, almost dropping both backpacks.

"Are you sure that's it? You seem a bit high strung."

"Me? I'm not high struuUUUUNNNNGGGG!" The masked head suddenly rose from behind a parked car on the other side of the street. Or was it just the sun reflecting off the hood? The whole world was hazy from the sweat in my eyes. I could feel my pulse slamming me in the temple. The head slowly went back down and disappeared behind the car. I gripped my chest.

"Rodney, you're scaring me," Jessica said.

You don't know what scary is! I almost screamed out loud. It felt like I was about to faint. Who was hiding behind that mask? Was it someone trying to ruin my date? If so, they were doing an excellent job. I couldn't stop my mind from racing. Was the person trying to do something worse than ruin a date? That thought was even more unnerving. Either way, I realized I'd better get my act together or this would be the final act of Jessica and Rodney. I forced a laugh. "Ha, I was just joking around. I'm like the king of relaxation. Nothing gets to this guy."

"I didn't realize you were joking. You're really good at acting scared and nervous."

"Don't forget cowardly," I added.

"Yeah, that too. You could win an Oscar."

"Ah, well, acting's one of my hobbies. I even did a scene once with the famous Broadway actor Victor Johnson."

Jessica ignored me and suggested we take the short-cut through the park. I met this with mixed emotions. If she was talking shortcuts, then she probably was tired of my jittering nerves and just wanted to get home. On the other hand, the straps from her backpack were beginning to cut off the circulation in my arms.

"The park sounds like a great ideeeeeEEEEE-AAAAAAA!" In the corner of my eye I saw the creepy clown mask pop up over a stockade fence that lined the sidewalk. It was just a few feet away! Part of me wanted to bolt but another, bolder part took over. Without thinking, I lifted Jessica's backpack and heaved it as hard as I could at the head—which ducked just in time. The backpack landed with a thud on the other side of the fence.

Jessica spun around. "What did you just do?"

I was breathing too hard to respond.

"Rodney, did you just throw my backpack over the fence?"

I stared down at my empty hands and back at Jessica. The look on her face told me she had finally decided I was crazy. And was I? Was I seeing things? "Huh?" I asked.

"What's the matter with you? You threw my bag over the fence. You're completely white. You're shaking. You're not answering me!"

"So you're not having a nice time?" My mouth was running off on its own. Jessica tilted her head and frowned. I better say something fast. Knowing I couldn't tell her the truth, I did my best to channel my inner Fernando. "Jessica," I said, "I've been waiting to spend time with you for so long, and now you're standing here and looking so pretty. I'm a little nervous . . ."

"A little nervous? You're soaking wet! Plus you just threw my bag over the fence!"

"Okay, very nervous. You're not just any girl, you know." Her glare softened slightly. "I'll get the bag," I added.

I had to do it, but as I approached the high fence all I could think of was the maniac waiting for me on the other side. My knees went shaky. There were no garbage cans around to stand on. I'd have to jump to reach the top of the wooden pickets. I had failed to impress Jessica with my cool, relaxed personality. At least I could redeem myself by showing her my superior physical abilities.

"Stand back," I said as I rubbed my sweaty palms against my pants, jumped, and managed to grip the scratchy top. I pulled hard to hoist myself up. I felt an instant burning strain in my arms and shoulders and only rose about an inch. My brain flashed back to Mr. Cramps, my demented athletics instructor from summer camp. I could almost hear him yelling at me, "Rathbone, those spindly arms of yours make me sick! You're a disgrace! You should be doing push-ups and pull-ups and sit-ups and chin-ups each and every morning!" As I struggled and groaned and the wood dug deeper into my hands, I wished I'd listened to him. I could feel a splinter biting into my palm as I attempted in vain to pull myself up. I just hung there as Jessica watched me gasp, flop, and struggle like a dying fish on a hook.

"Why don't you use the gate?" she asked.

Gate? I was almost blind by now from the sweat in my eyes. I looked over about ten feet and there it was. I wanted to smack my forehead but instead I dropped from the fence and said in my most dignified voice, "*Anyone* can use the gate, but if you insist . . ."

Pushing the gate open was one of the scariest things I've done. As it turned out, the creep was gone, the bag was sitting on the grass, and I looked like a complete moron. I retrieved it without incident and Jessica and I walked into the park. It was a somber, quiet walk. I had really blown it. We were getting close to her house and I figured this would be the final moments of my final date with her.

I was pleasantly surprised when she pointed to a bench and said, "You look a little tired after your, er, climb. Why don't we sit?"

"Sure," I said, secretly thrilled that I had more time. I was also happy that the bench was out of the sun near some shady woods. We both relaxed and I could feel myself cooling off. There was even a breeze that helped dry my sweaty hair. Everything was great, except I could tell Jessica was trying to put some words together. "What is it?" I asked.

She smiled. "I've always thought you were nice, Rodney, but you did act a little weird today. You said you were nervous. Do I really make you that nervous?"

I didn't know how to answer. She hadn't seen the evil clown head and talking about it would make me seem weirder than I already appeared. Maybe I could tell her about something else. "I'm sorry about my weirdo stunts," I began. "You don't make me that nervous. It's just that I have so many, uh, other high-pressure things going on in my life. I guess sometimes they get to me."

"What things? You can talk to me, Rodney."

I paused for a moment. The stinging had finally left my eyes and for the first time that afternoon I wasn't embarrassed to face her. She sure looked great sitting there, and there was a lot more to her than beautiful blue eyes and long blond hair. Most girls would have left me by now, but she was still here, genuinely concerned about me. Could I have found someone who'd actually listen to me? "I have a ton of strange problems," I managed.

She cringed back a little. "I heard you had a slimy contagious disease."

"I don't have a slimy contagious disease! That was just Rishi running his mouth."

"Well, then tell me."

I didn't want to overwhelm her with everything, so I figured I'd just tell her one problem. "You know that my mom is the new food critic for the *Cleveland Plain Dealer*, right?"

"Yeah, that's awesome!"

"Yeah, awesome," I replied sarcastically. "Anyway, you know that new restaurant in town, Mama's . . . ?"

I couldn't believe it. I found myself talking about the whole review situation with the Boss and about how tough and scary those guys were. I told her how we had to win every football game or they would come after me. I told her about the big dinner they were planning for the guys from Chicago and how I agreed to work opening night—even though I knew my parents wouldn't want me to. I must have gone on for twenty minutes. Even more amazing, she actually listened. She was the first person to ever take my concerns seriously.

When I finally finished she said, "You need to tell your parents! Actually, you should tell the police! This Boss guy sounds dangerous."

"Jessica, adults don't really listen to me. They certainly won't believe me, and the Boss made it clear that I'd better not tell anyone—or else."

"But what are you going to do if your mom gives Mama's a bad review?"

I didn't really have an answer. I picked up an acorn and flung it at a tree. "I've always wanted to see Mexico."

"Seriously, Rodney, I don't know how you live with that hanging over you."

"Well . . ." I was about to answer her when a branch snapped in back of us followed by some crunching sounds in the woods. This time we both jumped. We spun around and I thought I saw someone running off.

"Probably just a dog," Jessica said.

"Probably," I lied. My heart began to race. Had someone been listening to me spill my guts? Who could be listening? Was it the same crazy head I had seen all afternoon? Did the head belong to Cheese, or Willy, or maybe Toby? I fought hard to knock the horrible thoughts out of my mind. If the Boss found out I had been blabbing about him . . .

No one spooked us the rest of the way home. We paused at the end of Jessica's driveway. I felt a little awkward, unsure of what to say. I noticed her mom had come to the door and stood looking down at us. Trying to be polite, I smiled and waved. Jessica, on the other hand, frowned, as if to say, "Go away." Her mom just smiled and didn't budge.

"Well, this was fun, Rodney. Maybe we can, um, hang out again soon?"

I looked into her beautiful eyes and said, "That would be awful. No, I mean awesome, no, yes, I would love you, I mean not you, I would love to." I smacked my forehead and took a deep breath. "I can't think of anything I'd rather do."

She laughed quietly and took her backpack from me. My biceps, neck, and back all gave huge sighs of relief. "I'll see you tomorrow morning, Rodney." She turned and walked up to her front door. Her mom held it open for her and I watched as the best girl in the world disappeared into the house.

On the way home I pondered my long, crazy day. It was great that things had turned out good with Jessica but the mystery of the creepy head left me feeling jumpy and frightened. My mom broke my trance when she met me at the door.

"Rodney, I have great news!"

"What?" I asked. My mom's "great" news was never great, but even I wasn't prepared for what came next.

"It's Mrs. Lutzkraut. She's out!"

The world closed in around me. "How do you know?" I finally managed.

"Because she stopped by this afternoon. She just got

out today and came straight here to see you. I told her you were walking Jessica home. Isn't that nice? Rodney?"

I couldn't reply. I nodded dumbly and ran up to my room. I jumped on the bed and buried my face in the pillow. Too many thoughts were crowding my mind. Had the mystery surrounding the evil head been solved? Had that been Mrs. Lutzkraut behind the clown mask trying to ruin my date? Was she the noise in the woods behind the bench? If she had heard what I told Jessica about the Boss, how far would she go to use it against me?

As I pieced it all together, I was struck by an alarming thought: Either half of Garrettsville was after me or I was losing my mind. Or both. Lucky for me, I knew a room had just become available at Shady Pastures!

Chapter 13

THE STORM BEFORE THE STORM

Despite my mom's surprise Lutzkraut announcement, the days following my walk with Jessica turned out to be some of the best ever. Jessica and I spent a lot of time together and she was real easy to talk to—particularly with no masked lunatics making faces at me. Trevor and Josie seemed equally happy. Josh and Wendy were together all the time and even Kayla scowled less when Rishi was about. Fernando would be proud of us!

When Saturday rolled around we actually won another football game, which added to the excellent week I was enjoying. Trevor was great on defense while Josh delivered bone-jarring hit after hit. Of course, the pipsqueak hiding behind him with the ball got most of the credit—thanks to Rishi's constant tweets—but I didn't mind. As long as we were winning and the Boss was happy, I could deal with the extra attention.

Yes, I had allowed myself to enjoy the week by

keeping the darker thoughts out, but that could only last so long . . . especially with me. I knew that any day, at any moment, Mrs. Lutzkraut might pop back into my life. I also knew that something else I had been dreading was now only days away. Saturday night was the big grand opening of Mama's, and soon after that my mom would go to review it, and soon after that a horrible review of Mama's would appear in the newspaper, and soon after that the Boss would come after me . . .

I shuddered as I walked onto the football field for Monday practice. What *would* the Boss do to me? The air on the field felt still and heavy. The calm before the storm.

Apparently, I wasn't the only one feeling the pressure. Coach Laimbardi paced back and forth looking very agitated. He called us together.

"Gentlemen, do you know what's happening this Saturday?" I doubted he was referring to Mama's opening. "This Saturday is the biggest sporting event of your lives. Bigger than the Super Bowl, the Rose Bowl, the World Series, the NBA Finals, the Stanley Cup, the World Cup, the Kentucky Derby . . ."

My mind began to drift. I stared at a cloud high above the school building. The cloud began to look a little like the Boss smoking a cigar so I turned my attention back to Coach Laimbardi.

". . . Bigger than the Indianapolis 500, Wimbledon, the Masters, the Westminster Dog Show . . ."

But I couldn't get my mind off the Boss! He still hadn't paid us for putting up those flyers and now I was going to be working for him cleaning tables. The truth is that I was too afraid of the Boss to ask for the money he owed us ...

". . . Bigger than the Tour de France, the Summer Olympics, the Winter Olympics, the Iron Man, the French Open, the World Table Tennis Championships—"

"Uh, Coach?" Josh interrupted.

"Yes?"

"Are you saying it's a big game Saturday?"

"Of course it's a big game! It's bigger than all of them together! It's . . . it's . . . Windham!"

Just hearing the word "Windham" sent shivers down my spine. I hadn't seen the twin brutes Bart and Bruno since that first practice when I sent them flying. I knew that on Saturday I wouldn't be so lucky.

"That's right," Coach Laimbardi continued. "We have to beat the Windham Bombers! We have to, have to, have to win that game!" By now he was turning red. Coach Manuel brought him a cup of water but he knocked it away and kept going. "I have to win it once. Just one time. Bring your A game. Bring your AAA game! Pleeeeaaase win the game for me! The whole town will be here. With our recent success, we're only twenty-point underdogs. Victory is within reach. Can't you taste it? I have to beat Bill Belicheat once in my life . . ."

Coach Manuel turned to us. "You heard the coach. Big game Saturday. Now start practice!"

I wandered out to the huddle and knelt down. As Hector called out plays for us to run, I tried to piece together everything happening in my life. The Windham game was during the day on Saturday *before* Mama's opening. That meant if we lost, all the meals served that night would have to be free thanks to Rishi's stupid ad. The Boss would go broke and I'd go missing. If I made it to Sunday morning it would be a miracle! I took a deep breath. There was, however, a chance we would win Saturday—even with Bart and Bruno gunning for me. After all, we were on a roll. All I had to do was hide behind Josh during the day and bus tables for the boys from Chicago at night. *I can handle that*, I told myself. Maybe everything would be okay after all.

I stood up, let out a sigh of relief, and gazed into the stands. The second I saw her bright orange hair I knew that everything was not all right. Not by a long shot. Mrs. Lutzkraut sat in the middle of the yellow benches wearing a gold dress and holding a black G-Men flag. She saw me looking at her and gave a little wave.

As if seeing her wasn't bad enough, Hector, AJ, JJ, Phil, and Joe all waved back. "What are you doing?" I yelled. "Why are you waving at Mrs. Lutzkraut?"

Hector smiled. "She's our new tutor, Rodney. She's

helping us with reading and math and stuff. She's real nice."

"No she isn't. She—"

AJ interrupted. "Rodney, she really likes football. She asks us all sorts of stuff about it and about our games."

"Don't tell her anything. She's evil. I can't believe you guys. Is she tutoring the whole offense?"

"No," Hector said.

At least that was a relief.

"She's tutoring the defense, too."

I began to panic. "You guys can't let her tutor you! It's a trick of some kind."

They all laughed and looked at each other knowingly. "She said you'd say that," Hector explained.

"She's got you fooled. Trust me. She'll ruin everything!"

"She's not going to ruin anything," JJ tried to assure me. "She can only help us. For instance, she helps me memorize our playbook. Look, she's even waving our flag."

I was desperate. "Josh! Tell them they're wrong. Tell them about camp and how Mrs. Lutzkraut tried to ruin it."

"Camp," Josh repeated, staring off into space.

"Yes, camp. Tell them!"

"Well, at camp . . ."

"Yes???"

Josh grinned. "At camp we had fire!"

It was useless. My teammates wouldn't listen to me.

We practiced another play and I tried not to glance at Mrs. Lutzkraut, but something made me want to take one more look. Pretending I was stretching, I turned my body slightly toward the stands . . . but she was gone. I looked in every direction, from the school to the track to the woods and back again. Mrs. Lutzkraut was nowhere in sight. In less than a minute she had completely vanished—along with any hope that my great week could possibly continue.

"Why so glum, Rodney?" My mom stuck her head into the TV room where I was trying *not* to think about Mrs. Lutzkraut.

"Because everyone's too dumb to see the truth," I answered.

"I see. Well, maybe dinner tonight will cheer you up."

"What are you making?" my dad asked, turning down the volume on the Food Network. "Pot roast?" The prospect of a good meal was already working on him.

"No, we're going out on a review. With the Windbagg—"

"AHHHHHHHHHHH!" my dad and I whined in unison. "Not the Windbaggers!" I pleaded. Mr. Windbagger was one of the most annoying men in all of Ohio.

"Now, now. I have to review a restaurant, and besides, Fred and Ethel are very nice. Donald, you know Fred's

164

been trying to speak with you about that job opportunity. I think it's very important that you—"

"I am *not* going into business with Fred Windbagger," my dad said flatly.

"Donald, Fred's done very well for himself. This is not the job market to hold out for the ideal position . . ."

"I'd rather go hungry!" my dad lied.

"Donald, just listen to him. That's all I'm asking. Ethel thinks it would be a wonderful idea."

"Is Penny going?" I asked, noticing her walk by in her pajamas.

"No, we hired a babysitter—"

"But then why can't I stay—"

"Because, Rodney, Mr. Windbagger is a huge fan of yours. He's been to all your football games and specifically asked if you were coming. I think it's the least you can do to show up and thank him. We're leaving in twenty minutes, so go get dressed."

I groaned as I pulled myself off the couch. My dad shut off the TV and held his head for a minute. "Well," he announced, "at least we're in this together."

Mr. Windbagger frowned as he read the menu. We had met him and Mrs. Windbagger at the restaurant five minutes earlier and he had already complained that there was no bread on the table and the parking spaces were too small for his car. His frown deepened. "What kind of food is this anyway?"

My mom replied, "It's Asian Fusion. This restaurant is primarily focused on Japanese and Thai cuisine."

"Don't they eat steak in Taiwan? I don't see a T-bone on the menu."

"Actually," my mother explained, "the food is from Thailand, not Taiwan."

"Heck, I don't care if it's from Times Square, they should serve steak. Gloria, you want to review a good restaurant, you go to the Ponderosa. Now that's a good place. There's one over in Warren. *They* got a good T-bone."

"I'll keep it in mind," my mom said.

"Now let's see," he continued, studying the menu, "Ethel, what's that fancy dish I get down there at the Happy Wok?"

"Fried rice?"

"Yeah, that's it. Where's the fried rice?"

"I don't see any," my mom answered apologetically. "Maybe you'd like the Pad Thai? It's like Thai spaghetti."

"I guess. If I'm still hungry I can always grab a burger on the way home. So how's the job hunt going, Donald?"

My dad adjusted his knife and spoon on the tablecloth. He seemed to be having difficulty coming up with an answer. Eventually he managed, "Swell. I'm working part-time for now."

My mom cut in. "You know, Fred, it's been tough for Donald. He had gotten a wonderful position at Vanderdick Enterprises, but when the mall deal fell through they had to downsize their operation."

Mr. Windbagger nodded his head. "Tough one,

Donald. I read about that. Those darn tree-huggers ruin everything."

I felt my face redden. Evidently Fred Windbagger didn't know that in camp I had pretty much made sure they didn't cut down the forest to build houses and a mall. My dad spoke up. "Personally, I'm glad the deal was blocked. Saving the woods was the right choice." He winked at me and I felt better.

Not everyone shared his sentiment. "Baloney!" Mr. Windbagger exploded. "Donald, I think you've been eating too much of this seaweed stuff on the menu. Makes you soft. Remember, I'm looking for an assistant. I need a real go-getter. Ideas like saving some squirrels won't get you too far in the business world."

"I've always done fine," my dad responded, "and I haven't had to sacrifice my ideals."

"Ideals?" Mr. Windbagger shouted. "Would you rather have ideals or a Mercedes?" He laughed fairly loud and elbowed a man sitting behind him at another table. He repeated, "Ideals or a Mercedes? Mercedes, right?" The man made a nervous nod. Mr. Windbagger turned back to my dad. "See? *He* gets it. When I sell insurance I always speak the language people understand. Rodney, do you know what language I speak?"

"English?"

"I speak money. That's the international language. Right?" He laughed again.

"Perhaps we could order," my mom suggested, looking around for the waiter.

"Sounds good to me," Mr. Windbagger said. "Rodney, you like this stuff?"

"Not as much as a good T–bone and a baked potato."

Mr. Windbagger banged his hand on the table. "Donald, you may have some nutty ideas, but you're raising one heck of a boy here! You've been playing some great football, son. Been to all your games and seen you in all those ads for that restaurant. Ethel, what's the name of that restaurant?"

"Mama's," we all answered at once.

"Yeah, that's it," he agreed. "Gloria, are you going to review them on Saturday when they open?"

Mrs. Windbagger answered for my mother. "Fred, you remember what I told you. Gloria always waits a few weeks before she reviews a new restaurant. It gives them a chance to work out the kinks."

She was right. My mother never reviewed restaurants when they first opened. In fact, I had secretly been hoping that Mama's might close before my mom got down there. After all, with that horrible food, how long could they stay open? I took a sip of water and tried to let my worries about the Boss float away. . . .

"Actually," my mom said, "there's been so much buzz about Mama's that my editor wants me to review it right away. I'm going Saturday night."

"UGGGGGHHHHH!" I choked. Mr. Windbagger's meaty palm whacked me on the back and an ice cube shot across the table.

"Are you all right?" my dad asked.

I didn't even answer. I still hadn't told my parents I was working there that night. Plus I pictured Big Earl and Weasel serving up some slop, Cheese and Willy ordering the customers around, and the guys from Chicago causing problems. I was dead. Things couldn't get any worse!

"Well, look who it is," Mr. Windbagger said loudly.

A man and woman followed by two hulking sons were being shown to a table. As the boys turned around there was no mistaking their identity! I grabbed the menu and covered my face. They were identical twins . . . about twice my size . . . wearing mean expressions. . . .

"Come to eat your last supper?" Mr. Windbagger asked.

"Shhhh, Fred," his wife scolded. "You can't yell like that in a restaurant. Go over and talk quietly to your friend."

"That's not my friend," he said. Then he yelled, "Hey, Belicheat! Getting ready to lose on Saturday?"

Belicheat? Bart and Bruno's father was the Windham coach?

Belicheat turned in his seat to face Windbagger and said, "You Garrettsvillers are pathetic. You finally win a couple of games and you act like you're in the NFL playoffs."

"Keep talking, Belicheat. I got young Rodney Rathbone at my table and I can't wait to watch him run over your pathetic defense."

My mom shifted uncomfortably in her seat. Windbagger had used her last name. I shifted uncomfortably in my seat because I was about to poop my pants!

"Take a good look," Mr. Windbagger continued. Then, noticing me, he added, "Rodney, stop staring at that menu and let the coach take a look at you!" I slowly let the menu slide to the table.

"What do you think, boys?" Belicheat asked his sons. One of them took a sip of water and loudly crunched the ice in his mouth. The other picked up a fork and bent it into a U shape. "Let me introduce you to Bart and Bruno," Belicheat continued, not knowing we had already met. "We were a little late getting here tonight because they had to meet with the Notre Dame recruiter. It's pretty rare for recruiters to meet with middle school football players, but Bart leads the state in tackles, sacks, tackles for loss, and interceptions. Bruno, on the other hand, leads the county in unnecessary roughness penalties."

I was about to ask if I could be excused—from earth—but Mr. Windbagger wasn't done. "I hope none of them scouts will be at the game Saturday." I felt his hand grip my shoulder. "Those two altar boys of yours haven't had to meet Rodney here in the hole. Best running back Garrettsville's ever seen."

One of the twins said, "Dad, I don't see running back listed on the menu."

The other one added, "Guess we'll have to wait till Saturday. How do you like your running back cooked?"

"Rare," his brother answered with a smirk. "I like my running back bloody. It's also important that the meat is well tenderized."

For the first time in my life I knew how a cow felt and I didn't like it. Looking at the two brutes, I had little doubt they had every intention of making me the main course at Saturday's game—and they had the muscles to live up to their words.

It was all too much. My fate was sealed. Next Saturday was shaping up to be the worst day of my life. I suddenly needed air. "Excuse me, I'll be right back." I doubted the twin goons would get up and follow me . . . not with so many people around.

My mother looked concerned. "But we haven't ordered."

"Um, I'll take that Chinese spaghetti you mentioned."

I crossed the restaurant and headed for the doors. "Glad I brought Tums," was the last thing I heard from Mr. Windbagger as I pushed open the doors and headed outside.

The night had gotten cool and the air smelled faintly of burning leaves. I took a deep breath and tried to relax. Should I call Jessica? She was the one person I could talk to who would understand and give me advice. Should I run away? I needed a minute to think. I looked around and noticed a bench in a little garden surrounded by tall, trimmed hedges. I sat down and ran my fingers through my hair. After a minute I heard the restaurant door open. Were my parents looking for me? Were the twins looking for me?

"That *is* good news," I heard a man say. I assumed he was on a cell phone. Relieved that it wasn't the twins, I exhaled and was about to call Jessica but stopped when I heard the man's next words: "So you've managed to record almost all the G-Men's plays?"

Staying hidden in the shadows, I turned around and peeked through the bushes. It was Belicheat! He was about two feet away with his back toward me. After a pause I heard him continue on the phone. "That's more than I hoped for . . . Oh, I know I won't need their playbook, but what kind of coach would I be if I didn't dot my i's and cross my t's? . . . Hahahahah . . . Now *that's* what I call tutoring! . . . Hahahahahah . . . Great, see you tomorrow. Good work, Agent Orange!" He hung up and walked back into the restaurant.

For a few minutes longer I sat on the bench and debated my next move. I knew I had to head back in but I needed time to absorb everything. Thanks to old Windbagger, it was now a certainty that the two biggest, toughest kids in the state would take me apart on Saturday. If that wasn't enough, their dad was working with a certain orange-haired tutor named Mrs. Lutzkraut to learn our plays ahead of time! My mind felt like it was going to explode. This was all too much for a kid my age. It was only Monday night. What would Tuesday bring, an earthquake? I couldn't take it anymore. Eventually I managed to stumble back inside and sit down at the table.

"You were gone for a while, honey," my mom said. "Are you all right?"

I was pretty far from all right. I wasn't even sure of what to say. I was in a fog the rest of the meal. I vaguely remember nibbling on some food and trying not to make eye contact with the twins. The one time I did, either Bruno or Bart mouthed the word "you" while pointing down at his chicken. I remember my stomach doing flips as I watched him repeatedly stab the chicken with his bent fork.

I turned to Mr. Windbagger. "Did I hear you say you had Tums?"

It was the start of the toughest week of my life.

Chapter 14

TAKEN FOR A RIDE

"Rodney, what's gotten into you?" Rishi asked as we headed down the hall to lunch. "Aren't you aware that in two days you're playing Windham, and then it's opening night at Mama's?"

"Yeah, I'm pretty aware of it."

"Isn't that awesome? Why aren't you smiling from ear to ear? You've been moping around all week."

He sounded like my mom. "You don't have a clue, do you?" I finally asked.

While the few days since my dinner with the Windbaggers hadn't been a complete disaster, they hadn't exactly been incident-free. For starters, Mrs. Lutzkraut had hosted an afternoon get-together at her house on Tuesday for all the kids she was tutoring. Every G-Men player who ate her chocolate chip cookies wound up getting sick to their stomachs by the time they got home. Today was Thursday and some were still out. When I said to Hector, "See, she's trying to weaken the team before the big game," he just looked at me and shook his head.

"A bad batch of cookies, Rodney. It could happen to anyone."

Luckily I hadn't been invited to Mrs. Lutzkraut's little throw-up party, but on Tuesday night I had an encounter of my own that left me pretty shaken. My dad and I had driven over to the Home Depot in Streetsboro to pick up some paint he needed for my sister's room. While he examined all the colors I wandered up and down the aisles. Somewhere between kitchen cabinets and kitchen flooring I got the sense I was being followed. I spun around. For a second, all I saw were two enormous barrels taking up the aisle. Then I realized it was Bart and Bruno.

"That guy last night in the restaurant said you could beat us," one of them taunted. They both took a step in my direction. I couldn't tell which brother was which but it didn't really matter. By now I was pressed against a stainless-steel refrigerator with nowhere to run.

"How about we find out right here how tough you really are?" the other twin said, grabbing the front of my shirt and lifting me slightly off the ground. I guessed it was the twin who excelled at unnecessary roughness.

"Listen, fellas," I began, "you don't want to do this here—not in aisle nine. We'll just get in trouble." My mind was racing. *Say anything to stay alive!* "At Saturday's game we'll have plenty of time to find out who's really tougher!"

Did I just say that?

I felt my feet returning to the floor. "You got a deal," grunted twin #1.

"Yeah," the other one added. "That is, if we don't see you before then."

They both laughed like they were sharing a private joke and high-fived each other before walking off to join their dad. I didn't like that at all. Those two would have lots of chances to crush me on Saturday and make it look like an accident. They had probably been planning it for weeks! Wasn't that enough? Were they going to do something *before* Saturday's game?

And now I had Rishi asking me why I wasn't grinning from ear to ear. I realized he would never understand all the stuff on my mind and decided to just keep it to myself. "Only kidding," I said as we entered the cafeteria. "Everything's great."

He stopped and stared at me for a second. He looked a little confused, but then he starting laughing. "You almost got me, Rodney. That was a good one. Hey, I can't wait to tell you the great news I just got."

Oh no, not Rishi news! I prepared to bolt back down the hall before he could open his mouth but a voice stopped my feet cold.

"What news?" Jessica asked. She was standing behind us with Kayla and Samantha.

When Rishi saw them, his big smile stretched even wider.

"I'm glad you three are here. You got to hear this. I just got a call from *ESPN* magazine. Did you hear me? ESPN! They want to do a photo shoot and interview with my man, Rodney Rathbone."

"Really?" Jessica said.

"That's so cool," Samantha added.

Even Kayla looked at me with less annoyance than usual.

I wished I could share in the excitement, but I didn't want any additional unjustified appreciation. I wanted to keep out of the spotlight. It seemed like the world would never let that happen, and Rishi certainly wasn't helping.

"All right, Rodney," he said, "I've cleared up Friday afternoon's schedule. I just got off the phone with your father."

"Wait, what?"

"Can we come to the shoot tomorrow?" Jessica asked.

"Absolutely!" Rishi answered. "I'm sure I can get the three of you VIP status."

"There's Josh," I began, "we'd better tell him and the other players—"

"No," Rishi whispered, "not Josh and not Trevor. Just you. I was specifically told by *ESPN* not to bring them to tomorrow's shoot."

"Won't they notice a bunch of photographers showing up at practice?"

Rishi smiled. "They won't notice because it's not at the school. It's out at the Ledges."

"Nelson Ledges?" I gulped.

"You got it. They said it would be a really cool place to take the pictures."

I had heard a lot about Nelson Ledges from my friends—it was pretty close to town—and I could already picture it in my mind. I knew there were paths in the woods that led in and around a number of big rock formations. The place was a huge labyrinth full of caves and cliffs and waterfalls surrounding a lake. I remembered that Slim's mom had never let him go out there. She was afraid he'd fall into one of the ravines. From the sound of it, she was right. When I first moved to Garrettsville last year I had read that there were many drops in Nelson Ledges over one hundred feet, and that visitors had to stay on marked paths. It sounded like an odd location for a photo shoot. A creepy tingle rose up my spine.

"It'll be fun, Rodney," Jessica said.

"You bet it will be fun!" Rishi shouted. "It'll be the perfect way to begin the best weekend of your life!"

With Jessica and Rishi grinning at me, I fought hard to think of an excuse of why I couldn't go. Fortunately, good old Kayla quickly put an end to the plans. "How are we getting out there, brainiac? The Ledges is like five miles away. Don't think for a second that I'm going to ride my bike there and come back in the dark!"

I could kiss her, I thought . . . before quickly erasing the image.

Rishi smiled at her. "A bike? I have a car coming to school tomorrow to pick us up."

"Like a limo?" Samantha asked.

"Close," Rishi said. "Rodney, what does your dad drive again?"

"The same thing he's driven for ten years. A Honda."

"High-class all the way." He grinned.

The next day after school, the five of us stood outside the front entrance waiting for my dad to pick us up. I was happy that Jessica's parents had let her come along. It was fine that Samantha was coming too. And Kayla, well, at least Rishi would be happy.

My dad's Honda pulled up on time. I opened the back door for Jessica. Several greasy food wrappers tumbled out and the car smelled like French fries.

"Dad, couldn't you have cleaned out the backseat?"

My dad turned around. "Oh, sorry, son. Don't tell Mom. I don't want to listen to her recite my cholesterol counts again." Then, spotting Jessica, he added, "Hi, dear. Hope this is a nicer ride for you than coming back from Camp Wy-Mee!"

I cringed and wished he hadn't brought up about the time Jessica rode all the way home in silence because she was mad at me. Jessica looked at me and smiled, as if to say, "Don't worry, I know how dads are." Out loud she said, "Hi, Mr. Rathbone. Nice to see you. These are my friends, Kayla and Samantha."

"Nice to see you again!" my dad said to the girls. "I remember you both from the school dance at Baber Intermediate. Well, pile on in." As he said this I realized the car would be a little tight for us all. I smiled to myself. It would be nice to scrunch in close with Jessica. . . .

"Rodney, you and Rishi get up here with me. Let the girls have the back."

That daydream didn't last long! For the next five miles I had Rishi's elbow digging into my ribs. Turns out scrunching wasn't much fun.

As we pulled into the deserted Ledges parking lot, my chicken sense started tingling. Samantha must have been having similar thoughts. "Shouldn't there be a truck here or something?" she asked.

Kayla growled, *"Rishi."*

As usual, Rishi just smiled. "Have no fear. Look!" He pointed across the road to the entrance. Some teenager was holding an ESPN sign—except it didn't look very official. We got out anyway and my father started to join us.

"What are you doing?" I asked him.

"You didn't think your old man was going to drive off and miss all the excitement, did you?"

The last thing I needed was my dad directing a bunch of photographers on how to take pictures of me. I said, "I was kind of hoping I could handle this on my own."

He looked disappointed . . . but only for a second. "No problem, son! Those fries were awfully salty and I can't seem to get a milk shake out of my mind. Vanilla or chocolate? Oh, it's a tough decision." He started the car. "Text me when you want me to pick you up!" he called out as the Honda sped off down the quiet, wooded road. The brake lights flickered once before he rounded a bank and drove out of sight.

A chilly breeze blew across the parking lot and I couldn't help shivering. Something sure seemed strange about this photo shoot—but it was too late now. We crossed the road.

"You work for ESPN?" Kayla asked the kid with the sign. "What are you, like twelve years old?"

Before the kid could answer, Rishi spoke up. "Don't worry, Kayla. The woman I spoke to on the phone sounded real mature."

"I'm an intern," the kid added defensively. "See? I'm holding a clipboard and everything." He looked down as if reading something. "Mr. Rathbone?"

I didn't like this but just nodded.

He pulled out a walkie-talkie. "He's here. He's got some friends with him."

His walkie-talkie hissed for a second. A voice said, "All right. Send him up here to get his makeup done, but make sure his friends wait down there with you. I'll send someone down in five minutes to take them to the, uhh, interview."

Nervous pangs gripped my chest. "Wait, my friends can't go with me?"

The intern kid said, "You heard him. They'll be picked up in a few minutes."

"But I don't see why—"

"Listen, do you want to be interviewed or not?"

I was about to answer "or not" but Rishi cut in. "Oh, he does, he does . . ."

I looked at the girls. All three wore worried expressions. I noticed that the woods in back of them were beginning to grow dark as the late-afternoon sun dipped below the treetops. "I don't want to leave you guys," I said.

"Nonsense," Rishi insisted, "we'll be along in a minute. Go, go."

Jessica said, "Don't feel bad about us. It's not your fault. I'm sure we'll see you in a minute."

I had little choice after that but to walk into the woods . . . alone. I passed a big sign that said, DANGEROUS CLIFFS—STAY ON MARKED TRAILS ONLY. Beyond it was a smaller sign that explained the park's trail system. White Trails were the safest. After that there were various colors until you came to Red Trails. They were the most dangerous. I also noticed with alarm that the trail I was on led to the "Devil's Hole," which was right by something called the "Devil's Icebox." Did every trail in this place have to start with the word "Devil"?

I continued on, heading farther into the boulders and

cliffs. For a little while I could hear Kayla far below whining to Rishi. ". . . So, is standing in a parking lot your idea of VIP treatment? . . ." As the trail rose higher, however, her words grew fainter. I grew more nervous. I couldn't believe I was missing Kayla's complaints.

I got to the top of a bluff. Other than the wind rattling through dry leaves, it was quiet. The sun was definitely getting lower in the sky. I looked around and noticed an ESPN sign pointing down into a ravine. Unfortunately, the sign looked like it had been painted on the back of a pizza box. I strongly considered walking back out and telling everyone that I had gotten lost. There was something off about the whole setup and the idea of heading down into a dark chasm—alone—seemed about the worst thing I could do. It had also started to dawn on me how strange it was that no one had told me to bring a uniform, let alone a football.

"Hello," I called out. The only reply was my voice bouncing off the boulders. *That's it*, I told myself. *No way I'm heading down there.*

"Hey, Mr. Rathbone!"

I turned. The intern guy had followed me up the trail. "The interview team wants to know what's keeping you."

"Uhh, explain to me again why I'm being interviewed down there?"

"This is the Ledges. It's a famous place in these parts. The producer said it will make a real dramatic backdrop.

Now look, it's my job to see you go in there, so get moving."

For the first time there was a threatening tone to his voice. Being an official coward, I hurried ahead into the gorge. As the trail dipped lower into the chasm the air grew cooler and wetter. The rock sides were covered with a thick, slimy green moss. I was soon at least fifty feet down in the depths of the chasm. I looked up. There was no way to climb out other than the trail—which I suddenly noticed was marked RED! I went over a big tree root and wound around some boulders and under a ledge or two. Every now and then side passages branched off in different directions. I hoped I hadn't wandered off and gotten lost.

"You made it," a slick voice suddenly sounded from up ahead.

I didn't see anyone, but hearing a voice brought a wave of relief.

For a moment. Then I recognized the voice and my knees began to quake. How could I have been so dumb? I had walked straight into a trap and now found myself at the bottom of a gorge with no means of escape. I had even sent my dad away!

On the bright side, I no longer needed to worry about tomorrow's game or Mama's grand opening. It seemed pretty unlikely I'd be returning from Nelson Ledges anytime soon.

Chapter 15

IN THE DEPTH OF THE LEDGES

"So," I asked, "I take it the photo shoot is off?"

Toby stepped out from behind a bend in the trail. "I have to admit," he sneered, "I was getting a little worried that you wouldn't come. Sorry for doubting you." He let out an evil laugh. "How funny *was* that whole ESPN thing? I mean, why on earth would ESPN want to interview you of all people? Who'd be dumb enough to fall for that?" He paused and held his hand over his mouth. "Oh yeah, Rishi would!" He laughed some more and wiped a tear from his eye. "That guy cracks me up. He actually believes you're someone special."

Despite the fear coursing through my body, my anger rose when he insulted my best friend. "At least I can count on him . . ."

"To what?" Toby asked. "To always get you in trouble? Anyway, I've finally got you right where I want you, Ratbone. Last year you weaseled your way out of all my plans, and this year you've managed to win over my lame brother. He's athletic, but I've got the family's intelligence gene . . ."

He continued to ramble on. I was only half-listening. I knew that in addition to being evil, Toby was a big coward. Hey, it takes one to know one! That meant somebody else was probably lurking nearby to do his dirty work. But who? Josh and Trevor were now my friends, so they were out of the picture. I couldn't think of anyone else in Garrettsville strong enough, tough enough, or nasty enough to join him out here. Maybe Toby's plot wasn't as brilliant as he thought.

"Sorry to interrupt," I said, "but I think I'll be leaving now."

"Not so fast. My tutor has lined up a few surprises for you."

His tutor? I should have guessed Lutzkraut was behind this! It certainly explained the "mature" woman who had called Rishi about the photo shoot. My legs began to shake as my eyes swept the ravine for alternate escape routes. Toby noticed.

"Oh, there's no escape. I made sure of that." He snapped his fingers. Four kids wearing Windham Bombers sweatshirts came out from around the bend. They glared at me with folded arms.

I remembered Belicheat's phone call to Mrs. Lutzkraut. This wasn't good at all. I started inching back the way I'd come.

"Going somewhere?"

I spun around. Sure enough, Bruno and Bart were

blocking my way. At least this time their names were printed on their shirts! Bruno smirked, "I'm looking forward to the game tomorrow. I'll let you know how it turns out. And as for our little bet from the other night, looks like we'll be finding out right now how tough you are. Ain't that right, Bart?"

"Yep."

By now my legs were shaking so bad that a cloud of dust began to form around my feet. I noticed an opening to my right that separated two massive boulders. It wasn't much more than a wide crack.

"You're not going anywhere," Toby ordered. "I've waited a year for this moment. The time has finally come to get my revenge! Hahahaha! You're mine now and there's no way out. . . ."

"What about over there?" I asked, pointing to the crack I'd been eyeing.

Confusion flashed across his face. "What?"

I didn't wait to give him an answer. Instead, I sucked in my stomach and plunged between the rocks. I could hear Toby scream, "Get him!" as I scrambled frantically through the narrow channel. It was real tight and dark. I scraped my way through. I almost got stuck but pushed on, popping buttons off the front of my shirt. I realized this was one time being small was a definite asset. Bruno and Bart would have greater difficulty, and I knew Toby wasn't going anywhere without them.

After a few feet the passage began to open up and I

could move more quickly. I was increasing my lead, but once they squeezed through the opening I knew my pursuers would be right on me. I weaved in and out of the twisting passage. I came around one big turn and was faced with a horrific sight. The path ended at the foot of a massive slab.

I stood there gaping, breathing hard. The rocks around me rose straight up for at least thirty feet, too steep and high to climb. I was cornered. My chest tightened as I was gripped by an unbelievably powerful fear. I back-tracked a few feet, in case I had missed some passage. It was no good. The shouts from Toby and company were getting louder. They must have squeezed through and would soon be on me.

Yes, I've been in more bad spots than any kid I know, but hearing the approach of Bruno, Bart, Toby, and the other Windham players was the most scared I've ever been in my life.

Until I heard something near my feet go, "Pssst!"

"AGGHHH!" I screamed. Was I losing my mind? I glanced down into what looked like a black hole. Two eyes glowed back at me. Was it a zombie? Was it Gollum? I fell back against the wall. Whatever it was, the creature was coming out to get me . . .

"Rodney," it whispered.

. . . and it knew my name! I got ready to bolt back to Bruno and Bart, preferring their fists to whatever this beast had in store for me.

A gray hood popped out of the darkness. "Rodney, it's me . . . Pablo."

"Pablo?"

"Yeah, from school."

"You're not a zombie?"

"I don't think so. Are you being chased by those guys?"

"Huh? Oh, yeah."

"Then hide in here with me."

It sounded like a great offer. He slid back in and I squirmed my way in after him. The opening was super tight but inside the hole opened up a bit and was large enough for us both to sit. He lifted a couple of rocks and partially concealed the opening.

I wanted to ask him what he was doing in a hole in the middle of Nelson Ledges but noises from outside stopped me. I watched feet stomp by. I knew they'd be back once they reached the end. I just prayed they didn't see the hole. Sure enough, I heard a howl of confusion and anger. After another minute I heard the grumbling gang returning.

"I don't understand it. Where did they go?" Toby's voice whined.

"You said you picked the perfect place," Bart or Bruno barked at him. "You said there was no escape."

"There isn't any escape! I chose this spot after studying like three trail maps. I don't understand."

"Well apparently there *is* a way out! My dad and the

tutor aren't going to be happy about this. Let's get out of here."

I heard them walk off. After a minute I said to Pablo, "That was a close one."

"Guys!" Toby shouted from right above me. "Get back here. I heard a voice coming from this hole. I knew that coward Rodney was hiding! And he's talking to himself!"

Great. Like getting caught wasn't bad enough, now everyone would think I was crazy, too.

Pablo tugged on my sleeve. "Hurry," he whispered, "there's a passage at the back of the hole. It's real narrow and loaded with spiders but it does lead to an exit. That is, if we don't get stuck."

My brain launched into a frantic debate. Creepy, dark, tight passage full of spiders or Bruno and Bart's fists? Why couldn't I be wrestling with a simple choice like vanilla or chocolate milk shake?

A booming voice yelled, "We got you now, Rathbone!"

Okay, creepy passage it was. I motioned onward and Pablo started crawling. I went to follow but a hand reached in and grabbed my ankle. One of the twins was trying to yank me out! I kicked back hard and felt a crunch.

"Aghhh! My nose! You're dead, Rathbone!"

Under other circumstances, I would have been paralyzed by fear hearing those words, but not today. Pablo had disappeared into the dark before me. I wiggled after him on my hands and knees. Before I could stop myself, I slid down a wet, slick rock into pitch-blackness. At the bottom the passage leveled out. I heard Pablo scrambling along ahead.

"Wait up," I yelped in the dark. There was only enough room to wiggle on my stomach. I knew it would be impossible to turn around. Without Pablo I'd never get out alive.

"This way," he said.

I wanted to cheer, *Thank God for Pablo!*

"I think," he added.

"What do you mean, you 'think'?" I screamed. I felt like I was about to suffocate and realized I could now add claustrophobia to my long list of fears.

"I've never done this without a flashlight," he said, "but I'm pretty sure we're going in the right direction. Of course if we're not, then we could be in big trouble."

"What kind of trouble?" I asked.

"Ever read *Tom Sawyer*?"

"What?" I wheezed. I didn't think this was the time for a literary discussion.

"Well," Pablo continued, "there's this bad guy named Injun Joe who gets lost in a labyrinth of caves."

"What happens to him?"

"Oh, he never finds his way out and dies."

"He dies?" I almost screamed.

"Yeah, it was a real good book. Last time I crawled through here, I got home and found three spiders in my pants."

"Spiders?" He wasn't helping my panic level.

"Yeah, they weren't nearly as bad as this big millipede thing that—"

"You think you could change the subject?" I begged. By now I had thousands of little itches all over my body.

"Oh, okay. Hey, I just saw this real good show on the Discovery Channel. It was about earthquakes. I bet this passageway is the absolute worst place to be in an earthquake. There are millions of pounds of rock and dirt above us right now. It wouldn't take much to bring it all dow—"

"Ahhhhh! Ahh! I need to get out!" I shouted. "OUT!"

"Okay, relax, Rodney. There's the exit. See the light up ahead?"

He was right. With each slither, more light came pouring in. I'd never been so happy to see the sky peering through the cracks. I noticed the space around me getting higher and wider and suddenly we were in a big cave. I was able to stand up and it felt great.

"This is a cool cave, right?" Pablo asked.

I nodded and sat down on a boulder. As my heartbeat gradually returned to normal I noticed that the top of the cave opened up to the sky. One wall sloped gradually and wasn't too steep. Tree roots hung down almost like the rungs of a ladder. I looked over at Pablo and smiled. "So, do you mind my asking, what were you doing back there in that hole?"

"Oh. I heard people coming so I ducked into it."

"But what were you doing out here, at the Ledges, by yourself?"

Even in the dim light I noticed his face sag a bit. "I spend a lot of time out here," he said.

"Why?" I asked.

"Well, I like to walk here from town and explore. I sketch the cliffs, but I guess that's not the real reason."

I didn't ask what the real reason was. I figured if he wanted to tell me, he would. In school I had heard all kinds of stuff about Pablo. I knew that some of it was true and that some of it was just mean stuff kids say.

After a minute he decided to talk more. "You see, things aren't great at home. My mom's been away for years and my dad, well, he drinks a lot and, well, I don't like to spend much time there."

He didn't use many words but I got the picture. It also explained why he wore the same hooded sweatshirt to school every day. There was nobody at home to tell him not to. I realized that my parents may be clueless once in awhile, but I had it pretty good. I decided to change the subject. "Hey, Rishi's using your Borscht picture on Mama's website. You gotta be the best artist in the whole school."

His face brightened back up. "I was invited to take some art classes in Cleveland on Saturdays . . . but . . . my dad won't pay for them, and I have no money."

I thought of Mama's and busing tables tomorrow night. Maybe he could join us. "I may be able to get you a job."

"Really? You'd do that for me?"

"Hey, you just saved my life." We both laughed.

"Anyway," I said, "I'll try. Right now, let's concentrate on getting out of here."

We began our climb from the cave, taking our time and working together. At last, I gripped a root and pulled myself up and over. I felt a cool breeze blow across my back and head. It felt great to be surrounded by the late-afternoon light. I reached over the rim and pulled Pablo up. He looked past my shoulder and the expression on his face told me something was very wrong.

"Well, well, well," Toby's voice boomed from behind me. "How nice of you to drop in. Or should I say, climb out? Just in time, too. We were about to leave. How lucky."

Yeah, how lucky. Typical Rodney luck. I'd been so eager to escape from underground that I hadn't thought about what I was climbing into.

Toby continued, "I've waited—"

Bruno cut him off. "No more of your speeches. He's all mine. Look what he did to my nose." Then he turned to me. "You're dead, Rathbone!"

He began to advance. I was too exhausted to look for places to run. Anyway, Bart and the other Windham players had fanned out to cut off escape routes. This time I really was a goner.

"I'd leave him alone if I were you," a girl's voice called down through the woods. It sounded a lot like Jessica.

"Go away," another female voice joined eerily. I was pretty sure it was Samantha.

Bruno's eyes grew wider. "Who said that?"

Then, from much closer, a third girl yelled, "Touch him and you're dead." I was positive that voice belonged to Kayla.

Bruno spun around. "I'm not afraid of some weirdo ghost girls!"

"Did you just call me a weirdo?" Kayla's head popped up from behind a rock.

Bruno laughed nasally, looking a bit relieved. I saw white pieces of paper sticking out of his nostrils. "Get a load of this crazy one," he said to his brother.

"Now you're calling me crazy?" Kayla stepped around the rock and came closer.

"Yeah, you're crazy." Bruno laughed, smiling back at his brother.

Kayla howled and launched herself at him. She was a whirlwind of flying hair and flailing arms. Bruno fell back in alarm. In a second she was on him. He held up his hands to protect himself but soon yelped and took off—with Kayla hot in pursuit.

"Where are you going?" Toby screamed after him. "She's half your size!"

"I can't hit a girl," Bruno called back. "It's one of my dad's rules!"

We watched them go. I don't know if I was more shocked that Bruno had run off or that Kayla had actually stuck up for me.

"Bart," Toby said, "can you please take care of Rathbone once and for all?"

"My pleasure," he said with a grin.

"That would be a bad idea." This time the voice belonged to a boy. Rishi emerged from behind a tree holding up his phone.

"What now?" Toby whined.

"I'm filming this whole thing," Rishi said, "and I'm pretty certain none of these guys will be playing in tomorrow's game once their principal sees this footage."

"What?" several of the Windham players yelled.

"It was *his* idea!" Bart yelled, pointing at Toby.

All the other players yelled, "Yeah, it was Toby! Get him!"

"But, but, but," Toby blubbered. Seeing the charging Windham Bombers, it was Toby's turn to bolt. He ran off screaming through the trees. It was a beautiful sight.

The one Bomber who didn't join the pursuit was Bart. Something had caught his attention. He was standing next to Rishi. "So," he asked, "you're going to show this clip to my principal?"

"That's right," Rishi said, "and to our principal, Dr. Stone. Want to wave and say hi? As soon as I get back she's seeing it."

"So, you're not streaming it now?" Bart asked.

I could see where this was going and tried to warn him. "Rishi . . ."

"Well, the cell service is not the best out here," Rishi continued, smiling. Talking about video and photo technology was one of his favorite subjects. "I can upload later, and I can edit it, which . . . Hey!"

Bart grabbed the phone and hurled it with all his might into the depths of the gorge. "OOOps!" he laughed.

"That's a sixty-megapixel phone!" Rishi wailed.

Bart wasn't listening. Grunting, he shoved Rishi aside and moved in my direction. "I'm going to finally do what we set out here for." He came at me quickly, his two huge fists ready to . . .

"POLICE! FREEZE!"

This time it was an adult voice. Bart jumped and turned on his heels. Once again I had the pleasure of watching a Windham football player run off frantically into the woods.

Thank goodness the cops had arrived. I went to thank them but there weren't any. Instead, my dad appeared from behind a bush. "That was fun!" he said. "I felt just like Clint Eastwood. Did you see that kid take off?" Jessica and Samantha also came out from their hiding spots.

I was stunned, unable to comprehend what had just happened. "How . . . ?"

Everyone talked excitedly at once. From what I could make out, Rishi and the girls had become suspicious pretty soon after I left them and decided to come look-ing for me. They spotted the fake ESPN sign and saw me surrounded down in the ravine. When I disappeared into the crack between the cliffs, they didn't know what to do. Kayla, it turns out, was the one who suggested they shadow Toby and the Windham players.

"And Rishi here texted me," my dad added, "just as I was about to order a chocolate milk shake."

I gazed at them with tremendous appreciation—and relief. The bad guys had been scared off and we could see Kayla making her way back to us. She had on a rare big smile. She'd always been a pain in my butt but now I wanted to go up and hug her. Someone else must have been thinking the same thing. Rishi grabbed her and said, "My hero!"

"It's heroine, you numbskull!" she barked, but she was still smiling slightly and wasn't slashing at him.

Jessica asked, "Are you okay, Rodney? Why were those guys after you?"

"That's obvious," my dad said. "They're afraid of what he's going to do tomorrow! Oh, who's this, Rodney?"

In all the excitement I had forgotten about Pablo. He was hanging back near the rim of the cave. I motioned for him to join us. "Dad, this is Pablo. I think you're going to be seeing a lot of him over at our place."

"Oh, yeah? Great." Looking at Pablo he added, "You're always welcome in our home, son." My dad was like that sometimes. In one second he had sized up the situation. "And speaking of home," he continued, "we better be on our way. It's getting late."

Careful to stay on the White Trail, we hiked through

Nelson Ledges one last time back to the car. Once there, my dad looked at all of us. "Hmmm. We have one more than when we started. Rishi, why don't you and Pablo join me up front." He smiled at me. "Rodney, you wouldn't mind cramming in the back with the girls . . . would you?"

Yep, when it came to dads, mine was all right.

Chapter 16

LET THE GAMES BEGIN

All of Garrettsville sat behind me in the stands. In fact, the stands were so packed that the crowd had spilled over and people were surrounding the field.

Yes, everyone I knew had come out for the big game, but I didn't turn around. The fearsome-looking team on the opposite sideline held my attention. The last time I'd seen many of these players was yesterday at Nelson Ledges when they tore off into the woods. From their glares—and the way they kept shouting, "You're dead, Rathbone!"—I got the sense they weren't too happy.

"Isn't this great?" Rishi had suddenly joined me on the G-Men sideline. "They wouldn't be saying that stuff if you weren't the star player!"

"Lucky me. Hey, you're not allowed to stand here."

"I know, but I need to tell you something important. Yesterday, when we got back from Nelson Ledges—"

"You!" Coach Manual shouted, pointing at Rishi.

"Back in the bleachers. We're about to start the game."

"You better go," I said. "You can tell me during halftime."

"But . . ."

Coach Manual was still staring at us so Rishi took off—leaving me alone with my not-so-pleasant thoughts.

So far I had been able to avoid direct eye contact with the twins. They had been going over something with their father but now had joined the rest of the team. I noticed Bart's helmet turning slowly in my direction. I knew it was Bart by the number ninety-nine on his jersey. He was talking to one of the other players but scanning the G-Men carefully. Suddenly his massive head locked onto its target and came to a stop. I gulped. His eyes met mine and I watched his body tense. He took a step forward. My worst fears were coming true! He was actually going to walk straight across the field and clobber me in front of everyone.

Instead he gave me a friendly wave and kept talking to the kid next to him.

Huh? What was that about? Was the little wave part of some devious plot? I was completely confused. My mouth felt dry and I was about to grab some Gatorade when from behind me I heard, "We won't be able to stay and watch da game."

There was no mistaking the Boss's voice. I turned and found myself staring straight into Cheese's stomach. The Boss was dressed in a dark blue suit and standing next to

Willy. Coach Manuel walked over. "Hey, you can't . . ."

Cheese stared down at him. "We's can't what?"

"You can't, uh . . ." Coach Manuel was at a loss for words. "You can't believe what a good player Rodney is. Bye!" He ran off and hid behind Josh.

"As I was saying," the Boss continued, "da plane from Chicago arrives in an hour. We gotta go get ready for tonight. Know why we stopped by to see you?"

"To give me some words of encouragement?" I asked.

The Boss sneered. "To tell ya to win da game—or it's curtains for you."

The three of them turned and pushed their way through the crowd to the waiting limo.

"Was that guy an interior decorator?" Hector asked.

"What?"

"That guy. He was talking about curtains. Do you like home-improvement shows? I watch them a lot with my mom."

Great. I was basically dead meat if we didn't win today and all my quarterback could talk about was interior decorating! Unfortunately, the rest of the team was no better. Everyone was silent and pensive. How could we possibly beat Windham? The G-Men needed to get pumped up. There was only one person who could change their mood and say something inspirational.

I turned to Coach Laimbardi. He looked at me, yelped, "Gotta go!" and speed-walked his way to the end zone. Reaching a blue porta-potty he yanked open the door and disappeared inside. With my own stomach fluttering and gurgling, it wasn't the kind of inspiration I was hoping for.

I kept watching, eager for him to return. Time clicked off the scoreboard clock signaling that the game was about to start. He still didn't come out. What was going on? Eventually, I walked down the sideline. The crowd cheered my name. Josie and the cheerleaders waved their pom-poms as I neared the potty.

"Good planning, Rodney!" I heard my dad yell. "Take care of that now."

A bunch of people started laughing. Everyone was watching me and I didn't think things could get more embarrassing . . . until I saw the porta-potty was named Doodie Calls. I leaned in to speak. "Um, sorry to bother you . . ."

"You might want to find another place to go, son. This could be a while."

"It's Rodney, and we don't have a while! Coach, the game's going to start any minute. We need you to get us going. To motivate us. Are you coming out?"

"Uhhh, well, I'm having a little stomach issue. I don't understand it. It can't be nerves. I'm nervous before every game."

"Did you eat anything weird last night?"

"No. Last night I ate some of Mrs. Laimbardi's meat-loaf. Rodney, I really scored a touchdown when I married that one. She sure can cook. I remember when we—"

"How about today?"

"No, I never eat breakfast on game day. All I had were some G-Men cookies when I got here."

"G-Men cookies?"

"Yeah, they're shaped like footballs and say G-Men. That lady who's been tutoring the players gave them to me. Not bad. Now, I'm not saying she can bake as well as Mrs. Laimbardi, but . . ."

While he blabbed on about his wife's famous cheesecake, I looked into the stands. It didn't take long to spot Mrs. Lutzkraut's flaming red hair. She smiled at me, pretended to eat a cookie, and burst out laughing.

I had known that having her lurking about would cause me trouble. I also knew that she had shown our playbook to Belicheat. But I didn't see *this* coming. Without Coach getting us motivated and calling the plays, the game was hopeless.

"Rodney! Over here!" Several rows from Mrs. Lutzkraut, my mom was waving a pennant and nearly jumping out of her seat. She was completely caught up in the pre-game excitement. I'd never seen her cheer and yell about football. "Check out the float," she called to me, pointing down the field. Someone had driven over a giant football from last week's high school homecoming game. It had the words "G-Men" on both sides.

I smiled back at my mom and realized that her

enthusiasm was nothing compared to my dad. He and my old principal, Mr. Feebletop, were trying to get the wave started. Everyone loved it and was joining in. All of them—students, teachers, friends, families—believed we could win. The town's enthusiasm only made me feel worse. Once we lost, I'd have to deal with the Boss *and* a disappointed community.

I started to walk back to the team. The wave was now running the length of the crowd in full force. I noticed Mrs. Lutzkraut stand and throw her arms in the air with a big, fake smile on her face. She had timed the wave perfectly. She had timed everything perfectly. With Coach Laimbardi out of commission, the Bombers were bound to win. Her eyes met mine and again she made that cruel, twisted smile. I hated that it was going to end like this. Mrs. Lutzkraut, it appeared, had gotten her revenge.

Unless . . .

I looked from my teammates to the porta-potty and back to the team. A crazy idea began to form in my head. It was so crazy that it just might work. I turned my attention one last time to my former teacher, eager for her to see me. Now *I* was the one wearing a big grin— and she didn't seem to like it one bit.

"All right team," Coach Laimbardi yelled, "this is the day we've been waiting for—some of us our whole lives! Look across that field. See the confident looks behind their face masks? See Coach Belicheat grinning? See their fans in the away-stands laughing? How does that make you feel?"

There was a quiet grumble. Eventually Joe called out, "Sorry, coach, I didn't catch the last part."

"Oh. Let me try this." Through a vent near the top of the porta-potty Laimbardi asked, "Is this better?"

"Yes," we all agreed at once.

Minutes earlier I had enlisted the help of Josh and the entire offensive line. To the shock of everyone in the stands, we had dragged the porta-potty more than sixty yards to the middle of the sideline. As we pushed and pulled I saw Belicheat almost choke on his whistle. Mrs. Lutzkraut was equally stunned, though she would soon be right back to her old tricks.

"I was saying," Coach Laimbardi continued, "you boys aren't old enough to know this, but that man, that team, and those fans have been looking at us like that for years, and every year we've gone out on that field and gotten beat. The whole town of Garrettsville has suffered from continuous humiliation. Don't believe me? Look behind us. Everyone is here. It's the largest crowd we've ever had. They all know that this year is different. This is the year we beat the Windham Bombers! This is the year we restore our pride"—he banged against the porta-potty for emphasis—"and dignity!" *Doodie Calls* was vibrating wildly. "This is our game to win!"

"Yeah!" a bunch of my teammates yelled. They were getting pumped up. It was working.

"And how do I know we're going to win?" he called out.

We all shouted in unison, "How?" The excitement was building.

"Because your teammate, Rodney Rathbone, had the guts and bravery to guarantee it in the newspaper!" *Uh-oh.* "If he can stand up to Windham, we can *all* stand up to Windham. It's our destiny to win. Now go out there and show them what we're made of!"

"YEAH!" A sound like thunder filled the air as everyone banged on the blue plastic potty walls.

The kickoff team ran onto the field and the rest of us spread out to watch. I felt nauseas and wondered if coach had any room in his hideout. He must have seen me lingering through the vent holes. "What'd you think, Rodney?"

"Um, great speech, Coach."

"Thanks. Did you like how I tied you in there with the destiny thing?"

"Uh, yeah. Very inspiring."

"By the way, brilliant idea moving me to the middle of the sideline. I can do everything I need to do from here. *Everything.*"

Dealing with Coach's problems helped me put mine aside and I settled into watching the game. With Josie cheering him on, Trevor continued his inspired play. He tackled the Windham running back on first and second down and then swooped in and sacked their quarter-back on third. I was cheering along with everyone else until I remembered that Windham was now going to punt on fourth down. That meant I was about to . . .

"Offense, take the field!" the porta-potty yelled.

We ran out. As I headed to my huddle a big, thick arm grabbed me. It was Bruno. Was he going to tackle me before the play even started?

"Hey Rodney . . ." He paused. "Um, that was fun yesterday. We should do it again sometime. Good luck today." He smiled awkwardly and shambled off to join his defense.

"Rodney," Hector called.

"Huh?"

"You going to get in the huddle?"

"Uhh, yeah." My mind was on Bruno. Was he setting me up? There was no way he had fun yesterday. His nose was still bruised and swollen from where I'd kicked him! Maybe he was trying to get me to let my guard down. Once I did, wham, I'd be flattened.

"Rodney?" Hector called again.

"What?"

"Did you hear the play? We're running blue dive right on two. You ready?"

I lined up behind Josh.

"Hut, hut!" Hector yelled.

BLAHMMMM! The whole Windham line swarmed

inside the blocks. Somehow Hector managed to hand me the ball. I was supposed to run up the middle but all I saw were Windham players. Josh smashed into them and I did my best to follow him, picking up three or four yards before getting dragged down. The Windham players piled on top of me. It was hard to breathe and I felt like a bug squirming under a shoe.

"All right, get up," a voice commanded. "Come on, get off him." Who was this hero coming to my rescue? I felt the weight lifting and the air returning to my lungs. Once I could move, I turned my head and saw Bart. He was hoisting one of his own players out of the scrum. Noticing me staring in disbelief, he said, "Nice run, Rodney."

Another set of hands lifted me up. It was Bruno. "Hey, let me fix your shoulder pad." He tucked a flap back under my jersey. "There you go. Good as new."

I couldn't take it anymore! What were they up to? Next they'd be baking me a pie. "Uhh, thanks."

"Don't mention it."

More confused than ever I returned to the huddle—just in time for a new concern to surface. On the next two plays, it seemed that Windham knew exactly what we were going to do. Even though Mrs. Lutzkraut had shared our playbook with them, there was no way they could anticipate what play we were about to run. Or could they?

I sat down on the bench to give it some thought

just as a cheer erupted from the Windham sideline. The Bombers had kicked a field goal and we were now officially losing. I could almost hear Coach Laimbardi sigh from within the john.

The G-Men took the field on offense and I headed into the huddle. My eyes were glued to Hector. Was he wearing a microphone and giving Belicheat our plays? It had worked between Fernando and Trevor at Mama's Restaurant. Could Hector be doing the same thing? But I knew Hector. He would never do anything intentionally to hurt the team. Still, I watched closely as he ran back from the porta-potty after getting the play from Coach Laimbardi. Before telling us, he began tapping his helmet and waving his arm.

"What do you think you're doing?" I asked.

"Stretching," he answered a little nervously.

I pulled him aside. "You're signaling our plays."

His eyes widened. "Rodney, I'm not signaling. I'm, well, I'm signaling, but just to my tutor. I told you she helps me memorize all the plays. She said this would help me understand them better, you know, like a learning strategy."

I took a deep breath. "Hector, you can't do that."

"Why not, Rodney? I've had a lot of trouble remembering the playbook until I started working with Mrs. Lutzkraut. It doesn't hurt anything. You're one of her favorite students and she's our biggest fan." He continued blabbering on about how wonderful she was and

I knew it would be no use to persuade him otherwise. She was a master at fooling people. She had half of Garrettsville fooled, including my mom.

We had to run a play. Once again we were swarmed and I barely made it out of bounds alive. I had to do something quick. Should I tell Coach? Then a better idea hit. I walked over to Hector. "You realize you have to signal Mrs. Lutzkraut the reverse of what we're doing, right?"

"What are you talking about?"

"Well, she's facing us, so if you signal left, she thinks right, like a mirror. You see?"

He looked confused.

"What's the play, Hector?"

"A sweep to the right."

"Okay, tell her a sweep to the left."

"Are you sure?"

"Without a doubt. She'll be thrilled. *Remember*, I was one of her favorite students."

"Okay, Rodney."

As Hector tapped his helmet and shook his left leg, I looked into the stands. Sure enough, Lutzkraut was whispering into her phone, sending the play straight to Belicheat.

When Hector finally snapped the ball, the Windham defense flocked to our left. I bolted out to the right— into wide-open space. I was unaccustomed to so much empty green field around me and almost fell down. I regained my balance and rushed on. The Garrettsville bleachers erupted as I cruised down our sideline. I knew that somewhere out there Jessica and my family and all my friends were cheering me on. I had only the safety to beat. I watched him cutting the angle down. He'd be tough to get around. Then I noticed another Windham player gaining ground on me. It was number ninety-nine! The last thing I wanted was to get slammed by Bart. I braced for impact.

Blahm! I heard the crunch of pads smashing together—but didn't feel anything. I looked back and saw Bart lying on top of the Windham safety.

"You moron," Belicheat called to his son. "What did you do?"

"I missed!"

I was coasting toward the end zone. The sound of Belicheat cursing his son was a distant distraction. This was it. One more step. I was in the end zone! Was this really happening? After my embarrassing "Timeout Touchdown" in our first game I didn't allow myself to believe it—until the line judge blew his whistle, put two arms in the air, and shouted, "Touchdown!"

The crowd went crazy. The Garrettsville band started playing the fight song. The football float drove back and forth behind the end zone. Chants of "Rodney!" filled the air. While I jogged back up the field past the Windham bench I watched Belicheat yank an enormous clump of hair from the top of his head. My mouth couldn't help itself. "Love the new look. By the way, give

Mrs. Lutzkraut my best." I gestured to his phone. He looked at me for a second and growled before throwing the phone in the grass.

I have to admit, I felt pretty good sitting on the bench at halftime. We were winning seven-three and I hoped I had put an end to Mrs. Lutzkraut's devious signaling scheme. Best of all, Jessica had been the first one to run up to me when the second quarter ended. For a second I thought she was going to give me a kiss, and perhaps she was, but instead she smiled and asked if she could have my autograph. We both laughed as her friends and Dave and Slim and Rishi and even Pablo gathered around to congratulate me. They were all thrilled . . . except Kayla. "Lucky touchdown," she managed, refusing to smile. It was actually a relief after Bart and Bruno. At least *she* was acting like her old self.

Eventually Slim suggested they go and buy snacks and the group took off, wishing me good luck for the second half. Only Rishi remained behind. He plopped down next to me on the bench and started talking. "So, I heard Toby stayed away today. Far away!"

"Smart move." I laughed.

"But I see the twins showed up. So, how are they treating you, Rodney? Better than yesterday? Better than you could have ever imagined?"

Ah, I should have known he was behind it. "They've been nice. Too nice. What'd you do, Rishi?"

"Remember when one of them tossed my phone into the gorge?"

"Yeah. Throwing phones seems to run in the family."

Rishi laughed. "I saw that with Belicheat! Anyway, when I got home my dad reminded me that my phone is GPS enabled. We went back out to the Ledges and found it. This morning, when I saw Biff and Bluto pull up—"

"Bart and Bruno."

"Whatever. Anyway, I went over to them and held up the phone."

"What did they do?" I asked.

"Let's just say we came to an arrangement. I won't show the video to anyone as long as they leave you alone during the game. After all, I can't have anything happen to my number one client! What do you think?"

"I think you've been hanging around the Boss too much, but I like it."

"The funny thing is that there's actually no evidence!" Rishi was clearly enjoying himself. "Apparently," he laughed, "I never pressed 'record' during all the excitement yesterday. Can you believe—"

"Shhhh. Keep it down," I whispered.

"Why? Who's going to hear me? The twins are on the other side of the field."

"Hello, boys." We spun around. Mrs. Lutzkraut stood above us holding a hotdog in one hand and a plastic bag in the other. Fear gripped my chest. How long had she been standing there? "Such a marvelous game, Rodney. Something tells me the second half is going to be even better now . . . thanks to your friend Rishi. *A lot* better. Makes me think of a famous saying."

"Go team go?" Rishi suggested.

"Not quite. I was thinking, 'Loose lips sink ships.' It's an old expression that means be careful what you say, because you never know who's listening. The enemy might be lurking about. For example, Rodney, someone might be hiding in a park spying on you on a perfectly sunny afternoon. Which reminds me. Halloween is just around the corner. I thought you could use this."

She tossed the plastic bag into my lap and walked off. I looked inside.

"What is it?" Rishi asked.

I was too shocked to answer. He grabbed the bag and looked for himself. "What's the big deal, Rodney? You act like you never saw a clown mask before!"

Chapter 17

OUR NEW SECRET WEAPON

What a difference fifteen minutes can make. At the end of the first half I was on top of the world. I had scored a touchdown and Bart and Bruno were acting like a couple of teddy bears. Now I was about to take the field pretty certain that they had just found out Rishi was bluffing about his video.

If that wasn't bad enough, Mrs. Lutzkraut *wanted* me to know she was the one who had spied on Jessica and me that day. Yes, she was doing everything possible to rattle me—and it was working! If she had overheard me in the park, it meant she knew all about the Boss. It meant she knew that tonight's dinner with the Chicago gang had to go smoothly. And it meant she knew I had promised the Boss a good restaurant review from my mother.

"Rodney, Coach wants to see you!" Joe shouted.

Suddenly hearing my name brought me back to reality and the fact that we had a game to win. I ran over to the porta-potty. "How're you doing in there?" I asked.

"Maybe a little better but not good enough to come out. Listen, I'm really depending on you, Rodney. Every coach in Ohio will be laughing at me if we lose today's game. Someone told me they're already calling it #TheToiletBowl on Twitter. Please, Rodney, keep the team focused and pumped—and win one for Garrettsville!"

I promised I would try, but despite Coach Laimbardi's rousing pep talk the second half was nothing like the first. The twins were reinvigorated and eager to chase and crush me at every turn. It was clear why Notre Dame was interested in them. Only Josh was able to match their strength and ferocity. Why couldn't he have a nice big twin? Better yet, triplets! Three monstrous Joshes working for me! I had little time to dream. I spent every second running with one thought in mind. Survival!

The game wore on and while Bart and Bruno had yet to rip my head off, the outlook grew bleaker. We fell behind ten-seven and I sat out the end of the third quarter feeling pretty gloomy. It was beginning to look like all of Garrettsville would be at Mama's tonight demanding free food from the Boss. Just what I needed.

Someone else was also feeling down. Even from the bench I could hear the porta-potty whine to Coach Manuel, "Those two sons of his are wrecking balls and I can't think of anything else to do. Belicheat really is a much better coach than me. I'm never leaving this stinky john. I'll be buried in it in shame!"

"Interesting game so far, Rodney." Wendy Whizowitz had come over and was squirting a concoction into Josh's mouth. "Want some?" she asked. "I made it myself. It's much better than Gatorade and far more nutritional."

"Uh, okay." I figured at this point I had nothing to lose. She squirted some through my facemask into my mouth. "Aaarraah!" My mouth was on fire.

"Oh, that's the Tabasco sauce I added," Wendy explained. "It really gets Josh going."

"ArrrHHHOOOOOO!" he howled, kicking over the water jug.

"Great stuff," I croaked. "You should patent it."

"I might one day. I call it Wolf Juice because of Joshy's howl. What's going on with your coach?"

"Some sort of stomach issue."

She seemed to think for a minute. "I might have something for that."

"Another special formula? You're brilliant!" I shouted. "You're like the best scientist."

"I wouldn't go *that* far." She reached into her purse and pulled out a bottle of Pepto-Bismol.

"Hey, that'll work." Not wanting to waste another minute, I ran over and knocked on old *Doodie Calls*. "Coach, I have something for you."

The door cracked open and I slid the bottle in. I heard a couple of gulps and moments later the door banged wide open. From the Garrettsville stands a cheer erupted as the coach emerged into the sunshine, whacked himself in the stomach, and shouted, "I feel like a new man! Perfectly regular. Take that, Belicheat! Good work, Rodney."

My lips cracked into a smile. I don't know if my happiness was from having our coach back or from his pink Pepto-Bismol mustache. "Actually," I told him, "you have Wendy to thank for your, er, regularity. She had the bottle in her bag."

"Excellent work." He smiled at her and then paused. "I'm sorry, we can't have friends on the team bench."

Wendy ignored him. "Have you considered running a reverse? I've noticed they're over-pursuing. It's actually rather interesting. On average, they're 3.2 meters out of containment position. As I noted on my tablet, this happens on 83 percent of the plays run to the left. Now, running to the right is interesting on a whole other level. If you use the distributive property . . ."

Coach Laimbardi rubbed his head. "Got any aspirin in that bag of yours?"

Again Wendy ignored him, instead going into tremendous detail about how the distributive property could be used to our advantage.

"*Who* are you again?" Coach asked.

"I'm Wendy Whizowitz."

"The reverse is a good idea. You got any more clever schemes?"

"Well, I've written a whole book of plays." She held up a binder.

"May I?" Coach Laimbardi asked. Wendy handed over the book. Coach began to read. His eyes grew wider and wider. He licked away the pink mustache as he read and eventually bit down on his bottom lip. "You wrote all these?"

"Yes. Last night during the *PBS NewsHour*."

"I love this single-wing counter-sweep on page sixty-three."

"Oh, that one. Yes, I conceived it from Heisenberg's uncertainty principle."

"Heisenberg?" Coach asked. "I've heard of Heisman . . ."

Wendy smiled. "Besides Plato, there's nothing I'd rather read."

"I like Play-Doh," Josh said.

Wendy smiled at him. "See? We have so much in common."

"Well isn't that *just darling*!" The unmistakably sarcastic voice came from several feet away on the track. My heart began to race. With her usual fake smile, Mrs. Lutzkraut asked Coach Laimbardi, "May I approach the bench?"

"Uh, sure," he answered, "as long as you're not packing any cookies."

The second she joined us she dropped the nice act. "This girl," she hissed, pointing at Wendy, "is NOT allowed to be here during the game. You should know better." Somehow Lutzkraut had noticed that the school's smartest student was coaching the coach.

Laimbardi tried to be reasonable. "I really don't see the harm in—"

"Don't see the harm?" Lutzkraut exploded. "What if a football should strike her? She's not covered by the school's insurance policy like members of the team. It's a lawsuit waiting to happen!"

Coach Laimbardi stared at her long and hard. "That's where you're wrong," he finally answered. "Wendy Whizowitz *is* a member of the team. She's our new offensive coordinator."

I snuck a peak at Wendy, who was smiling proudly. "Congratulations," I whispered.

Coach Laimbardi wasn't through with Mrs. Lutzkraut. "In fact," he continued, "the only one standing here who *doesn't* belong on the team is you! Now please return to the bleachers at once or I'll be forced to call over Dr. Stone."

"Well!" Mrs. Lutzkraut snapped, shooting him a nasty look before marching back to her seat.

"Now, where were we?" Coach resumed. "Oh, yes. Is there any way we can turn this game around, Whizowitz?"

"Sure," she said, smiling and adjusting her glasses. "I think the first thing is to keep those two gigantic defensive ends away from Rodney."

"She's a genius!" I shouted to no one in particular.

And she was. Wendy immediately gave us a crash course on her wild yet brilliant plays. She was amazing. While her designs were light-years beyond even the NFL, she made it easy for us to grasp. Armed with her schemes, we stormed back on the field and started to gain ground.

After each advance I looked over at Coach Belicheat. His face was getting redder by the second. I didn't need to glance at Lutzkraut to know how she felt about our new secret weapon.

For the first time all second half I began to believe we had a chance to turn the game around. You could feel the home crowd's excitement as I made my way down the field on runs. I tried to stay focused but this was a once-in-a-lifetime moment and I wanted to savor it. From the corner of my helmet I watched proudly as Mr. Feebletop and my dad high-fived each other. My mom was standing and shouting my name. It seemed everyone was shouting my name, including Jessica and all my friends and hundreds of people I didn't even know.

The funny thing is that Josh, not me, was actually carrying the team. Wendy had put him in a position to take on the twins one at a time, and I was able to slide through without getting creamed. While the importance of Josh's blocks may have been lost on the casual fan, Belicheat eventually recognized the problem. "Take him on together!" he barked at his boys, jerking his head in Josh's direction. "Before they score!"

They took their father's order to heart. Completely ignoring the game, and me, the two brothers launched themselves full force at Josh. I watched them charge and collide with my big friend. The impact sounded like two freight trains ramming an aircraft carrier. A tremendous amount of dust from the dry field burst into the air. I couldn't see and tripped over Hector's ankle but I was more worried about Josh than the run. I waded into the cloud and found the three of them on the ground. "Josh!" I called, "are you all right?"

"That tickled," he said.

Staggering to his feet, Bart whined, "Hitting him is like running into a brick wall."

Unlike his brother, Bruno was no complainer. Instead he turned to his father. "Mommy!"

"Football's fun." Josh giggled. "I don't want the game to end. How many more innings, Rodney?"

I knew this wasn't the time to educate him on the game's finer points. "Uh, this is it, Josh. The last inning. Now, give them everything you've got!"

I pointed him in the right direction and we continued to move the ball down the field, picking up one first down after another. While our progress looked good, I couldn't help but notice the clock. It was clicking down—quickly! I even tried to run out of bounds to stop it.

"Nice try, Rathbone," Belicheat shouted, "but there's no time left for you to win. Your team and your lousy coach will never beat me."

I was afraid he was right. With under a minute on the clock we were still over thirty yards from the end zone— and stuck with a quarterback who refused to throw the ball.

"Time out!" Coach Laimbardi hollered. We went to the sideline and gathered around. I never saw him look so serious. "We only have time for one play," he explained. "Hector, I know you haven't thrown a pass all season, but we can't win by running the ball. You're going to have to throw it into the end zone."

"No thanks, man. Not with those two monsters running around!"

In a somber tone Laimbardi announced, "Well, then that's that. I might as well walk over to Belicheat and congratulate him on—"

"Actually, sir, we can still win."

Everyone turned to face the girl in our midst.

"How?" Laimbardi asked.

"I might have just the play," Wendy explained.

We all leaned in. "Well, let's hear it," Coach Laimbardi whispered nervously, a drop of sweat rolling down his forehead.

Wendy took a deep breath. "You see, we have a lot of ground to cover and no time. I think there's only one logical choice. We need to run the *Triple Reverse Statue of Liberty Fumblerooski.*"

Coach's face lit up. "Of course! The old *Triple Reverse Statue of Liberty Fumblerooski.*"

"You've heard of it?" Wendy asked excitedly.

"No."

"Well, it's bound to work. Everyone, watch what to do. Now Joe, you're going to get things started by . . ."

In record time, Wendy explained the craziest, most complicated play I'd ever heard in my life. The second she was done we ran onto the field and took our positions. I wish I could fully describe it but I never fully understood it. And I didn't even see the whole thing. What I *did* see was Joe snap the ball and Hector fumble it. But that was on purpose. JJ picked it up and ran right. He flipped it to Trevor, who flipped it to me. I flipped it to Hector, who wound up his arm to throw but at the last second let Josh take the ball. While they were doing that, I pretended I was hurt and limped to the sideline.

"Good!" Mrs. Lutzkraut called down to me. "Serves you right!" By now she was unable to control herself and didn't seem to care.

I had a fake, pained look on my face, but just before I stepped out of bounds I gave her a big thumbs-up and started sprinting.

"Stop him!" she screeched.

I reached the ten-yard line as Josh threw the ball. He was the only one strong enough to throw it that far. In all the confusion created by the play, I was wide open and now stepping into the end zone. The ball hung in the air for what seemed like a long time. In a weird slow-motion voice I heard Belicheat howl, "Nooooo!"

Which was followed by Lutzkraut shrieking, "Drop it!" The voice sounded awfully close and I spun around to see her charging out of the stands, her crazy red hair as wild as the look in her eyes.

"The ball, Rodney!" people were shouting.

Huh? Every G-Men player and fan was pointing. I

turned back just in time to snatch the ball before it hit the ground.

"Touchdown!" the ref yelled as the clock ran out.

"We win!" Coach Laimbardi roared. Trevor dumped an enormous jug of Gatorade over his head but I don't think Laimbardi even felt it. He was too busy jumping up and down with Coach Manuel shouting, "We beat Windham! We beat Windham!"

The home crowd went bananas and the next few minutes were pure chaos. I was swept up on shoulders and praised, cheered, thanked, and applauded from every direction. I finally broke away to run over and congratulate Coach Laimbardi. Before I could say anything he started shaking my hand.

"Rodney, you've made me a very happy man." His voice choked up. "I knew from that first day of school that you've got what it takes. You're a great athlete and a real team player. I'll never forget what you did for me here today." The look he gave me was one of pure joy. He was savoring the greatest victory of his life.

Before I could say, "You're welcome," someone shouted, "The float's out of control!"

I looked up in time to see it go in reverse right under the goalpost, the giant football on top crunching flat and flopping over the driver's windshield. Brown crepe paper flew everywhere. Next it lurched forward and started going in circles. I couldn't see who was driving but they sure were bad. When the float turned and headed straight for Coach Laimbardi and me, I had an idea who was behind the wheel. Mrs. Lutzkraut had tried to run me over with a bulldozer at summer camp! Was she up to her old tricks? I watched as the huge "G-Men" football veered wildly from side to side. It circled past us one last time and swooped back in our direction.

"Take cover, Rodney!" Coach Laimbardi shouted. "It's heading straight for the . . ."

BOOM!!!

Like a massive blue missile, *Doodie Calls* soared into the air and flew halfway across the field before landing near the Windham bench. Unfortunately for Belicheat and most of the Bomber players, including Bart and Bruno, it exploded on impact.

"EEEeeewwWW!" hundreds of people screamed in unison. It wasn't a pretty sight. Coach Laimbardi put his hand on my shoulder. "Glad we're not on the Windham bus later."

I turned my attention from the opposite sideline back to the float. It sat silent and empty where it had collided with the porta-potty . . . its driver's door wide open.

"Where'd she go?" I wondered out loud. People were swarming everywhere. Once or twice I thought I saw her but there was too much confusion. If it *had* been Mrs. Lutzkraut behind the wheel, she had managed to escape.

"What a show!" Rishi ran up to me grinning from ear to ear holding his phone in the air. "I caught the whole thing on video, especially your awesome touchdowns."

Then, as though reading my mind, he added, "Don't worry, I pushed 'record' this time."

My other friends soon joined us along with my parents and Penny and even the Windbaggers. They all congratulated me and spoke at once about the great Garrettsville win over Windham. My dad went on and on about how the game was destined for football legend. He began stopping strangers. "My son scored both G-Men touchdowns!"

"Okay, I've got to go now." I laughed. "Time to celebrate with my teammates." I was getting more embarrassed by the second.

We all said good-bye and as I headed back to the school building I realized that the battle was only half won. I still had to survive tonight at Mama's Restaurant—a night that might be all the more difficult thanks to a certain former teacher. But that was later. For now, the unthinkable had happened. I, Rodney Rathbone, had helped Garrettsville Middle School win the biggest game in its history.

As I pulled open the gym door and was greeted by shouts of "Rod-ney!" I realized it was even more than my school team winning. My home team had won. For the first time since leaving New York, I was finally home.

Chapter 18

SPATS HOULIHAN

"Rodney, I couldn't be prouder," my dad announced from his big chair in the living room. He had been sitting there, smiling, since getting back from the game. "This is the greatest day of my life!"

"What about the day I was born?" Penny asked, momentarily lowering her iPad.

"Yeah, that was good," he added absently, "but I've been waiting my whole life to beat the Windham Burgers!"

"What are you talking about?" Penny snapped. "We've only lived here a year. And it's Bombers, not Burgers."

"Oh . . . right. Guess I've got Freddy Burgers on my mind. Hey, what do you say we all celebrate Rodney's big victory by heading over to The Brick for dinner?"

I felt a rush of nervousness to my stomach. A couple of days earlier I had told my parents about my plans to bus tables tonight at Mama's and they weren't exactly thrilled.

In fact, it kind of felt like they were saying "no" so I had dropped the subject.

"I'd like to go with you tonight, Dad," I began, "but you know, well, I have to work at Mama's Restaurant."

The glory left his face. "I told you, Rodney, I don't like you hanging out down there. I've heard the owner isn't a nice guy."

He was right about that, but there was no backing out now. "I've promised to help," I explained, "and besides, Rishi says we're going to make a lot of money. It's the grand opening."

My dad didn't look impressed. "Money isn't everything."

I was about to say, "Well, maybe not to you," but decided to let it go. He was having too good a day. Instead I just said, "I've promised to help, and I don't want to be a quitter." I knew that would do it. My dad was always going on about finishing what you started.

"All right, son, but be careful."

I suddenly remembered the review. "Hey, aren't you and Penny still going with mom later to review Mama's for the newspaper?"

His face perked up. From the other room my mom called, "Yes, we are, and the Windbaggers are picking us up at seven-fifteen."

His face sagged—until he got an idea. "Rodney, want me to drive you to Mama's? We could leave right now. I'm sure your mom and Penny wouldn't mind heading over there with Fred and Ethel . . ."

"Nice try, Dad," I said, patting his shoulder, "but Mr. Singh is taking us."

Poor dad. Even on the greatest day of his life, there was no escaping Mr. Windbagger!

Two hours later, Rishi, Josh, and I walked in through the front door of Mama's. As my eyes adjusted to the dim lighting, I heard someone start clapping slow and loud. Cheese was pounding his big palms together.

The Boss turned around from the back of the restaurant and joined in with Cheese. I thought of my dad and how he might be wrong about the Boss. "Nice win today, Rodney," the Boss called out. "I have to admit, I was a bit nervous."

"Nervous?" Rishi scoffed. "There was never any doubt. Windham didn't stand a chance. And," he said, raising a finger in the air, "I estimate my marketing plan has given you one hundred times the exposure you would have had. I think you'll see quite a return on your investment. Maybe it's time we speak about compensation . . ."

"You believe dis kid?" Cheese said.

Willy walked in carrying a stack of menus. "What'd he do?"

"He's shaking down the Boss for money. Now. Right before da big opening."

"Unbelievable," the Boss agreed. "We're running around trying to make everything perfect before my Chicago friends arrive and dis one brings up money."

Money was the one subject that could instantly put the Boss in a bad mood. I was afraid Rishi might remind him that he hadn't paid us a penny yet, but even Rishi sensed this wasn't the time.

"Anyways," the Boss continued, looking madder by the second, "football star or not, I've been waiting for you to show up for an hour now. And where's that fourth kid you promised?"

It was a good question. We had offered to pick up Pablo at his house but he said he would just meet us here. I got the sense he didn't like people seeing where he lived. "Uh, our friend is running late," I explained, wondering if he would show up at all.

The Boss wiped his forehead with the back of his hand. "Well, let's hope he comes soon. We got a lot of work to do. You"—he pointed at Josh—"we got tables to bus. You ever bus before?"

"Sure," Josh said. "Every day." The Boss looked relieved until Josh added, "I ride one to school."

The Boss growled and ran his hands angrily through his hair. He must have been wearing a lot of gel or something because it stuck straight up. Josh laughed. "Nice hair."

We all gasped. The Boss's eyes narrowed. He took a step toward Josh. It was so silent in the restaurant I could hear the clock ticking on the wall. When the phone suddenly rang I almost bolted out the door. Everyone was too busy watching the Boss to move. The phone kept ringing until the bartender I had seen that first day walked out from the office and answered it.

"Yeah . . . yeah, okay, I'll tell him." He hung up. "Boss, that was Toothpick."

The Boss's face went white. He forgot about Josh. "What'd he want?"

"He said they just landed in Cleveland. Should be here within the hour. And that Spats is starving."

The Boss turned to Rishi and me. "Okay, let's hustle. You two are busboys tonight. Willy and Cheese will be waiting tables. I need you to fill people's water and take away their dirty plates and stuff. Right now you can start by setting the tables. And you, knucklehead," he said to Josh, "I've got a special job for you. Weasel and Big Earl left a ton of dirty dishes in the kitchen yesterday. I guess they's was testing recipes or something. Can you handle washing dishes?"

"Sure," Josh grunted.

As the two disappeared through the swinging door into the kitchen I heard the Boss ask, "You're positive, right? You're not going to say you ride a dish to school or something . . ."

Once they were gone, Rishi and I had a chance to talk. As we put the silverware and glasses on the tables, I whispered, "I don't like this. The Boss seems super nervous. What if people don't show up? What if he finds out my mom hates the food? He'll blame me for everything. I'm finally enjoying Garrettsville and I'll have to move to another town. I mean . . ." I stopped talking and stared at Rishi.

"What?" he asked. "I'm listening."

It sure didn't look like it. He had a big smile on his face and was busy doing some weird thing with the napkins. "I'm folding them into swans!" he said proudly. "For the plates."

"Swans? That looks like a crumpled-up ball. The Boss is going to have a fit!"

"Some things take imagination, Rodney."

I pointed to a corner of the napkin. "Is that the beak?"

"Clearly that's a wing."

My stomach started gurgling. I was surrounded by crazy people, including my best friend! "Rishi, stop doing that. No one's going to know it's a . . ."

Cheese was walking by so I shut my mouth. He took a few steps past us, slowed down, and came back. This was it.

"Hey!" he hollered. "It's one of dem big white birds! One of dem swan things. Willy, check it out. Dis guy's a regular Margaret Steward."

For the next five minutes, Rishi taught Cheese and Willy how to fold napkins into animals. I, on the other hand, kept waiting for the Boss to see them and go ballistic.

CRASH!

I jumped. It sounded like a plate breaking on the kitchen floor. I heard Josh laugh. "Oops!"

Willy and Cheese scattered as the Boss yelled "Careful!"

before bursting out of the kitchen. He glared at Rishi and me and came over to the table we were setting. "Hurry up. People are going to be here any minute." Then he flashed one of his not-so-happy smiles and warned, "We're about to find out if all them dumb ads and flyers was worth it. If no one shows up, all I can say is I'm glad you two will be right here where I can find you."

As he walked away he brushed against the table, knocking Rishi's swan napkin on its side. For the first time it actually looked real to me—a big dead duck in the middle of a plate! I gulped. This was going to be some night.

We had just finished with the final table when the front doors swung open. Before I could stop him, Rishi stepped forward to greet a middle-aged couple. "Welcome to Mama's. My name is Rishi. I'll be the maître-d' this evening . . ."

The Boss stepped in front of him. "This *busboy* will fill your glass with water and keep your table clean. If he don't, we'll lock him in the freezer overnight."

The lady laughed at what she assumed was a joke.

Over the next ten minutes, more people began to arrive. Suddenly it felt like hundreds of people were showing up at once! Willy and Cheese tried to seat everyone as fast as they could but a line was forming outside. When one man complained that he had reserved a table by the window, Cheese said, "Oh yeah? How's about I *toss* you through da window?"

While Cheese's customer service left something to be desired, one thing was certain—I could stop worrying whether people would show up for the opening. Of course, once they tasted the cabbage spaghetti they'd probably never come back, but for now the Boss would be happy.

A hand gripped my shoulder. It was the Boss. He was anything but happy. His face was whiter than before and his eyes were bulging. "There he is," he whispered. "Spats Houlihan. All the way from Chicago. And he brought backup."

Four men and a couple of women walked in, cutting straight to the front of the line. "Is Spats Houlihan the one with the toothpick in his mouth?" I asked.

"Use your brain!" the Boss scolded. "The one with the toothpick is Toothpick. Toothpick Tudeski. He's Spats's right-hand man. Real mean. Spats is the bald one with the white things over his shoes. The other two mugs with the squashed faces are a couple of tough guys from the old neighborhood. Oh no! Big Mouth is talking to them!"

Sure enough, Big Mouth Singh had put down his pitcher of water and was busy running his mouth. The Boss and I hurried to the front of the restaurant.

"Welcome to Mama's!" the Boss said.

Spats ignored the greeting and pointed at Rishi. "Who's dis kid?"

"Him? That's just one of our busboys. He—"

"He seems to know an awful lot about our operation.

236

Says we should expand into Pittsburgh. How would he know about that? You been talking in front of him?"

Beads of sweat covered the Boss's forehead. "No! Nothing like that. Just a lucky guess on his part."

"Not so lucky for you," Spats answered. "Makes me wonder if it was a mistake letting you take over Ohio."

I was beginning to see that there was nothing friendly about the Boss's Chicago "friends."

Spats looked at his watch. "Are we ever going to sit or are we eating standing up?"

Before the Boss could answer, Willy started shouting at a young couple waiting in line. "I don't care if you just got married! You, sit at that table, and you, sit back there where we got room. See the open seat next to them brats?"

As the woman ran crying from the restaurant the Boss pulled me aside. "Rodney, I don't trust Willy or Cheese to wait on Spats. I've always thought you had smarts. A bright kid. Just tuck in your shirt and be Spats's waiter tonight. We have to keep him happy."

Keep him happy? I'd hate to see him mad!

The Boss looked at me. "Be his waiter and there's an extra twenty in it for you. Here."

I was finally going to get some money from the Boss! Instead he shoved a pad and pen into my hand.

"But—"

"But nothing." He turned to Spats. "Rodney will show you to your table."

Toothpick Tudeski stared at me and shifted the tooth-pick from one side of his mouth to the other. "He's just a kid," he said. "He better not mess up."

"That's right," Spats added. "I'm expecting everything to be perfect. I didn't come all this way to get no gravy spilled on me."

My knees began to shake as I said, "Follow me."

The Boss had set up a special section for them toward the back of the restaurant. It was partially hidden by a heavy curtain and felt like a private room. We were halfway there when a girl called, "Rodney!" I turned around. All the commotion of the place and my con-cerns melted away. Jessica wore a light blue dress that matched her eyes. She was sitting with her parents and looked better than I'd ever seen her before. She hadn't told me she was coming. "Rodney, you walked right by us . . ."

I realized that Spats and his group had come to a stop, waiting for me. The Boss was watching. I looked into Jessica's big blue eyes. "I'm busy."

It wasn't exactly the response she was expecting. It wasn't even what I meant to say. "Well!" she declared, folding her arms and turning away from me.

Spats looked angrily at his watch again. The Boss kept jerking his head in the direction of their table. I had to say something. "Uh, Jessica, I meant—"

"He meant good-bye," Toothpick cut in.

I had no choice but to continue walking them to their

table. As I left I heard Jessica's dad ask, "*That's* the boy you've been talking about?"

Rishi ran up to me holding a basket of bread and a pitcher of water. "Here. The Boss said it was for your table. Isn't this fun, Rodney?"

After finally getting Jessica to like me again I had just blown it—and six people were expecting me to serve them without making any mistakes. "Fun" was the last word on my mind.

I handed out the menus and started to fill the water glasses. Spats, Toothpick, and the two guys with the dented faces were eyeing me suspiciously, but I wanted to look back at Jessica. I turned and was about to mouth the words, "I'm sorry."

"Watch it, kid!" Spats yelled. I spun around and saw in horror that I had missed his glass and splashed water all over his tie. "Dis is one hundred percent rayon!" he barked.

"I'm so sorry, Mr. Hooligan," I blubbered. I reached out with a swan to blot up the liquid.

"It's Houlihan," he corrected me.

My heart was pounding. "Sorry, Mr. Hoodlum."

"HOULIHAN!" he screamed. Half the restaurant looked over. He swatted my hand away from his tie. "You seem pretty nervous, kid. I don't like nervous people."

"Me? Nervous? I'm not nervous. I'm like this all the time. I have a, uh, medical condition. Uh, Jitteritus it's called. Not contagious, so no worries. Inherited actually.

239

I come from a long line of jitterers on my mother's side. Say, how about them Bears?"

Toothpick pointed his toothpick at me and said to Spats, "Maybe he works for the Feds and that's why he's nervous. We should check to make sure he's not wearing a—"

"Leave him alone," one of the two women said. "He's just a kid. And he's a cute kid at that." Despite all the chaos, her words made me smile and glance her way. She had long black hair, wore a lot of makeup, and was pretty. She saw me looking at her and smiled back.

"You making eyes at my lady?" Spats spat.

"Who, me? Eyes? Oh no, I was looking at the painting." I pointed to a large picture of Moscow just behind the woman's shoulder. "It's beautiful, isn't it? I love the way the sunlight hits the Kremlin. Anyway, let me go get some more butter for the bread. Can't have too much butter, right?"

"You just tell Francis that we're hungry. I want to see what my investment tastes like. And shut that curtain so we can have some privacy!"

I nodded, shut the curtain, and headed straight to the Boss. He was standing just outside the kitchen door and held up his hands as if to ask, "How's it going?"

"Well, Francis . . ."

His eyes locked onto mine. I thought I was a goner.

CRASH! Another dish could be heard smashing in the kitchen, followed by an "Oops!" from Josh.

"Careful!" the Boss yelled through the swinging doors. "One more and it comes out of your salary."

Before he had a chance to yell at *me*, I grabbed some butter off a side table and rushed back to Spats, pulling the curtain behind me. Everyone was studying their menus and talking like I wasn't even there. I took out my pad and pen and stood quietly against the wall until they were ready to order.

"Dis is a disaster," Spats was saying to Toothpick. "Look at this menu. Who ever heard of meatballs and sauerkraut for an appetizer?"

"No way people are coming back to this place," Toothpick agreed, flipping through the pages. "Tonight, sure, they're curious . . . but Mama's will be shut by next week and you can kiss your money good-bye."

Spats didn't like that. "You can kiss *him* good-bye if he don't pay me back."

"With all due respect," Toothpick continued, "I never understood why you backed this guy. He's been broke for years now. Borrows money from his mother in the morning and loses it at the racetrack by dinner."

As I stood there listening, everything became clear to me—but it didn't make me feel any better. A lot more was riding on tonight and my mom's review than I had realized. These guys were much tougher than the Boss. In fact, I was beginning to see that the Boss was a big fake. He bullied us around and wore fancy suits like he had a lot of money but . . .

"You!" Spats barked.

My pen went flying across the room.

"How long you been standing there?"

"Uh," I stammered, "I was waiting to take your orders."

"Been spying on us, huh? This isn't good—for you!"

All four men started to rise. I was about to dive under the table when a hand reached in and pulled open the curtain. "THERE you are!" a voice boomed. "Been looking all over for you!"

I was never so happy to see Mr. Windbagger.

"I'll say it again, Rodney, one heck of a game today!" He came into the room and shifted his attention to Spats and the rest at the table. "I'm sure you all know who your waiter is. That's my boy, Rodney Rathbone!" He grabbed Toothpick's water glass, took a gulp, and raised it up. Toothpick's mouth dropped open and his toothpick fell to the floor but Mr. Windbagger was taking no notice. He said, "A toast—to Rodney leading Garrettsville in our big win against Windham!"

Everyone stared at him in shock.

"Now don't be shy, come on, come on . . ." Mr. Windbagger ran around the table sticking a water glass in each person's hand. He stopped behind Spats and gave him a hearty slap on the back. "You too, pops!"

I covered my ears.

Toothpick jumped to his feet and reached for his pocket. "Okay, who do you work for?"

Mr. Windbagger reached for *his* pocket—and pulled

out a business card. "Proud to say I run my own agency, Windbag Insurance." He started pumping Toothpick's hand. "Fred Windbagger here from Garrettsville, USA. I'm a guest tonight of Rodney's mother, Gloria Rathbone."

At hearing my mom's name, Spats turned in his seat and stared up at me. It was the first time I saw him smile. "Of course, you're Gloria Rathbone's son. Gloria Rathbone of the *Cleveland Plain Dealer*. Francis mentioned you."

Toothpick, who still didn't know what was going on, asked what he should do about Mr. Windbagger.

"What you should do," Spats said, "is listen to what this good man suggests we do."

A minute later the Boss appeared in the room. Nothing could have prepared him for what he found. Everyone was standing, glasses raised high, shouting, "To Rodney, the world's greatest waiter!"

"And running back!" Mr. Windbagger added, whacking Spats again.

"And running back!" they all agreed. "Here's to Rodney Rathbone!"

The Boss was so stunned I had to pour him a glass of water.

After a minute Mr. Windbagger said, "Great meeting you all. Rodney, be sure to stop over at our table and say hi. Oh, and most important"—he turned to Spats and the group—"did everyone get one of my cards? Not sure what line of work you nice people are in, but there's no such thing as too much life insurance!"

Chapter 19

THE HUNGER GAMES

If the night had ended at that moment, making up with Jessica would have been my biggest problem. Unfortunately, I was about to learn of another problem from the Boss. "Meet me and Cheese in the kitchen," he said so only I could hear. "Willy can take care of Spats and his crew." He hurried away.

"So," Spats asked before I had a chance to leave, "your mom's one of dem two women sitting with that crazy guy who was just here?" He stared across the dining room in her direction.

I nodded my head "yes."

"Good." He leaned over and whispered something in Toothpick's ear.

"Um, I have to go now," I said. "Great meeting you all."

My first order of business was apologizing to Jessica. The Boss would have to wait a minute. As I walked across the dining room to her table I saw a lot of people I knew and said hello to a few, including the Boss's mother, who was all dressed up for the occasion. I couldn't help notice, however, that everyone was frowning and grumbling about how long it was taking for the food to come out.

"Do you know when my order will be ready?" a woman asked as I passed by.

"Any minute," I said. "I'll check with the chefs."

"Thank you, son. It's taking forever."

What was going on with Big Earl and Weasel? I was beginning to guess they might be the reason the Boss wanted to see me in the kitchen, but right now I had trouble of my own. Jessica had spotted me coming and turned her head in the other direction. I was two tables away from her when Coach Laimbardi called out, "Rodney, come over here a second and meet my wife!"

He and Coach Manuel were sitting in a booth with their wives. I shook hands with both women and said to Mrs. Laimbardi, "I've heard so much about you. I'm not sure our desserts will live up to your cheesecake."

She laughed. "Oh, yes, Vince just loves his sweets." She patted Coach Laimbardi's hand. They all seemed real nice, including Coach Manuel's wife. It was a welcome change from Spats and Toothpick.

Coach Laimbardi said, "Rodney, I still feel like I'm floating after today's game. Pull up a chair, we need to celeb—"

"Rodney!" the Boss ordered from the kitchen door.

"Gotta go," I said to Coach. "I'll join you when I get a chance."

I ran over to Jessica's table and started to say "sorry" but had only gotten "so" out before the Boss called me a second time.

"So?" Jessica asked. "That's all you can say?" Her parents frowned and shook their heads.

I tried one last time. "Jessica, and Mr. and Mrs. Clearwater, I promise I'll make it up to you but we're very busy and I have to help out in the kitchen."

Jessica's father reached out and grabbed my arm. "Can you at least get us some bread? I'm starving to death!"

"Dad!" Jessica blushed, looking prettier than ever.

"Of course," I said, seeing my chance to set things right. "No problem." I gave Jessica a wink and was thrilled to see her smile back. "I'll be right out!"

I tore off into the kitchen—and was shocked by what I found. Josh was standing knee-deep in a pile of broken dishes . . . but there was nothing strange about that. I was shocked because no one was cooking.

"Where are the chefs?" I asked the Boss.

"Exactly!" he yelled. "Where are the chefs?"

Cheese shrugged. "Haven't seen them in an hour."

Besides the fact that restaurants tend to get bad reviews when they forget to serve food, I felt sorry for all those people sitting around in the dining room. I gave it some thought. "Did anyone check the freezer? I know Big Earl naps in there sometimes."

Cheese stomped into the walk-in freezer. He emerged ten seconds later, alone and shivering. "It's freezin' in there!"

I was about to say "Duh!" but bit my tongue. I could tell from the panicked look on the Boss's face this wasn't the time for jokes. "What about out back?" I suggested. "Sometimes Weasel hangs out in the alley."

Before waiting for the Boss to say anything, Cheese disappeared through the screen door. This time he had better luck.

"Put me down!" Weasel whined as Cheese returned to the kitchen. He was dangling in Cheese's left hand. Cheese's right hand gripped Big Earl.

"Where do you want dem?" Cheese asked the Boss.

"You can throw them in that pot of boiling water for all I care."

For a second I thought Cheese might do it. Instead he let them go as the Boss approached and started yelling, "Where were yous? Everyone's waiting for their dinner! Have you made the borscht? The meatballs? Stuffed the cabbage?"

Big Earl shrugged like he didn't care. "I don't know how to make that food."

"What?" the Boss hollered. "We went over the whole menu!"

"Yeah, all that weird stuff," Weasel mumbled. "I only make scrambled eggs."

"This is a disaster!" The Boss stuck his head in his

hands. "I'm ruined! You two are going to get me in real hot water with Chicago!"

Josh looked over into the pot of boiling water and scratched his head.

"Anyway," the Boss continued, "get going and cook the things we talked about!"

"Hey, you can't yell at us," Weasel cut in. "We just got a real good job offer from some lady outside."

The Boss snapped his fingers and Cheese's weighty hand clamped down on Weasel's shoulder. Weasel glanced at it nervously. The Boss's voice went smooth, quiet, and frightening. "I can yell at whoever I want, see? Whenever I want. Now, what lady are you talking about?"

"I don't know, some old lady with red hair. She just left. She said she'd pay us double what you're giving us. She said we should quit now without notice. After all, she reminded us, we're respected chefs."

An old lady with red hair! I'd spent the afternoon hoping that the clown mask had just been a scare tactic to throw me off in the game, but now I knew for certain. Mrs. Lutzkraut had heard me in the park that day and was trying to make sure Mama's got a bad review. Anything to get me in trouble.

"Respected chefs?" the Boss was screaming. He kicked the stove and threw the garbage pail against the wall. "You two idiots are fired! Cheese!"

"Boss?"

"Get rid of dem!"

Big Earl and Weasel didn't need any encouragement from Cheese. Making like his eggs, Weasel scrambled through the door with Big Earl close on his heels.

Once again, Mrs. Lutzkraut had gotten her way. Like some evil wizard or witch, she didn't even need to be present to accomplish her goals! Mama's Restaurant was now without its chefs. I shook my head and watched the Boss pace around the kitchen breathing hard. Josh watched the pot on the stove. "Bubbles!" He laughed.

The happy outburst brought the Boss back to his senses. He turned to me. "See that, Rodney? That's how you handle a problem. Do it fast and hard. It's never a good idea to think too much." He straightened out the front of his suit—and suddenly smacked his forehead so hard that his head snapped back into some hanging pots. For a few seconds they swung and clunked into each other. "What am I going to do?" he cried. "I just fired our chefs!"

Evidently it took a few minutes for news to reach his brain, but now that it had arrived the Boss looked truly frightened. "Cheese, go out front and try to keep the customers happy. I'll think of something."

As Cheese walked by me he said, "Oh, I'm supposed to tell you that your bratty friends are here."

I guessed that wasn't the exact wording but I got the idea. After the football game, Wendy, Kayla, Dave, and Slim had said they would try to get their parents to drive them over to Mama's tonight. They all wanted to see Josh, Rishi, and me dressed as waiters . . . even though I told them we were just busing tables. In all the excitement I hadn't noticed them. "Where are they sitting?" I asked Cheese.

"They only wanted Cokes so I stuck 'em at that broken table off the dining room."

The dining room!!! I suddenly remembered Jessica's father and the bread. Now Jessica would be *really* mad at me—and for good reason. I turned to the Boss. "Where's that bread I saw before? That the bakery delivered?"

He pointed without looking to the corner of the kitchen. Most of the trays were empty but there were two loaves left. I grabbed one, cut it into slices, threw it in a basket, and rushed through the swinging doors.

I was halfway to Jessica's table when I noticed the flowers.

Some guy in a suit was placing the biggest, craziest floral arrangement I'd ever seen right on top of my mom's table. All around her, people began sneezing and blowing their noses. Eyes were watering. The whole restaurant smelled like a giant florist. My mom looked worried and was waving me over excitedly. As I got closer to her table I noticed a silk banner hanging from some roses: WE'LL MISS YOU, FIDO.

"Rodney, do you know anything about this?" my mom asked.

I guessed it was my mom. I couldn't really see around the flowers. "I have an idea who might have sent them,"

I said, remembering Spats whispering to Toothpick. "By the way, where's dad?"

"He's with Rishi. Now Rodney, you know it's supposed to be a secret when I review a restaurant!"

"Nice going," Penny added, "and who are your creepy friends over there?" She motioned toward Spats's table.

"Um, just some people I have to wait on tonight."

"Very nice people, actually," Mr. Windbagger told his wife. "Salt of the earth type. Say, is that for us, Rodney? The little miss and I are starving over here." He was eyeing the breadbasket.

"Um, sure." I placed it on the table, praying that Jessica and her parents weren't watching. Just then the front door opened and Pablo walked in, looking shy and a little scared. "Excuse me," I told my mom. "I have to go."

"But Rodney . . . the flowers . . ."

I met Pablo at the door. He wasn't exactly dressed up. In fact, he was wearing his trademark gray hoodie, his jeans were covered in grease, and I noticed his hands were black. "What's that smell?" he asked.

"Just some flowers. Listen, where have you been?"

He looked sad. "Sorry I'm late, Rodney. The chain on my bike broke on the way here and it took a while for me to fix it."

"That's okay," I said. "You can wash in a second, but right now we better go see the Boss. Everything's going wrong tonight."

As we headed toward the kitchen I noticed Rishi and my dad hooking up wires to a big TV that hung across the back wall. I was about to ask what they were doing when I heard, "Pssst!" from Spat's table. I went over to investigate.

"So," Spats asked, "did your mom like the flowers? If that don't get us a good review, I don't know what will!"

I was about to say, "Good food wouldn't hurt," but I had already been down that road with the Boss. Instead I just thanked him.

Toothpick looked like he was ready to eat the table-cloth. "Where's da food we ordered from Willy?"

Not wanting to be the bearer of bad news, I said, "Should be out in a minute," and turned to join Pablo, who was talking with Rishi and my dad.

Rishi was grinning like a fool, which usually spelled trouble for me. "Rodney, check it out! I came up with a great way to keep people occupied while they're waiting for dinner. Your dad and I just hooked it up." He clicked a remote and I was shocked to see today's football game against Windham appear on the TV. "You like it? It's plugged into my phone. I edited it so people can watch the highlights."

I doubted that anyone but Coach Laimbardi and my dad would enjoy it, but at least it would keep people's minds off their stomachs! "Great," I said.

Still looking at the TV, Rishi asked, "Oh, did you see the gang? They're sitting in the corner. Josh just went over to say hi to Wendy."

"I'll go over in a minute. Listen, we have a big problem. Mrs. Lutzkraut fixed it so we don't have any chefs in the kitchen. All these people will freak out when they realize there's no food coming—especially those tough guys from Chicago. Rishi?"

"Here comes the part where Coach Belicheat throws his phone in the grass!"

I shook my head. "Let me know how it ends."

As Pablo and I headed back to the kitchen, he said something that was to change the events of the night—in lots of ways. "If you need someone to cook," Pablo volunteered, "I'm pretty good at it. I'm the one who cooks for my family. You know, with my mom gone and all . . ."

"Yeah? Do you think you can cook for *this* many people?" I motioned to the hungry diners . . . and found myself staring into Jessica's angry eyes. The bread! "Wait right here," I told him as I dashed over to where she and her mom were sitting.

"Forget something?" Jessica asked.

"I'm so sorry. All this stuff is going on. I'll get some bread and come right back. I promise!"

"Promise?"

"Promise! Hey, where's your dad?"

It was Jessica's mom who answered this time. "He went out for pizza. Said he couldn't take it anymore."

I felt awful . . . until Jessica giggled. "He's really in the men's room." Both she and her mom started laughing and I realized that Mrs. Clearwater had the same fun sense of humor—and smile—as her daughter.

"Good one." I laughed. "See you in a minute."

I grabbed Pablo and headed into the kitchen, eager to tell the Boss that I might have a solution to his chef problem.

"Who's this?" the Boss barked, eyeing Pablo up and down. "Like I don't got enough on my mind."

"This is my friend Pablo," I said, not liking the way the Boss was acting in front of him. "He's the fourth guy who's helping out tonight. He designed the menu."

"Yeah, well, he might be good with a crayon but I don't need someone like him moping around and scaring customers away."

I motioned for Pablo to pop back into the dining room. Once he was gone I said, "I think you got bigger problems with the customers right now. You don't have a cook, remember?"

"You're right, and I'm probably a goner, but I don't intend to spend my final moments with someone like dat kid."

"What's your problem with Pablo?" I demanded. It came out a lot louder than I expected. I could feel my face turning red, either from anger or fear or both.

"Not that I gotta explain myself to a runt like you, but I'm running a classy joint here. That kid ain't classy. Let's just say he's from the wrong side of the tracks."

"And what's the right side?" I asked. "Where you

come from?" My voice felt like it belonged to someone else. I wanted to tell it to shut up before it got me tossed in the freezer.

"You better watch it," the Boss warned.

"Or what?" My heart was racing. All I could think about was how right my dad had been about the Boss. He was turning out to be a real creep. What came out of my mouth next probably shocked the Boss as much as it did me. "Either Pablo stays, or we all walk out, right now! Me, Rishi, and Josh! See how good you manage!"

I couldn't believe I said it. I got ready to bolt if the Boss went nuts.

It sure looked like it was going in that direction. He eyed a big soup pot. Was he going to clobber me with it? The two of us stood staring at each other listening to the water boil. After a minute his eyes fell to the floor. He was in trouble and he knew it. "All right. Your friend can stay."

"And . . ."

"And what?"

"And you have to apologize to him."

By now I was sure some prizefighter had taken over my body. In my whole life I had never stood up to anyone like this—especially to a full-grown bully like the Boss. He stared at me and shook his head. "You're really pushing it kid, but fine, send him in."

"Pablo!" I yelled.

He came back in. Before the Boss could open his

mouth, Pablo said in his quiet voice, "Sorry about the way I look. The chain broke on my bike on the way here. I'll go wash up." He started to turn around.

"Wait," the Boss called, "there's a sink back here you can use. And listen, sorry about before. This is my big opening and my two cooks just quit. I'm a little jumpy."

"Yeah, I understand," Pablo answered, "but I think I can help. I know my way around a kitchen pretty well. I can cook anything."

The Boss smiled. "Well, go wash your hands, put an apron on, and . . ." Suddenly he paused and sagged down onto a milk crate. "What am I saying? I'm going to have a twelve-year-old be my chef?" He stuck his face into his hands and moaned.

"What's the matter, Francis?" the Boss's mother asked, entering the kitchen.

The Boss jumped up and put on a fake smile. "Nothing! Everything's great. Are you having a good time?"

"Yes, honey, but it looks like the customers are getting tired of watching football. They want to eat."

"Watching football?" the Boss grumbled. "Who put on the TV?"

His mom looked concerned. "Why are you so upset, sweetie puffs?"

"Cause I got a whole crowd of people and no chefs. I fired them . . . by accident."

"That wasn't too smart now, was it, Francis?" She

picked an apron off of a hook on the wall.

"Whadaya doin'? You know how I feel about you working in the kitchen."

"Honey, someone has to cook dinner for those people."

The Boss sighed. "I guess you're right."

"I could use some help though," she said.

Louder than I'd ever heard him before, Pablo told her all about how he could cook. "Let me help!" he suggested.

"Really? How wonderful. What's your name?"

"Pablo."

Mama smiled and patted him on his head. Then she looked at the stack of orders Willy and Cheese had left on the counter. It was almost a foot high. "I'm afraid Pablo and I are going to need a bit more help to get these dinner orders turned around. Maybe you could ask your Chicago friends if they want to—"

"No!" the Boss shouted. "I mean, I wouldn't bother them. They're not exactly the kitchen type."

It was finally my turn to speak up. "I have an idea. It's our only chance! Wait here a second."

I was about to charge into the dining room, but this time I remembered. I grabbed the last loaf of bread and tossed it like a football to Mr. Clearwater as I flew past Jessica's table. A minute later I was back in the kitchen—with Josh, Wendy, Slim, Dave, and Kayla.

Mama smiled and clasped her hands. The Boss looked

annoyed. "What's this, tryouts for *Annie*? I got a restaurant to run. These kids can't be back here."

"These kids," I said, "are your new junior chefs!"

My friends had jumped at the idea of helping out with the cooking—especially Slim, who had licked his lips and shouted, "I always wanted to see a restaurant kitchen!"

Mama seemed to love the idea. "All right, everyone. Wash your hands and come right back. We have a lot of prep to do." She had already begun placing large containers of meats and sauces and vegetables on the counters. Luckily, Weasel and Big Earl had begun thawing most of the food before Mrs. Lutzkraut tried to ruin everything.

"Can I help too?" a familiar voice called from the door.

Mama answered, "Only if you promise not to get any sauce on that beautiful blue dress. Better grab an apron, sweetie."

Jessica gave me a big smile and joined the group. They all stood on one side of the counter with Mama and Pablo on the other. Mama began, "You can call me Mama or you can call me Chef. Got it?"

"Got it!" everyone cheered.

"And I think you all know my partner this evening, Chef Pablo."

Pablo smiled and bowed. They all clapped.

"Okay, good then. Pablo will show you two boys

258

how to peel potatoes. And you," she asked Wendy, "have you ever stuffed a cabbage? Now, I'll need you two girls to start seasoning the meat . . ."

Seeing that Mama was firmly in charge and that things were heading in the right direction, the Boss left to return to the front of the restaurant. As he passed me he looked down and smiled. "Thanks for saving my butt, kid. A lot is riding on tonight with Spats and me. You have no idea."

"Actually I do," I told him. "Now get out there before he thinks you forgot about him."

"You ain't half bad," he said before disappearing through the swinging doors.

I turned back to see if Mama needed anything else. She was talking to the one junior chef who was still mesmerized by boiling water. "I'm sorry," Mama asked, "but what's your name?"

"Josh."

"Well, Josh, stop gazing into that pot . . . you're making me nervous. Do you know anything about beets?"

Josh jumped and spun around. "Yes! Beets make your poo—"

"He just loves beets," I interrupted.

"How nice, so do I," Mama said. "Tonight everyone's going to eat a lot of beets."

"Hahahahaha!" Josh grabbed his stomach and pounded the counter.

Mama watched him and smiled. "A happy kitchen

makes tasty food! So, how is everyone doing?"

I looked around the busy kitchen. I had never seen my friends so quiet. Even Kayla! They were all busy slicing and dicing and mincing and chopping. Giant pots of sauce began simmering on the burners. Pablo carefully checked each one, adding salt or spices where needed. Before long the kitchen erupted with wonderful smells. I smiled. "See you guys in a minute," I called out. "Just going to check if Rishi needs help."

I walked back into the dining room and saw that the football game was still on. My dad, Mr. Windbagger, and the two coaches were having a great time. The same couldn't be said for the rest of the customers, who were frowning and sighing. I guess I couldn't blame them. They were starving—and half were probably Windham fans—but I definitely didn't mind seeing myself on that giant TV catching the game-winning touchdown.

"Way to go, Rodney!" my dad called over to me.

I gave him a thumbs-up but was busy watching what came next. I was being hoisted on some shoulders. And there I was congratulating Coach Laimbardi in the middle of the celebration. And there was the G-Men float going crazy up and down the field . . . which would mean . . .

I started looking frantically for Rishi. He wouldn't! I ran over to Spats's table and asked the Boss, "Have you seen Rishi?"

"No, why?"

Please tell me he wouldn't be dumb enough to include . . .

AHHHHhhhhhhhhh!!!!!! The restaurant erupted into a horrified scream. I joined in as I watched the porta-potty explode near the Windham bench. The sound of chairs falling backward filled the air as half the restaurant bolted outside gagging. The Boss grabbed his chest like he was having a heart attack.

"Is this some kind of joke?" Spats yelled at him. "You think you can ruin me by making sure this place fails? First you make people wait two hours for food and now this?"

The Boss was shaking his head "no" but was too stunned to defend himself.

"Toothpick!" Spats ordered, keeping his angry eyes fixed on the shaking Boss, "Take this idiot 'round back and . . ."

The pretty woman with the long black hair leaned forward. "Toothpick's puking on the sidewalk."

At that very moment, with the most horrid timing ever, Willy and Cheese marched in from the kitchen with the first of the appetizers. Cheese proudly announced, "Here comes da food, everybody!"

One lady blurted, "Who can eat after that?"

She was right, but the plates were delivered to her table, and instead of gagging she poked with a fork at what looked like some meatballs covered in wet leaves. Her nostrils twitched. Tentatively, she cut into the ball and took a nibble. The moment of truth. "This is di . . ." She paused, getting the attention of the other diners at her table. She soon had the attention of the whole restaurant and the customers returning from outside.

Di what? I frantically wanted to know. Disastrous? Disgusting? Demented?

"Di what?" the Boss screamed, seeing that Toothpick was back.

"This is . . . delicious. I've never had a meatball taste so good."

"You got to try this soup," a man sitting across from her said. "It's sweet, it's spicy, it's creamy, it's . . . Oh, I have to order another bowl. Waiter!"

As the food was brought out from the kitchen, all you could hear was the sound of knives and forks clinking on plates. I saw nodding heads and everyone began eating with gusto—even the people still recovering from Rishi's video recap. I couldn't believe it. How could anyone eat after that?

Rishi appeared at my side. "As usual I saved the day. Look at my timing. The video finished just as the food arrived."

"Maybe we could have done without the big finish."

"What? That's the best part," he said, smiling. "Okay, time to fill more water glasses."

"I'll join you in a second," I said.

Things looked like they had calmed down at Spats's table, now that the food had arrived and everyone was busy stuffing their faces. The Boss got up to leave.

"Where do you think *you're* going?" Spats ordered. Maybe things hadn't calmed down.

"Um, thought I'd check on the kitchen . . ."

"You ain't going nowhere. This is the best meal I ever tasted. Everyone in the joint is loving it. As far as I'm concerned, you can open ten more restaurants! Now sit. Stay with us. Tonight, you're da guest of honor." Spats raised his glass in the air and shouted, "To Francis!" Everyone at the table joined in.

While I knew the Boss hated people hearing his real name, he sure looked happy—and relieved. He noticed me watching. So only I could see, he raised his glass a little and nodded his head at me. For the second time that night, I was being toasted at Spats's table.

As I dashed around clearing plates, I learned just how chaotic working in a busy restaurant could be. It seemed like in every direction there was something that needed to be done. I sprinted around grabbing dirty plates, filling water, wiping crumbs from tablecloths, and replacing Toothpick's toothpicks. All the while, people I knew surrounded me and said hello. It was hard being polite and making small talk while getting everything accomplished.

But even though I was sweating and my feet hurt, I was aware of something else. It seemed that everyone liked the food. I mean really liked it. All over I heard people saying, "This is delicious," and going "Mmmmmmm!"

At one point Mr. Windbagger called me over and said,

while licking his bowl, "I don't know what this goulash goop is, but man is it good. Ethel, forget the Ponderosa. We're coming here from now on."

My mom said, "Rodney, do you see the bald man at the table over there?"

"Who, Spats Houlihan?"

"No. Who's Spats Houlihan?"

"Oh nobody, I just made up the name, haha."

She gave me a funny look. "I'm talking about Michael Symon. He's Cleveland's most famous chef. He must have heard about the Russian-Italian menu. It's never been done before. Rodney, you're working in one of the most innovative restaurants in America."

"You're saying you like it?"

"Like it? The food has more than lived up to the hype. It's probably the best restaurant in Ohio."

"So you're going to give Mama's a good review?" I finally asked.

My mom smiled. "I would, of course," she began, "but after those flowers arrived at the table I realized that they knew who I was. I called my editor and he agreed that I shouldn't review it. Plus with you working here, and all the advertisements with your face on them, well, it just didn't feel right."

"You mean we have to pay for this!" my dad shouted.

"Yes, Donald, we'll have to pay for dinner, like everyone else. I already told Fred and Ethel that they would be our guests."

My dad sunk down in his seat. Wiping his face with a napkin, Mr. Windbagger said, "Thanks, Donald. Think I'll order another one of them blini desserts."

My mom looked at me. "I hope you're not disappointed that I decided not to review Mama's."

Oddly enough, I realized my dad was probably a lot more disappointed than I was. So much had happened over the past few hours that I no longer cared or worried about the Boss or Spats or even Mrs. Lutzkraut. To be honest, I only had one thing on my mind—Jessica.

My family started to get up to leave. My dad said to me, "I'll pick you up once I drop everyone off."

"Yep. Thanks."

I said good-bye to them and the Windbaggers and continued clearing plates. Most of the restaurant began to finish their desserts and head home. There was one table still finishing. I went up to them. Jessica had returned from the kitchen and was sitting with her parents.

"So, did you like everything?" I asked.

Mr. Clearwater looked at me. His face wasn't angry or anything, but it wasn't warm and inviting either. "Eventually," he said, "once the food finally arrived."

I knew he was pretty serious and strict. I remembered how he'd sent my friend Greg home when he wanted to practice for our Robin Hood play last year. I'd been happy about that, but now it was my turn to face him. It was now or never.

"Mr. Clearwater, I was wondering if it would be

okay for me to take Jessica out to dinner one night next week."

Mrs. Clearwater smiled at her daughter. Jessica blushed, shifted in her seat, and looked nervously at her dad.

"Rodney, I think my daughter is a little young to be going to dinner with boys."

My stomach dropped.

"That being said, I guess a dinner would be all right. As long as I can drive both ways and sit at the next table . . ."

"Daaaaad!" Jessica whined.

"All right, a table on the other side of the room."

Jessica made a face but I said, "I think that sounds great."

I saw a large shadow begin to form over the table and realized Cheese had come up in back of me. I turned around.

"Dat was cute wit da dad. Listen, Boss wants to talk to you. In his office. Now. Wit Rishi."

I said good-bye to Jessica and her parents, grabbed Rishi, and walked into the office. Like that first time we met him, the Boss was sitting behind his big wooden desk. I couldn't believe only a couple of months had passed. Not even.

"You two did real good tonight," the Boss said. "Spats loved everything. Da place was packed and we got enough reservations to last us till New Year's. I think we can finally talk about money."

Rishi elbowed me.

"Yup, we made a boatload tonight." He slid an envelope across the desk. "That's for you and your friends. There's going to be plenty more where that came from."

Rishi blurted, "Now we're talking!"

I sat there looking at it. The envelope looked full. A number of things I wanted to buy flashed across my mind, but then I thought about the things my dad was always telling me . . . about what really mattered in life. "You can keep my share," I said. "Buy something nice for your mother with it."

"Rodney, what are you doing?" Rishi hollered.

I ignored Rishi and continued talking to the Boss. "We helped you out and I'm glad Mama's will be a hit, but all I want now is to go back to being a normal student. I think the restaurant business will have to get along without me."

The Boss frowned. I couldn't tell if he was insulted, confused, or just tired from the long night. "If dat's really what you want, I ain't gonna twist your arm." He picked up the cash envelope and handed Rishi some money. "Dis is for you and the other guys. As for your friend here, I think he's making a mistake."

"We'll see," I said, but as I stood to leave, I felt real good about my decision.

Once outside the office I said to Rishi, "Sorry, but I can't do all this anymore. There are a lot of other things I want to focus on."

He paused, then his eyes widened. "Hey, yeah, me too!

I'm thinking Hollywood. I'm going to make some calls tomorrow. I see big things for us, Rodney. Big things!"

I laughed. Good old Rishi. While he rambled on about the movies, I collected Josh and Pablo. The Boss had told Pablo he could leave his bike in the kitchen and get it tomorrow.

"Ready to go?" my dad asked. He had just returned to take us home.

"You bet," I said.

As we walked to the car, he looked over at me. "So how does it feel to be a real working Joe?"

"I wouldn't know," I said. "I'm retired."

Rishi told my dad about how I had turned down the money. "What do you think of that, Mr. Rathbone?"

My dad didn't answer right away. It was only after we had dropped everyone off and gotten out of the car that he looked at me across the Honda's roof, smiled, and said, "Good job tonight, son. Real good job."

Chapter 20

A NIGHT AT THE BRICK

"Cheers!" I said.

Jessica's glass of Sprite clinked with my root beer. She looked out from our booth at the wooden tabletops and brick walls. Some guys at the bar were arguing about a game on the TV. "This is, uh, nice," she said.

"Hey, it may not be fancy but wait until you try a Freddy Burger. You haven't lived until you've tasted one!"

"What's so special about it?"

"Who knows? It comes with ketchup, mustard, pickles, relish, mayonnaise, onions, and cheese, but just knowing the ingredients doesn't mean anyone can make it. My dad tried to duplicate it once. It tasted like a shoe."

She laughed. "I didn't know you ate shoes."

"Ah yeah, delicious."

I was having a great time with Jessica. It felt like I was finally picking up where I had left off with her before heading to summer camp.

The waitress who had brought our drinks came back to the table. "You kids finish deciding yet?"

"Sure," Jessica said, putting down the menu, "I'll have a Freddy Burger. And hold the mayonnaise, please."

"How do you want it cooked?"

"Well done."

"I'll have the same," I said, "but make mine medium rare."

The waitress nodded and walked off.

"You like it bloody?" Jessica asked.

"I prefer to think of it as juicy. And what's with the well done? You'd probably like my dad's shoe recipe," I teased. It was fun to joke around with her. "Besides, I like mayonnaise."

"That's just gross," she said. She took a sip of her Sprite. "Actually, I kind of figured you were going to take me to Mama's tonight."

It had been exactly a week since the grand opening. "I've decided to leave Mama's behind," I explained.

She nodded. "Probably a good idea. That owner seemed real bossy. What was his name again?"

"Uh, the Boss."

"Yeah, a real mean guy."

I wasn't sure about that. When Pablo had gone back to pick up his bike the next morning, he said the Boss talked to him for like an hour. Pablo told him all he wanted to be an artist and about the art lessons on Saturdays. The Boss told him stuff about when he was growing up, and how tough it was without money. Three days later a letter arrived at Pablo's house. Someone had paid for him to go to the art school for a whole year.

"Okay, Rodney," Jessica continued, "so you're leaving the restaurant business. What now? Football season is over. Mrs. Lutzkraut is . . . well I don't know where she is, but I doubt she'll be bothering you again."

I didn't say anything. I knew deep down Mrs. Lutzkraut wasn't going anywhere.

Jessica asked again, "So then what's next for you?"

I was sure I could count on Rishi to get me in trouble before long, but I also kept that thought to myself. I got the feeling Jessica wanted to hear something else from me—and I couldn't wait to tell her. "Well, there's this girl I like. Maybe I could spend more time with her."

She smirked. "Who is this girl?"

"She's blonde . . ."

"Yeah?"

"And she's got blue eyes . . ."

"Yeah?"

"And the happiest day of my life was when she kissed me last year after graduation."

A man three tables away dropped his newspaper sharply. Mr. Clearwater stared at me and I tightened up. *Uh-oh*, I had forgotten he was there.

"Daaad," Jessica whined, "Rodney was only kidding."

"Yeah," I said. "Just kidding!"

He let out a breath and went back to his paper.

For the next few minutes Jessica and I limited the conversation to Kayla and Rishi and other silly stuff. Finally the waitress returned with our Freddy Burgers. I saw in a second that Jessica would be happy. I, on the other hand, couldn't believe my eyes. Both burgers were burnt to a crisp.

"I asked for medium rare!" I cried. I had never seen them mess up an order before.

The waitress looked concerned. "I'm sorry about that, honey. We just hired two new guys in the kitchen and everything they touch comes out horrible. I would offer to get you a new burger but it would probably be even worse." She turned to leave, adding, "One of them keeps bragging that all he cooks is eggs. We don't even serve eggs!"

"Do you know their names?" I asked, although I was pretty certain I knew the answer.

"Let's see . . . one is called Woodchuck or something and the other one is Big . . . Big . . ."

"Big Earl?"

"Yeah, I believe you're right. Are they friends of yours?"

"Not exactly," I said.

"Well, let me know if you need anything else." She smiled, gave a check to whoever was sitting in the booth behind Jessica, and disappeared to the front of the restaurant.

I stared at my plate and shook my head. For days I had been looking forward to a Freddy Burger. I imagined Mrs. Lutzkraut watching me through a big crystal ball and laughing. She had gotten Mama's cooks fired last Saturday and her evil was still causing me problems. "I hate well-done burgers," I complained.

Jessica giggled. "Look at tough Rodney Rathbone . . . ready to cry over a burger!"

I smiled at her. "Maybe I'm not that tough after all."

"Yeah, right," she said.

"Maybe I got everyone fooled."

She began speaking to me in a tone like a kindergarten teacher. "Rodney, we don't have to go through all your tough-guy adventures. I mean, the whole town knows you took out Josh on your very first day last year."

"It wasn't me," I answered back. "It was a baseball. It hit him in the nose and rolled under a bush. Nobody saw it."

"A baseball?" she laughed. "Who'd ever believe something so ridiculous?"

I shrugged. She was right. If an author had used that in a book they'd never be taken seriously.

Jessica continued, "Besides, I saw you fight Josh with my own eyes. Remember when you gave him a karate kick at the end-of-year dance?"

"I slipped on the wet floor."

"What about the time you took me off that ravine in

273

that big sled? What about the McThuggs? What about Old Man Johnson?"

She was recounting all my daring acts from last year.

"All luck," I said.

She rolled her eyes. "Okay, then what about at summer camp? When I came up that day, everyone kept talking about how you won all the competitions and beat that snotty rich kid. What was his name again?"

"Todd Vanderdick." Just thinking of his name made me want to puke. "He had it in for me from the first day of camp," I explained. "It only got worse when I stopped his dumb father from developing Camp Wy-Mee. But I'm telling you, Jessica, it was luck that I beat him. My canoe took a wrong turn."

It felt great to finally be getting everything off my chest.

"Okay, if you really are telling the truth, why are you telling me?"

I looked into her big blue eyes. I was about to tell her that I liked her so much that it didn't matter if she knew I was secretly a coward. As I went to open my mouth I thought, *This might be the happiest moment of my life.*

"Yes, Rodney," a kid's voice snickered from the booth in back of Jessica, "why are you telling her?"

My heart started pounding. I knew that voice from somewhere. I saw two legs swing around from the booth as the person started to rise. In a flash I noticed pink socks under fancy brown pants. As the figure rose I saw a yellow shirt followed by—Todd Vanderdick! He looked down at me and sneered. "Actually, my dad and I would both like to know."

I felt the restaurant begin to spin. My ears were ringing. I was about to faint. This couldn't be happening. Todd Vanderdick and his father—dressed in matching outfits—were now standing at the side of our booth. And they had just heard me confess everything to Jessica! Todd looked at her and introduced himself. "I'm the snotty rich kid you mentioned."

"Uh, pleased to meet you."

"My dad's buying me a red Ferrari when I turn sixteen."

"That's nice," she said, smiling politely.

I tried to speak. "Wha . . . Wha . . . What are you doing in Garrettsville?"

"Oh, we'll be spending a lot of time here," Mr. Vanderdick announced with a sickening grin. "I'm funding construction of the new Business Studies Center at Hiram College. Just five minutes from here. They're naming it Vanderdick Hall . . . and my company's building it. Why, it's almost like Todd and I will be moving to Garrettsville!"

"Yeah," Todd said directly to me, "and I can't wait to meet your friends and tell them everything I just learned about you."

My perfect date with Jessica had turned into a perfect nightmare. Things couldn't get any worse in my life. I had finally hit rock bottom.

"Actually, Todd," Mr. Vanderdick said with a sly grin,

"I believe our friend Helga Lutzkraut had Rodney as a student last year. I'm sure she would be only too happy to help you locate his friends. Heck, she probably knows his enemies as well!"

You could hear the two of them laughing all the way out to the parking lot. I stared down at the table. When would I ever learn? I always underestimated just how low rock bottom can get.

And then I heard a girl's voice that reminded me just how lucky I was. "What creeps!" Jessica laughed. "They were even worse than I pictured! And what's with those loafers they both had on?"

I had to smile.

"Listen, Rodney," she continued, "I wouldn't worry about that jerk Todd. If he comes around again he'll be laughed right out of town."

I wasn't sure I agreed with her, but it sure felt great knowing she was trying to make me feel better. And it was working. For the next ten minutes all we did was make fun of Todd and his fake rich accent. By the time Jessica and her dad and I were ready to leave, I was feeling pretty good—considering Todd Vanderdick was back in my life.

As we passed the kitchen and walked outside I heard a loud banging of pots and pans followed by, "What do you mean we're fired? You can't fire us! We's is respected chefs!"

I looked up at the gigantic autumn moon hanging over the town and smiled. Just another night in Garrettsville.

How to Beat the Bully, Book Three: *Revenge of the Bully*

by Scott Starkey

About the Book

All Rodney wants is a peaceful first day at his new middle school. Of course, that's not going to be easy with a best friend like Rishi! Before they can even enter the building, Rishi gets Rodney drafted onto the school football team. Forced to compete with kids twice his size—including the team bully—Rodney is soon tackling more than football problems. The toughest guy in town needs his help and won't take no for an answer, a certain former teacher is up to her old tricks, and Rodney's girlfriend, Jessica, is still mad after her surprise visit to Camp Wy-Mee.

Everyone is out for revenge in this funny and exciting third novel in the How to Beat the Bully series. With fast-moving action on and off the football field, including an underground chase through pitch-black caves, *Revenge of the Bully* keeps readers hooked—and laughing—at every step.

Exploring *Revenge of the Bully* through Writing and Research

1. In *Revenge of the Bully*, Rodney has moved from elementary school to middle school. What is it about this transition that Rodney finds challenging? What does he hope will be different about middle school from his previous school experience?

2. At the opening of *Revenge of the Bully,* Rodney shares, "The front doors of Garrettsville Middle School loomed before me. I paused and tried to swallow but my mouth was too dry." Based on your personal experience, are first days of school always difficult? What are the biggest challenges for students to overcome?

3. Describe Rodney. What makes him an interesting character? Is he the type of friend you would want? Why or why not?

4. What makes Josh's attack on Toby so unusual? How does this action on the first day of school help set the stage for the relationship between Rodney and Josh?

5. Rodney has a gift of finding ways to turn bad situations

around to his advantage. How is he able to accomplish this? What are some specific examples from the *Revenge of the Bully* you liked best?

6. After Coach Laimbardi recruits Josh to play football, Rishi announces that Rodney is "tougher" and "faster," and Coach L immediately states, "I've been looking for players like you" to Rodney and Josh. In what ways is this typical behavior for Rishi? Do you find his enthusiasm for celebrating Rodney's "accomplishments" to be a benefit to their friendship? Would you want a friend like Rishi?

7. After their first encounter, Toby's brother, Trevor, tells Rodney, "Now I see what he's been talkin' about. You just come waltzin' in here like you own the place, thinking you're the baddest. Thinking you can take my spot! Thinking all the cheerleaders are gonna like you! I don't care what you did in that nursery school last year, you're in middle school now and I'm going to be real happy showing you just how *bad* bad can be." Do you believe Rodney is wise to fear Trevor? In what ways does he operate much like his younger brother, Toby? How does the relationship between Trevor and Rodney change throughout the course of the book?

8. In *Revenge of the Bully*, what are the most impressive obstacles Rodney overcomes? Which of these hurdles did you like best?

9. Describe Rodney's relationship with Jessica. What makes it particularly challenging? Do you think she reacts appropriately to the attention Rodney receives from others?

10. In what ways does Rodney's mom's new career as a food critic cause potential drama for Rodney? Did you find the resolution to this satisfying?

11. Why does Rodney work so hard to convince Josie to consider a second date with Trevor? Do you feel she is being overly critical of Trevor?

12. After learning that Mrs. Lutzkraut has been released, Rodney thinks, "I was struck with an alarming thought: either half of Garrettsville was after me or I was losing my mind. Or both." Do you agree with Rodney's assessment?

13. Throughout the novel, author Scott Starkey uses clever chapter titles such as "Fernando Knows Best" to whet the reader's appetite and introduce the action of that chapter. Considering the various chapters, which chapter title in *Revenge of the Bully* was your favorite? What about it did you like best?

14. How does knowing that Mrs. Lutzkraut is obsessed with seeking revenge against him impact Rodney? Why

do you think she is unable to let her preoccupation with Rodney go?

15. After getting a promise from Fernando that he'd come help him, Rodney explains, "I trusted Fernando and began to feel better about things. For the first time all day, I actually relaxed . . ." What is it about Fernando that puts Rodney at ease? Does Fernando's presence actually help Rodney solve his problems?

16. Consider the cast of characters in the novel: Who did you like the most? The least? Of all of the characters, who did you feel was most similar to you due to his/her personality or experiences?

17. In what ways is Rodney and Rishi's work for The Boss problematic? Though he is a tough character, what does seeing him interact with his mother indicate about The Boss/Francis?

18. Like both *How to Beat the Bully Without Really Trying* and *The Call of the Bully, Revenge of the Bully* is told by Rodney in first person. How would this third installment of Rodney's story be different if another narrator was telling it? Do you think changing the point of view would make the story better or worse?

19. Explain the significance of the novel's title. Do you

think the title is appropriate for this installment of Rodney Rathbone's adventures?

Extended Writing and Research

1. In *Revenge of the Bully*, Rodney, his friends, and his classmates change throughout the course of the novel. Based on your observations, which character do you believe demonstrates the greatest growth? Compose a short persuasive essay offering your position on this issue. While considering your selected character's experiences, use textual evidence to provide specific examples to support your case.

2. Throughout the course of the novel, readers are offered great insight about Rodney's point of view based on the events of *Revenge of the Bully*. Assume the role of one of the secondary characters from *Revenge of the Bully* and draft a diary entry detailing what you experienced and witnessed. To prepare, create an outline using the five Ws (who, what, when, where, and why). Remember to write in first person and give special attention to sensory imagery (what you saw, smelled, heard, etc.)

Extension Activities

1. Making thematic connections. Consider the following themes of *Revenge of the Bully*: bravery, ingenuity,

friendship, and perseverance. Select one of the themes and find examples from the book that help support this theme. Create a sample Life Lesson Chart using the model at: http://www.readwritethink.org/files/resources/lesson_images/lesson826/chart.pdf

2. One of the central themes of *Revenge of the Bully* is friendship. Journal a response to the following:

- Describe what it means to be a friend.

- What is the value of friendship?

- What can we learn about ourselves from our friends?

- What does Rodney learn about himself from his friends like Rishi, Fernando, or Jessica? Use evidence from the story to support your response.

3. A strength of Starkey as a writer is his ability to offer richly descriptive scenes. Select a favorite scene from *Revenge of the Bully* and create either a digitally or manually illustrated graphic novel for that scene. Using a digital comic strip creator (http://www.makebeliefscomix.com/Comix/ or http://infinitecomic.com/ for example), begin by using the strips to create storyboards for their scene. Select original art, images, and graphics.

Alternatively, assume the roles of two of the characters with each one's personality and voice and interact with one another by creating an extension of a scene from one of the novels.

This guide was created by Dr. Rose Brock, a teacher and school librarian in Coppell, Texas. Dr. Brock holds a Ph.D. in Library Science, specializing in children's and young adult literature.

Did you LOVE reading this book?

Visit the Whyville...

IN THE MIDDLE BOOK HIVE

Where you can:

- Discover great books!
- Meet new friends!
- Read exclusive sneak peeks and more!

Log on to visit now!
bookhive.whyville.net

ALL ABOARD
FOR THE ADVENTURE
OF A LIFETIME!

"READERS SHOULD THRILL TO THIS ROUSING TALE AS IT BARRELS AHEAD AT FULL SPEED."
—PUBLISHERS WEEKLY

THE BOUNDLESS

KENNETH OPPEL

INTERNATIONAL BESTSELLING AUTHOR OF AIRBORN

The Boundless is the most magnificent train ever built.
Magic and danger loom around every bend.
And the hardest trick is staying alive!

Just because you're a kid,
it doesn't mean you
can't solve crimes.

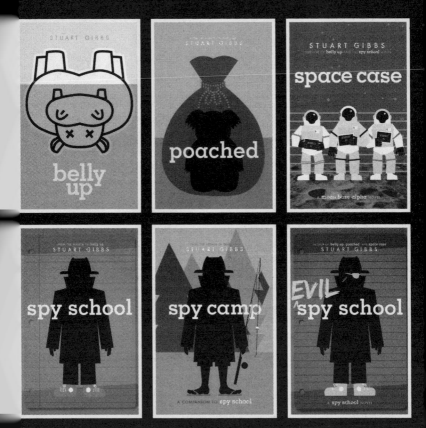

But it probably means you
won't solve them well.

Mystery, murder, mayhem.
That's no excuse to be rude.

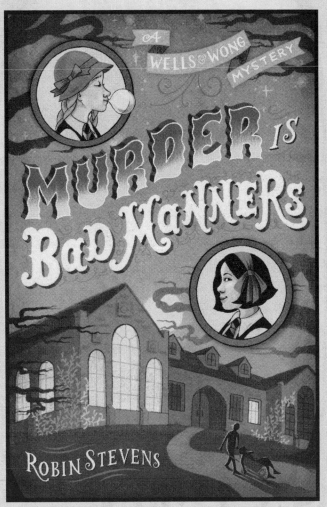